And from beloved authors

JUDITH STACY

"Judith Stacy is a fine writer with
both polished style and heartwarming sensitivity."
—Bestselling author Pamela Morsi

"...lovable characters that grab your heartstrings...
a fun read all the way."
—*Rendezvous* on *The Blushing Bride*

"...a delightful story of the triumph of love."
—*Rendezvous* on *The Dreammaker*

and

MARY BURTON

"This talented writer is a virtuoso,
who strums the hearts of the readers and
composes an emotional tale."
—*Rendezvous*

"Watch for more from this talented author..."
—*Romance Reviews Today*

"Mary Burton is a delightful surprise
for western romance fans...."
—*Affaire de Coeur*

DIANA PALMER

has a gift for telling the most sensual tales with charm and humor. With over 40 million copies of her books in print, Diana Palmer is one of North America's most beloved authors and is considered one of the top ten romance authors in America.

Diana's hobbies include gardening, archaeology, anthropology, iguanas, astronomy and music. She has been married to James Kyle for over twenty-five years, and they have one son.

JUDITH STACY

gets many of her story ideas while taking long afternoon naps. She's trying to convince her family she's actually working, but even after more than a dozen novels, they're still not buying it.

Judith is married to her high school sweetheart. They have two daughters and live in Southern California.

MARY BURTON

lives in Richmond, Virginia, with her husband and two children. *Snow Maiden* is her sixth historical romance.

DIANA PALMER

JUDITH STACY · MARY BURTON

A HERO'S
Kiss

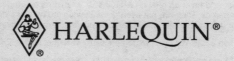

HARLEQUIN®

TORONTO · NEW YORK · LONDON
AMSTERDAM · PARIS · SYDNEY · HAMBURG
STOCKHOLM · ATHENS · TOKYO · MILAN · MADRID
PRAGUE · WARSAW · BUDAPEST · AUCKLAND

If you purchased this book without a cover you should be aware
that this book is stolen property. It was reported as "unsold and
destroyed" to the publisher, and neither the author nor the
publisher has received any payment for this "stripped book."

ISBN 0-373-83562-0

A HERO'S KISS

Copyright © 2003 by Harlequin Books S.A.

The publisher acknowledges the copyright holders
of the individual works as follows:

THE FOUNDING FATHER
Copyright © 2003 by Diana Palmer

WILD WEST WAGER
Copyright © 2003 by Dorothy Howell

SNOW MAIDEN
Copyright © 2003 by Mary Taylor Burton

All rights reserved. Except for use in any review, the reproduction or
utilization of this work in whole or in part in any form by any electronic,
mechanical or other means, now known or hereafter invented, including
xerography, photocopying and recording, or in any information storage
or retrieval system, is forbidden without the written permission of the
publisher, Harlequin Enterprises Limited, 225 Duncan Mill Road,
Don Mills, Ontario, Canada M3B 3K9.

All characters in this book have no existence outside the imagination of
the author and have no relation whatsoever to anyone bearing the same
name or names. They are not even distantly inspired by any individual
known or unknown to the author, and all incidents are pure invention.

This edition published by arrangement with Harlequin Books S.A.

® and TM are trademarks of the publisher. Trademarks indicated with
® are registered in the United States Patent and Trademark Office, the
Canadian Trade Marks Office and in other countries.

Visit us at www.eHarlequin.com

Printed in U.S.A.

CONTENTS

THE FOUNDING FATHER   9
Diana Palmer

WILD WEST WAGER   137
Judith Stacy

SNOW MAIDEN   283
Mary Burton

Dear Reader,

I am thrilled to present you with the prequel to my LONG, TALL TEXANS series for Silhouette Books. In "The Founding Father" you will meet Big John Jacobs, the founder of Jacobsville, Texas. He attracted a railroad line to his small ranching property with the help of a gutsy young debutante who preferred John and cold beans to a titled European and caviar. Camellia Ellen is a fiercely independent young woman who flowers when given a chance to escape the rigorous, correct society of her time. She and John begin as enemies but become husband and wife, and spend many happy years together.

I have often wished that I had the opportunity to show how Jacobsville began. It has been fun revisiting the Texas of more than a century ago and dabbling in the subject that I took my degree in—history! I hope you enjoy the characters, and the story.

I am still your biggest fan,

Diana Palmer

THE FOUNDING FATHER

Diana Palmer

For Susan James

CHAPTER ONE

IT TOOK A LOT TO MAKE BIG John Jacobs nervous. He was tall, rawboned, with deep-set green eyes the color of bottle glass, and thick dark brown hair. His lean, rough face had scars left over from the War Between the States. He carried scars both inside and out. He was originally from Georgia, but he'd come to Texas just after the war. Now he lived in one of the wildest parts of southeast Texas on a ranch he'd inherited from his late uncle. He was building up the ranch frugally, heading cattle drives to Kansas and buying livestock with the proceeds. What he had was very little to show for fifteen years of hard work, but he was strong and had a good business head. He'd tripled his uncle's land holdings and bought new bulls from back East to breed with his mangy longhorns. His mother would have been proud.

He noted the deep cut on his left hand, a scar from a knife fight with one of a band of Comanches who'd raided his property for horses. John and his hired help had fought them to a standstill and put them on the run. His ranch was isolated and he had good breeding stock. Over the years he'd had to fight roaming Comanche raiders and renegades from over the Mexican border, as well as carpetbaggers. If it hadn't been for the military presence just after the war ended, courtesy of the Union Army, lawlessness would have been even worse.

John had more reason than most to hate Union officers. But in the part of Texas where his ranch was located, to the southeast of San Antonio, the peace had been kept during Reconstruction by a local commandant who was a gentleman. John had admired the Union officer, who'd caught and prosecuted a thief who stole two horses from the ranch. They were good horses, with excellent bloodlines, which John had purchased from a Kentucky thoroughbred farm. The officer, who rode a Kentucky thoroughbred of his own, understood the attachment a rancher felt to his blood stock. John had rarely been more grateful to another human being. Like John himself, the officer was fearless.

Fearless. John laughed at his own apprehension over what he was about to do. He didn't mind risking his life to save his ranch. But this was no fight with guns or knives. It was a much more civilized sort of warfare. In order to win this battle, John was going to have to venture into a world he'd never seen close up. He wasn't comfortable with high society folk. He hoped he wasn't going to embarrass himself.

He removed his dress hat and ran a big hand through his sweaty brown hair. He'd had Juana cut it before he'd left the 3J Ranch. He hoped it was conservative enough to impress old man Terrance Colby. The railroad magnate was vacationing in Sutherland Springs, not far from the 3J. The popular resort boasted over one hundred separate springs in a small area. John had ridden out there to speak to Colby, without a single idea of how he was going to go about it. He had figured the details would work themselves out if he made the trip.

He was uneasy in company. He'd had to pawn his grandfather's watch to buy the used suit and hat he was wearing. It was a gamble he was taking, a big one. Cattle were no good to anyone if they couldn't be gotten to market. Driving cattle to the railheads in Kansas was becoming ever more dangerous. In some areas, fear of Texas tick fever had caused armed blockades of farmers to deter Texas cattle from entry. If he was going to get his cattle to market, there had to be a more direct route. He needed a railroad spur close by.

Colby owned a railroad. He'd just announced his intentions of expanding it to connect with San Antonio. It would be no great burden to extend a line down through Wilson County to the Jacobs' ranch. There were other ranchers in the area who also wanted the spur.

Old man Colby had a daughter, Camellia Ellen, who was unmarried and apparently unmarriageable. Local gossip said that the old man had no use for his unattractive daughter and would be happy to be rid of her. She got in the way of his mistresses. So Big John Jacobs had come a courting, to get himself a railroad…

It started raining just as he got to town. He cursed his foul luck, his green eyes blazing as he noted the mud his horse's hooves was throwing up and splattering onto his boots and the hem of the one good pair of pants he owned. He'd be untidy, and he couldn't afford to be. Terrance Colby was a New York aristocrat who, from what John had heard, was always impeccably dressed. He was staying at the best hotel the little resort of Sutherland Springs could boast, which was none too luxurious. Rumor was that Colby had come here on a hunting trip and was taking the waters while he was in the area.

John swung down out of the saddle half a block from the hotel Colby was staying at, hoping to have a chance to brush the mud off himself. Just as he got onto the boardwalk, a carriage drew up nearby. A young woman of no particular note climbed down out of it, caught the hem of her dress under her laced shoe, and fell face-first into a mud puddle.

Unforgivably, John laughed. He couldn't help it. The woman's companion gave him a glare, but the look he gave the woman was much more expressive.

"For God's sake, woman, can't you take two steps without tripping over your own garments?" the man asked in a high-pitched British accented voice. "Do get up. Now that we've dropped you off in town, I must go. I've an engagement for which you've already made me late. I'll call on your father later. Driver, carry on!"

The driver gave the woman and Big John a speaking look, but he did as he was instructed. John took note of the stranger, and hoped to meet him again one day.

He moved to the woman's side, and offered her an arm.

"No, no," she protested, managing to get to her feet alone. "You're much too nicely dressed to let me splatter you. Do go on, sir. I'm simply clumsy, there's no cure to be had for it, I'm afraid." She adjusted her oversized hat atop the dark bun of her hair and looked at him with miserable blue eyes in a pleasant but not very attractive face. She was slight and thin, and not the sort of woman to whom he'd ever been attracted.

"Your companion has no manners," he remarked.

"Thank you for your concern."

He tipped his hat. "It was no trouble. I wouldn't have minded being splattered. As you can see, I've already sampled the local mud."

She laughed and her animated face took on a fey quality, of which she was unaware. "Good day."

"Good day."

She moved away and he started into the barbershop to put himself to rights.

"John!" a man called from nearby. "Thought that was you," a heavyset man with a badge panted as he came up to join him. It was Deputy Marshal James Graham, who often stopped by John's ranch when he was in the area looking for fugitives.

They shook hands. "What are you doing in Sutherland Springs?" John asked him.

"I'm looking for a couple of renegades," he said. "They were hiding in Indian Territory, but I heard from a cousin of one of them that they were headed this way, trying to outrun the army. You watch your back."

"You watch yours," he retorted, opening his jacket to display the Colt .45 he always wore in a holster on a gunbelt slung across his narrow hips.

The marshal chuckled. "I heard that. Noticed you were trying to help that poor young woman out of a fix."

"Yes, poor little thing," he commented. "Nothing to look at, and of little interest to a man. Two left feet into the bargain. But it was no trouble to be kind to her. Her companion gave her no more help than the rough edge of his tongue."

"That was Sir Sydney Blythe, a hunting companion of the railroad magnate, Colby. They say the girl has a crush on him, but he has no use for her."

"Hardly surprising. He might have ended in the mud puddle," he added on a chuckle. "She's not the sort to inspire passion."

"You might be surprised. My wife is no looker, but can she cook! Looks wear out. Cooking lasts forever. You remember that. See you around."

"You, too." John went on into the barbershop unaware of a mud-covered female standing behind the corner, trying to deal with wiping some of the mud from her heavy skirt.

She glared at the barbershop with fierce blue eyes. So he was that sort of a man, was he, pitying the poor little scrawny hen with the clumsy feet. She'd thought he was different, but he was just the same as other men. None of them looked twice at a woman unless she had a beautiful face or body.

She walked past the barbershop toward her hotel, seething with fury. She hoped that she might one day have the chance to meet that gentleman again when she was properly dressed and in her own element. It would be a shock for him, she felt certain.

A short while later John walked toward the Sutherland Springs Hotel with a confidence he didn't really feel. He was grateful for the marshal's conversation, which helped calm him. He wondered if Colby's daughter was also enamoured of the atrocious Sir Sydney, as well as that poor scrawny hen who'd been out riding with him? He wasn't certain how he would have to go about wooing such a misfit, although he had it in mind.

At thirty-five, John was more learned than many of his contemporaries, having been brought up by an educated mother who taught him Latin while they worked in the fields. Since then, he'd been educated in other ways while trying to keep himself clothed and fed. His married sister, the only other survivor of his family, had tried to get him to come and work with her husband in North Carolina on their farm, but he hadn't wanted to settle in the East. He was a man with a dream. And if a man could make himself a fortune with nothing more than hard work and self-denial, he was ready to be that man.

It seemed vaguely dishonest to take a bride for monetary reasons, and it cut to the quick to pretend an affection he didn't feel to get a rich bride. If there was an honest way to do this, he was going to find it. His one certainty was that if he married a railroad tycoon's daughter, he had a far better chance of getting a railroad to lay tracks to his ranch than if he simply asked for help. These days, nobody rushed to help a penniless rancher. Least of all a rich Northerner.

John walked into the hotel bristling with assumed self-confidence and the same faint arrogance he'd seen rich men use to get their way.

"My name is John Jacobs," he told the clerk formally. "Mr. Colby is expecting me."

That was a bald lie, but a bold one. If it worked, he could cut through a lot of time-wasting protocol.

"Uh, he is? I mean, of course, sir," the young man faltered. "Mr. Colby is in the presidential suite. It's on the second floor, at the end of the hall. You may go right up. Mr. Colby and his daughter are receiving this morning."

Receiving. Go right up. John nodded, dazed. It was easier than he'd dreamed to see one of the country's richest men!

He nodded politely at the clerk and turned to the staircase.

The suite was easy to find. He knocked on the door confidently, inwardly gritting his teeth to gear himself up for the meeting. He had no idea what he was going to give as an excuse for coming here. He didn't know what Ellen Colby looked like. Could he perhaps say that he'd seen her from afar and had fallen madly in love with her at once? That would certainly ruin his chances with her father, who would be convinced that he only wanted Ellen's money.

While he was thinking up excuses, a maid opened the door and stood back to let him inside. Belatedly he swept off his hat, hoping his forehead wasn't sweating as profusely as it felt.

"Your name, sir?" the middle-aged woman asked politely.

"John Jacobs," he told her. "I'm a local landowner," he added.

She nodded. ''Please wait here.''

She disappeared into another room behind a closed door. Seconds passed, while John looked around him uncomfortably, reminded by the opulence of the suite how far removed he was from the upper class.

The door opened. ''Please go in, sir,'' the maid said respectfully, and even smiled at him.

Elated, he went into the room and stared into a pair of the coldest pale blue eyes he'd ever seen, in a face that seemed unremarkable compared to the very expensive lacy white dress worn by its owner. She had a beautiful figure, regardless of her lack of beauty. Her hair was thick and a rich dark brown, swept up into a high bun that left a roll of it all around her head. She was very poised, very elegant and totally hostile. With a start, John recognized her. She was the mud puddle swimmer from the hotel entrance.

He must not laugh, he must not...! But a faint grin split his chiseled lips and his green eyes danced on her indignant features. Here was his excuse, so unexpected!

''I came to inquire about your health,'' he said, his voice deep and lazy. ''The weather is cold, and the mud puddle was very large....''

''I am...'' She was blushing, now apparently

flattered by his visit. "I am very well. Thank you!"

"What mud puddle?" came a crisp voice from the doorway. A man, shorter than John, with balding hair and dark blue eyes, dressed in an expensive suit, came into the room. "I'm Terrance Colby. Who are you?"

"John Jacobs," he introduced himself. He wasn't certain how to go on. "I own a ranch outside town..." he began.

"Oh, you're here about quail hunting," Colby said immediately. He smiled, to John's astonishment, and went forward to shake hands. "But I'm afraid you're a few minutes too late. I've already procured an invitation to the Four Aces Ranch to hunt antelope and quail. You know it, I expect?"

"Certainly I do, sir," John replied. And he did. That ranch was the sort John wanted desperately to own one day, a huge property with purebred cattle and horses, known all over the country—in fact, all over the world! "I'm sure you'll find the accommodations superior."

The older man eyed him curiously. "Thank you for the offer."

John nodded. "My pleasure, sir. But I had another purpose in coming. A passerby mentioned that the young lady here was staying at this hotel.

She, uh, had a bad fall on her way inside. I assisted her. I only wanted to assure myself that she was uninjured. Her companion was less than helpful,'' he added with honest irritation.

''Sir Sydney drove off and left me there,'' the woman said angrily with flashing eyes.

Colby gave her an unsympathetic glance. ''If you will be clumsy and throw yourself into mud puddles, Ellen, you can expect to be ignored by any normal man.''

Ellen! This unfortunate little hen was the very heiress John had come to town to woo, and he was having more good fortune than he'd dreamed! Lady Luck was tossing offerings into his path with every word he spoke.

He smiled at Ellen Colby with deliberate interest. ''On the contrary, sir, I find her enchanting,'' he murmured.

Colby looked at him as if he expected men with nets to storm the room.

Ellen gave him a harsh glare. She might have been flattered by the visit, but she knew a line when she heard one. Too many men had sought access to her father through her. Here was another, when she'd hoped he might like her for herself. But when had that ever happened? Disappointed, she drew herself up to her full height. ''Please excuse me. I am in the middle of important work.'' She lifted her chin and added deliberately, ''My father's dog is having her bath.''

She turned and stalked toward a door between rooms, while John threw back his head and laughed with genuine glee.

Colby had to chuckle, himself, at his daughter's audacity. She never raised her voice, as a rule, and he'd long since come to think of her as a doormat. But this man pricked her temper and made her eyes flash.

''An interesting reaction,'' he told John. ''She is never rude, and I cannot remember a time when she raised her voice.''

John grinned. ''A gentleman likes to think that he has made an impression, sir,'' he said respectfully. ''Your daughter is far more interesting with a temper than without one. To me, at least.''

''You have a ranch, you said?'' Colby asked.

John nodded. ''A small one, but growing. I have begun to cross breeds to good effect. I have a longhorn seed bull and a small herd of Hereford cattle. I hope to raise a better sort of beef to suit Eastern tastes and ship it to market in Chicago.''

The older man sized up his guest, from the worn, but still useful, shoes and suit and the well-worn gunbelt and pistol worn unobtrusively under the open jacket.

''You have a Southern accent,'' Colby said.

John nodded again. "I am a Georgian, by birth."

Colby actually winced.

John laughed without humor. "You know, then, what Sherman and his men did to my state."

"Slavery is against everything I believe in," Colby said. His face grew hard. "Sherman's conduct was justified."

John had to bite his tongue to keep back a sharp reply. He could feel the heat of the fire, hear his mother and sister screaming as they fell in the maelstrom of crackling flames....

"You owned slaves?" Colby persisted curtly.

John gritted his teeth. "Sir, my mother and sisters and I worked on a farm outside Atlanta," he said, almost choking on memories despite the years between himself and the memory. "Only rich planters could afford slaves. My people were Irish immigrants. You might recall the signs placed at the front gates of estates in the North, which read, No Colored Or Irish Need Apply."

Colby swallowed hard. He had, indeed, seen those signs.

John seemed to grow another inch. "To answer your question, had I been a rich planter, I would have hired my labor, not bought it, for I do not feel that one man of any color has the right to own another.'' His green eyes flashed. ''There were many other small landowners and sharecroppers like my family who paid the price for the greed and luxury of plantation owners. Sherman's army did not discriminate between the two.''

''Excuse me,'' Colby said at once. ''One of my laundresses back home had been a slave. Her arms were livid with scars from a mistress who cut her when she burned a dress she was told to iron.''

''I have seen similar scars,'' John replied, without adding that one of the co-owners of his ranch had such unsightly scars, as well as his wife and even their eldest daughter.

''Your mother and sisters live with you?'' Colby asked.

John didn't reply for a few seconds. ''No, sir. Except for a married sister in North Carolina, my people are all dead.''

Colby nodded, his eyes narrow and assessing. ''But, then, you have done well for yourself in Texas, have you not?'' He smiled.

John forced himself to return the smile and forget the insults. ''I will do better, sir,'' he said with unshakeable confidence. ''Far better.''

Colby chuckled. ''You remind me of myself, when I was a young man. I left home to make my fortune, and had the good sense to look toward trains as the means.''

John twirled his hat in his big hands. He wanted to approach Colby about his spur, which would give him the opportunity to ship his cattle without having to take the risk of driving them north to railheads in Kansas. But that would be pushing his luck. Colby might feel that John was overstepping his place in society and being ''uppity.'' He couldn't risk alienating Colby.

He shifted his weight. ''I should go,'' he said absently. ''I had no intention of taking up so much of your time, sir. I wanted only to offer you the freedom of my ranch for hunting, and to inquire about the health of your daughter after her unfortunate accident.''

''Unfortunate accident.'' Colby shook his head. ''She is the clumsiest woman I have ever known,'' he said coldly, ''and I have found not one single gentleman who lasted more than a day as a suitor.''

''But she is charming,'' John countered gallantly, his eyes dancing. ''She has a sense of humor, the ability to laugh at herself, and despite her companion's rudeness, she behaved with dignity.''

Colby was listening intently. ''You find her... attractive?''

''Sir, she is the most attractive woman I have ever met,'' John replied without choosing his words.

Colby laughed and shook his head. ''You want something,'' he mused. ''But I'm damned if I don't find you a breath of fresh air, sir. You have style and dash.''

John grinned at him. ''Thank you, sir.''

''I may take you up on that invitation at a later date, young man. In the meantime, I have accepted the other offer. But you could do me a favor, if you're inclined.''

''Anything within my power, sir,'' John assured him.

''Since you find my daughter so alluring, I would like you to keep an eye on her during my absence.''

''Sir, there would not be adequate chaperones at my ranch,'' John began quickly, seeing disaster ahead if the old man or his daughter got a glimpse of the true state of affairs at the Jacobs' ranch.

''Oh, for heaven's sake, man, I'm not proposing having her live with you in sin!'' Colby burst out. ''She will stay here at the hotel, and I have told her not to venture out of town. I meant only that I would like you to check on her from time to time, to make sure that she is safe. She will be on her own, except for the maid we have re-tained here.''

''I see.'' John let out the breath he'd been holding. ''In that case, I would be delighted. But what of her companion, Sir Sydney?'' he added.

''Sir Sydney will be with me, to my cost,'' Colby groaned. ''The man is an utter pain, but he has a tract of land that I need very badly for a new roundhouse near Chicago,'' he confessed. ''So I must humor him, to some extent. I assure you, my daughter will not mourn his absence. She only went to drive with him at my request. She finds him repulsive.''

So did John, but he didn't want to rock the boat.

''I'm glad you came, young man.'' Colby of-fered his hand, and John shook it.

''So am I, sir,'' he replied. ''If you don't mind, I would like to take my leave of your daughter.''

''Be my guest.''

''Thank you.''

John walked toward the open door that con-tained a maid, Miss Ellen Colby and a very mad wet dog of uncertain age and pedigree. It was a shaggy dog, black and white, with very long ears. It was barking pitifully and shaking soapy water everywhere.

''Oh, Miss Colby, this doggy don't want no

bath,'' the maid wailed as she tried to right her cap.

''Never you mind, Lizzie, we're going to bathe her or die in the attempt.'' Ellen blew back a strand of loose hair, holding the dog down with both hands while the maid laved water on it with a cup.

''A watering trough might be a better proposition, Miss Colby,'' John drawled from the doorway.

His voice shocked her. She jerked her head in his direction and loosened the hold she had on the dog. In the few seconds that followed, the animal gave a yelp of pure joy, leaped out of the pan, off the table, and scattered the rugs as it clawed its way to the freedom of the parlor.

''Oh, my goodness!'' Ellen yelled. ''Catch her, Lizzie, before she gets to the bedroom! She'll go right up on Papa's bed, like she usually does!''

''Yes, ma'am!''

The maid ran for all she was worth. Ellen Colby put her soapy hands on her hips and glared daggers at the tall green-eyed man in the doorway.

''Now see what you've done!'' Ellen raged at John.

"Me?" John's eyebrows arched. "I assure you, I meant only to say goodbye."

"You diverted my attention at a critical moment!"

He smiled slowly, liking the way her blue eyes flashed in anger. He liked the thickness of her hair. It looked very long. He wondered if she let it down at bedtime.

That thought disturbed him. He straightened. "If your entire social life consists of bathing the dog, miss, you are missing out."

"I have a social life!"

"Falling into mud puddles?"

She grabbed up the soaking brush they'd used on the dog and considered heaving it.

John threw back his head and laughed uproariously.

"Do be quiet!" she muttered.

"You have hidden fires," he commented with delight. "Your father has asked me to keep an eye on you, Miss Colby, while he's off on his hunting trip. I find the prospect delightful."

"I can think of nothing I would enjoy less!"

"I'm quite a good companion," he assured her. "I know where birds' nests are and where flowers grow, and I can even sing and play the guitar if asked."

She hesitated, wet splotches all over her lacy

dress and soap in her upswept hair. She looked at him with open curiosity. "You are wearing a gun," she pointed out. "Do you shoot people with it?"

"Only the worst sort of people," he told her. "And I have yet to shoot a woman."

"I am reassured."

"I have a cattle ranch not too far a ride from here," he continued. "In the past, I have had infrequently to help defend my cattle from Comanche raiding parties."

"Indians!"

He laughed at her expression. "Yes. Indians. They have long since gone to live in the Indian Territory. But there are still rustlers and raiders from across the Mexican border, as well as deserting soldiers and layabouts from town hoping to steal my cattle and make a quick profit by selling them to the army."

"How do you stop them?"

"With vigilance," he said simply. "I have men who work for me on shares."

"Shares?" She frowned. "Not for wages?"

He could have bitten his tongue. He hadn't meant to let that slip out.

She knew that he'd let his guard down. She found him mysterious and charming and shrewd.

But he had attractions. He was the first man she'd met who made her want to know more about him.

"I might take you for a ride in my buggy," he mused.

"I might go," she replied.

He chuckled, liking her pert response. She wasn't much to look at, truly, but she had qualities he'd yet to find in other women.

He turned to go. "I won't take the dog along," he said.

"Papa's dog goes with me everywhere," she lied, wanting to be contrary.

He glanced at her over his shoulder. "You were alone in the mud puddle, as I recall."

She glared at him.

He gave her a long, curious scrutiny. He smiled slowly. "We can discuss it at a later date. I will see you again in a day or two." He lifted his hat respectfully. "Good day, Miss Colby."

"Good day, Mr....?" It only then occurred to her that she didn't even know his name.

"John," he replied. "John Jackson Jacobs. But most people just call me 'Big John.'"

"You are rather large," she had to agree.

He grinned. "And you are rather small. But I like your spirit, Miss Colby. I like it a lot."

She sighed and her eyes began to glow faintly as they met his green ones.

He winked at her and she blushed scarlet. But before he could say anything, the maid passed him with the struggling wet dog.

"Excuse me, sir, this parcel is quite maddeningly wet," the maid grumbled as she headed toward the bowl on the table.

"So I see. Good day, ladies." He tipped his hat again, and he was gone in a jingle of spurs.

Ellen Colby looked after him with curiosity and an odd feeling of loss. Strange that a man she'd only just met could be so familiar to her, and that she could feel such joy in his presence.

Her life had been a lonely one, a life of service, helping to act as a hostess for her father and care for her grandmother. But with her grandmother off traveling, Ellen was now more of a hindrance than a help to her family, and it was no secret that her father wanted badly to see her married and off his hands.

But chance would be a fine thing, she thought. She turned back to the dog with faint sadness, wishing she were prettier.

CHAPTER TWO

JOHN RODE BACK TO HIS RANCH, past the new-fangled barbed wire which contained his prize longhorn bull, past the second fence that held his Hereford bull and his small herd of Hereford cows with their spring calves, to the cabin where he and his foremen's families lived together. He had hundreds of head of beef steers, but they ranged widely, free of fences, identified only by his 3J brand, burned into their thick coats. The calves had been branded in the spring.

Mary Brown was at the door, watching him approach. It was early June, and hot in south Texas. Her sweaty black hair was contained under a kerchief, and her brown eyes smiled at him. "Me and Juana washed your old clothes, Mister John," she said. "Isaac and Luis went fishing with the boys down to the river for supper, and the girls are making bread."

"Good," he said. "Do I have anything dry and pressed to put on?" he added.

Mary nodded her head. "Such as it is, Mister

John. A few more holes, and no amount of sewing is gonna save you a red face in company.''

"I'm working on that, Mary," he told her, chuckling. He bent to lift her youngest son, Joe, a toddler, up into his arms. "You get to growing fast, young feller, you got to help me herd cattle."

The little boy gurgled at him. John grinned at him and set him back down.

Isaac came in the back door just then, with a string of fish. "You back?" He grinned. "Any luck?"

"A lot, all of it unexpected," he told the tall, lithe black man. He glanced at Luis Rodriguez, his head vaquero, who was short and stout and also carrying a string of fish. He took Isaac's and handed both to the young boys. "You boys go clean these fish for Mary, you hear?"

"Yes, Papa," the taller black boy said. His shorter Latino companion grinned and followed him out the door.

"We have another calf missing, *señor*," Luis said irritably. "Isaac and I only came to bring the boys and the fish to the house." He pulled out his pistol and checked it. "We will go and track the calf."

"I'll go with you," John said. "Give me a minute to change."

He carried his clothing to the single room that

had a makeshift door and got out of his best clothes, leaving them hanging over a handmade chair he'd provided for Mary. He whipped his gunbelt back around his lean hips and checked his pistol. Rustlers were the bane of any rancher, but in these hard times, when a single calf meant the difference between keeping his land or losing it, he couldn't afford to let it slide.

He went back out to the men, grim-faced. "Let's do some tracking."

THEY FOUND THE CALF, butchered. Signs around it told them it wasn't rustlers, but a couple of Indians—Comanches, in fact, judging from the broken arrow shaft and footprints they found nearby.

"Damn the luck!" John growled. "What are Comanches doing this far south? And if they're hungry, why can't they hunt rabbits or quail?"

"They all prefer buffalo, *señor,* but the herds have long gone, and game is even scarce here. That is why we had to fish for supper."

"They could go the hell back to the Indian Territory, couldn't they, instead of riding around here, harassing us poor people!" John pursed his lips thoughtfully, remembering what he'd heard in Sutherland Springs. "I wonder," he mused aloud, "if these could be the two renegades from Indian Territory being chased by the army?"

"What?" Isaac asked.

"Nothing," John said, clapping him on the shoulder affectionately. "Just thinking to myself. Let's get back to work."

THE NEXT DAY, HE PUT ON his good suit and went back to the Springs to check on Ellen Colby. He expected to find her reclining in her suite, or playing with her father's dog. What he did find was vaguely shocking.

Far from being in her room, Ellen was on the sidewalk with one arm around a frightened young black boy who'd apparently been knocked down by an angry man.

"...he got in my way. He's got no business walking on the sidewalk anyway. He should be in the street. He should be dead. They should all be dead! We lost everything because of them, and then they got protected by the very army that burned down our homes! You get away from him, lady, he's not going anywhere until I teach him a lesson!"

She stuck out her chin. "I have no intention of moving, sir. If you strike him, you must strike me, also!"

John moved up onto the sidewalk. He didn't look at Ellen. His eyes were on the angry man, and they didn't waver. He didn't say a word. He simply flipped back the lapel of his jacket to disclose the holstered pistol he was carrying.

"Another one!" the angry man railed. "You damned Yankees should get the hell out of Texas and go back up north where you belong!"

"I'm from Georgia," John drawled. "But this is where I belong now."

The man was taken aback. He straightened and glared at John, his fists clenched. "You'd draw on a fellow Southerner?" he exclaimed.

"I'm partial to brown skin," John told him with a honeyed drawl. His tall, lithe figure bent just enough to make an older man nearby catch his breath. "But you do what you think you have to," he added deliberately.

"There," Ellen Colby said haughtily, helping the young man to his feet. "See what you get when you act out of ignoble motives?" she lashed at the threatening man. "A child is a child, regardless of his heritage, sir!"

"That is no child," the man said. "It is an abomination...."

"I beg to disagree." The voice came from a newcomer, wearing a star on his shirt, just making his way through the small crowd. It was Deputy Marshal James Graham, well known locally because he was impartially fair. "Is there a problem, madam?" he asked Ellen, tipping his hat to her.

"That man kicked this young man off the sidewalk and attacked him," Ellen said, glaring daggers at the antagonist. "I interfered and Mr. Jacobs came along in time to prevent any further violence."

"Are you all right, son?" the marshal asked the young boy, who was openmouthed at his unexpected defense.

"Uh, yes, sir. I ain't hurt," he stammered.

Ellen Colby took a coin from her purse and placed it in the young man's hand. "You go get yourself a stick of peppermint," she told him.

He looked at the coin and grinned. "Thank you kindly, miss, but I'll buy my mama a sack of flour instead. Thank you, too," he told the marshal and John Jacobs, before he cut his losses and rushed down the sidewalk.

Graham turned to the man who'd started the trouble. "I don't like troublemakers," he said in a voice curt with command. "If I see you again, in a similar situation, I'll lock you up. That's a promise."

The man spat onto the ground and gave all three of the boy's defenders a cold glare before he turned and stomped off in the opposite direction.

"I'm obliged to both of you," Ellen Colby told them.

John shrugged. "It was no bother."

The deputy marshal chuckled. "A Georgian defending a black boy." He shook his head. "I am astonished."

John laughed. "I have a former slave family working with me," he explained. His face tautened. "If you could see the scars they carry, even the children, you might understand my position even better."

The deputy nodded. "I do understand. If you have any further trouble," he told Ellen, "I am at your service." He tipped his hat and went back to his horse.

"You are a man of parts, Mr. Jacobs," Ellen told John, her blue eyes soft and approving. "Thank you for your help."

He shrugged. "I was thinking of Isaac's oldest boy who died in Georgia," he confessed, moving closer as the crowd melted away. "Isaac is my wrangler," he added. "His first son was beaten to death by an overseer just before the end of the war."

She stood staring up into his lean, hard face with utter curiosity. "I understood that all Southerners hated colored people."

"Most of us common Southerners were in the fields working right beside them," John said coldly. "We were little more than slaves ourselves, while the rich lived in luxury and turned a blind eye to the abuse."

"I had no idea," she said hesitantly.

"Very few northern people do," he said flatly. "Yet there was a county in Georgia that flew the Union flag all through the war, and every attempt by the confederacy to press-gang them into the army was met with open resistance. They ran away and the army got tired of going back to get them again and again." He chuckled at her surprise. "I will tell you all about it over tea, if you like."

She blushed. "I would like that very much, Mr. Jacobs."

He offered his arm. She placed her small hand in the crook of his elbow and let him escort her into the hotel's immaculate dining room. He wondered if he should have told Graham about the Comanche tracks he'd found on his place. He made a note to mention it to the man when he next saw him.

ELLEN LIKED THE LITHE, rawboned man who sat across from her sipping tea and eating tea cakes as if he were born to high society. But she knew that he wasn't. He still had rough edges, but even those were endearing. She couldn't forget the image she had of him, standing in front of the frightened boy, daring the attacker to try again. He was brave. She admired courage.

"Did you really come to see my father to inquire about my welfare?'' she asked after they'd discussed the war.

He looked up at her, surprised by her boldness. He put his teacup down. "No," he said honestly.

She laughed self-consciously. "Forgive me, but I knew that wasn't the real reason. I appreciate your honesty."

He leaned back in his chair and studied her without pretense. His green gaze slid over her plain face, down to the faint thrust of her breasts under the green and white striped bodice of her dress and up to the wealth of dark hair piled atop her head. "Lies come hard to me," he told her. "Shall I be completely honest about my motives and risk alienating you?"

She smiled. "Please do. I have lost count of the men who pretended to admire me only as a means to my father's wealth. I much prefer an open approach."

"I inherited a very small holding from my uncle, who died some time ago." He toyed with the teacup. "I have worked for wages in the past, to buy more land and cattle. But just recently I've started to experiment with crossing breeds. I am raising a new sort of beef steer with which I hope to tempt the eastern population's hunger for range-fed beef." His eyes lifted to hers. "It's a long, slow process to drive cattle to a railhead up in Kansas, fraught with danger and risk, more now than ever since the fear of Texas fever in cattle has caused so much resistance to be placed in the path of the cattle drives. My finances are so tight now that the loss of a single calf is a major setback to me."

She was interested. "You have a plan."

He smiled. "I have a plan. I want to bring a railroad to this area of south Texas. More precisely, I want a spur to run to my ranch, so that I can ship cattle to Chicago without having to drive them to Kansas first."

Her eyes brightened. "Then you had no real purpose of inviting my father to hunt quail on your ranch."

"Miss Colby," he said heavily, "my two foremen and their families live with me in a one-room cabin. It looks all right at a distance, but close up, it's very primitive. It is a pretend mansion. As I am a pretend aristocrat." He gestured at his suit coat. "I used the last of my ready cash to disguise myself and I came into town because I had heard that your father was here, and that he had a marriageable daughter." His expression became self-mocking when she blinked. "But I'm not enough of a scoundrel to pretend an affection I do not feel." He studied her quietly, toying with a spoon beside his cup and saucer. "So let me make you a business proposition.

Marry me and let your father give us a railroad spur as a wedding present.''

She gulped, swallowed a mouthful of hot tea, sat back and expelled a shocked breath. ''Sir, you are blunt!''

''Ma'am, I am honest,'' he replied. He leaned forward quickly and fixed her with his green eyes. ''Listen to me. I have little more than land and prospects. But I have a good head for business, and I know cattle. Given the opportunity, I will build an empire such as Texas has never seen. I have good help, and I've learned much about raising cattle from them. Marry me.''

''And…what would I obtain from such a liaison?'' she stammered.

''Freedom.''

''Excuse me?''

''Your father cares for you, I think, but he treats you as a liability. That gentleman,'' he spat the word, ''who was escorting you stood idly by when you fell in a mud puddle and didn't even offer a hand. You are undervalued.''

She laughed nervously. ''And I would not be, if I married a poor stranger and went to live in the wilds where rustlers raid?''

He grinned. ''You could wear pants and learn to ride a horse and herd cattle,'' he said, tempting her. ''I would even teach you to brand cattle and shoot a gun.''

Her whole demeanor changed. She just stared at him for a minute. "I have spent my entire life under the care of my mother's mother, having lost my own mother when I was only a child. My grandmother Greene believes that a lady should never soil her hands in any way. She insists on absolute decorum in all situations. She would not hear of my learning to ride a horse or shoot a gun because such things are only for men. I have lived in a cage all my life." Her blue eyes began to gleam. "I should love to be a tomboy!"

He laughed. "Then marry me."

She hesitated once again. "Sir, I know very little of men. Having been sheltered in all ways, I am uneasy with the thought of…with having a stranger…with being…"

He held up a hand. "I offer you a marriage of friends. In truth, anything more would require a miracle, as there is no privacy where I live. We are all under the single roof. And," he added, "my foremen and their families are black and Mexican, not white." He watched for her reactions. "So, as you can see, there is a further difficulty in regard to public opinion hereabouts."

She clasped her hands before her on the table. "I would like to think about it a little. Not because of any prejudice," she added quickly, and smiled. "But because I would like to know you a little better. I have a friend who married in haste at the age of fifteen. She is now twenty-four, as I am. She has seven living children and her husband treats her like property. It is not a condition which I envy her.''

''I understand,'' he said.

The oddest thing, was that she thought he really did understand. He was a complex man. She had a sudden vision of him years down the road, in an elegant suit, in an elegant setting. He had potential. She'd never met anyone like him.

She sighed. ''But my father must not know the entire truth,'' she cautioned. ''He has prejudices, and he would not willingly let me go to a man he considered a social inferior.''

His thin lips pursed amusedly. ''Then I'll do my utmost to convince him that I am actually the illegitimate grandson of an Irish earl.''

She leaned forward. ''Are there Irish earls?''

He shrugged. ''I have no idea. But, then, he probably has no idea, either.'' His eyes twinkled.

She laughed delightedly. It changed her face, her eyes, her whole look. She was pretty when she laughed.

''There is one more complication,'' he said in a half-serious tone.

''Which is?''

His smile was outrageous. ''We have lots of mud puddles at the ranch.''

"Oh, you!" she exclaimed, reaching for the teapot.

"If you throw it, the morning papers will have a more interesting front page."

"Will it? And what would you do?" she challenged brightly.

"I am uncivilized," he informed her. "I would put you across my knee and paddle your backside, after which I would toss you over my shoulder and carry you home with me."

"How very exciting!" she exclaimed. "I have never done anything especially outrageous. I think I might like being the object of a scandal!"

He beamed. "Tempting," he proclaimed. "But I have great plans and no desire to start tongues wagging. Yet."

"Very well. I'll restrain my less civilized impulses for the time being."

He lifted his teacup and toasted her. "To unholy alliances," he teased.

She lifted hers as well. "And madcap plots!"

They clicked teacups together and drank deeply.

IT WAS UNSEEMLY FOR THEM TO be seen going out of town alone, so Ellen was prevented from visiting John's ranch. But he took her to church on Sunday—a new habit that he felt obliged to acquire—and promenading along the sidewalk after a leisurely lunch in the hotel.

The following week, John was a frequent visitor. He and Ellen became friends with an elegant Scottish gentleman and his wife who were staying at the hotel and taking the waters, while they toured the American West.

"It is a grand country," the Scotsman, Robert Maxwell, told Ellen and John. "Edith and I have been longing to ride out into the country, but we are told that it is dangerous."

"It is," John assured him grimly. "My partners and I have been tracking rustlers all week," he added, to Ellen's surprise, because he hadn't told her. "There are dangerous men in these parts, and we have rustlers from across the border, also."

"Do you have Red Indians?" Maxwell exclaimed. His eyes twinkled. "I would like to meet one."

"They're all in the Indian Territory now, and no, you wouldn't like to meet one," John said. "The Comanches who used to live hereabouts didn't encourage foreign visitors, and they had a well-deserved reputation for opposing any people who tried to invade their land."

"Their land?" the Scotsman queried, curiously.

"Their land," John said firmly. "They roamed

this country long before the first white man set foot here. They intermarried with the Mexican population...."

Maxwell seemed very confused, as he interrupted, "Surely there were no people here at all when you arrived," he said.

"Perhaps they don't know it back East, but Texas was part of Mexico just a few decades back," John informed him. "That's why we went to war with Mexico, because Texas wanted independence from it. Our brave boys died in the Alamo in San Antonio, and at Goliad and San Jacinto, to bring Texas into the union. But the Mexican boys fought to keep from losing their territory, is how they saw it. They considered us invaders."

Ellen was watching John covertly, with quiet admiration.

"Ah, now I understand," the Scot chuckled. "It's like us and England. We've been fighting centuries to govern ourselves, like the Irish. But the British are stubborn folk."

"So are Texans," John chuckled.

"I don't suppose you'd go riding with us, young man?" Maxwell asked him wistfully. "We should love to see a little of the area, and I see that you wear a great pistol at your hip. I assume you can shoot any two-legged threats to our safety."

John glanced at Ellen and saw such appreciation in her blue eyes that he lost his train of thought for a few seconds.

Finally he blinked and darted his green gaze back to the foreigners, hoping his heartbeat wasn't audible.

"I think I'd like that," John replied, "as long as Ellen comes with us."

"Your young lady," the Scotswoman, Nell Maxwell, added with a gentle, indulgent smile.

"Yes," John said, his eyes going back to Ellen's involuntarily. "My young lady."

Ellen blushed red and lowered her eyes, which caused the foreign couple to laugh charmingly. She was so excited that she forgot her father's admonition that she was not to leave the hotel and go out of town. In fact, when she recalled it, she simply ignored it.

THEY RENTED A SURREY and John helped Ellen into the back seat before he climbed up nimbly beside her. He noted that it was the best surrey the stable had, with fringe hanging all the way around, and the horses' livery was silver and black leather.

"I suppose this is nothing special for you," John murmured to her, looking keenly at the horses' adornments, "but it's something of a treat for me."

Ellen smoothed the skirt of her nice blue suit with its black piping. "It's a treat for me, too," she confessed. "I had very much wanted to drive out in the country, but my father only thinks of hunting, not sightseeing, and he dislikes my company."

"I like your company very much," John said in a deep, soft tone.

She looked up at him, surprised by the warmth in his deep voice. She was lost in the sudden intensity of his green eyes under the wide brim of his dress hat. She felt her whole world shift in the slow delight it provoked.

He smiled, feeling as if he could fly all of a sudden. Impulsively his big, lean hand caught hers on the seat between them and curled her small fingers into it.

She caught her breath, entranced.

"Are you two young people comfortable?" Maxwell asked.

"Quite comfortable, thank you, sir," John replied, and he looked at Ellen with possession.

"So am I, thank you," Ellen managed through her tight throat.

"We'll away, then," Maxwell said with a grin at his wife, and he flicked the reins.

The surrey bounded forward, the horses obviously well chosen for their task, because the ride was as smooth as silk.

"Which way shall we go?" Maxwell asked.

"Just follow the road you're on," John told him. "I know this way best. It runs past my own land up to Quail Run, the next little town along the road. I can show you the ruins of a log cabin where a white woman and her Comanche husband held off a company of soldiers a few years back. He was a renegade. She was a widow with a young son, and expecting another when her husband was killed by a robber. Soon after, the Comanche was part of a war party that encountered a company of soldiers trailing them. He was wounded and she found him and nursed him back to health. It was winter. She couldn't hunt or fish, or chop wood, and she had no family at all. He undertook her support. They both ran from the soldiers, up into the Indian Territory. She's there now, people say. Nobody knows where he is."

"What a fascinating story!" Maxwell exclaimed. "Is it true?"

"From what I hear, it is," John replied.

"What a courageous young woman," Ellen murmured.

"To have contact with a Red Indian, she would have to be," Mrs. Maxwell replied. "I have heard many people speak of Indians. None of what they say is good."

"I think all people are good and bad," Ellen

ventured. "I have never thought heritage should decide which is which."

John chuckled and squeezed her hand. "We think alike."

The Maxwells exchanged a complicated look and laughed, too.

THE LOG CABIN WAS POINTED OUT. It was nothing much to look at. There was a well tucked into high grass and briar bushes, and a single tree in what must once have been the front yard.

"What sort of tree is that?" Mrs. Maxwell asked. "What an odd shape."

"It's a chinaberry tree," John recalled. "We have them in Georgia, where I'm from. My sisters and I used to throw the green berries that grow on them back and forth, playing." He became somber.

"You have family back in Georgia?" Ellen asked pointedly, softly.

He sighed. "I have a married sister in North Carolina. No one else."

Ellen knew there was more to it than just that, and she had a feeling the war had cost him more than his home. She stroked the back of his callused hand gently. "Mama died of typhoid when I was just five. So except for Papa and Grandmother, I have no one, either."

He caught his breath. He hadn't thought about

her circumstances, her family, her background. All he'd known was that she was rich. He began to see her with different eyes.

"I'm sorry, about your family," she said quietly.

He sighed. He didn't look at her. Memories tore at his heart. He looked out beyond the horses drawing the surrey at the yellow sand of the dirt road, leading to the slightly rolling land ahead. The familiar *clop-clop* of the horses' hooves and the faint creak of leather and wood and the swishing sound of the rolling wheels seemed very loud in the silence that followed. The dust came up into the carriage, but they were all used to it, since dirt roads were somewhat universal. The boards that made the seats of the surrey were hard on the backside during a long trip, but not less comfortable than the saddle of a horse, John supposed.

"Do you ride at all?" he asked Ellen.

"I was never allowed to," she confessed. "My grandmother thought it wasn't ladylike."

"I ride to the hounds," Mrs. Maxwell said, eavesdropping, and turned to face them with a grin. "My father himself put me on my first horse when I was no more than a girl. I rode sidesaddle, of course, but I could outdistance any man I met on a horse. Well, except for Robert," she conceded, with an affectionate look at her husband. "We raced and I lost. Then and there, I determined that I needed to marry him."

"And she did," he added with a chuckle, darting a look over his broad shoulder. "Her father told me I must keep her occupied to keep her happy, so I turned the stables over to her."

"Quite a revolution of sorts in our part of the country, I must add," Mrs. Maxwell confessed. "But the lads finally learned who had the whip hand, and now they do what I say."

"We have the finest stable around," Maxwell agreed. "We haven't lost a race yet."

"When I have more horses, you must come and teach my partners how to train them," John told Mrs. Maxwell.

"And didn't I tell you that people would not be stuffy and arrogant here in Texas?" she asked her husband.

"I must agree, they are not."

"Well, two of them, at least," John murmured dryly. "There," he said suddenly, pointing out across a grassy pasture. "That is my land."

All three heads turned. In the distance was the big cabin, surrounded by pecan and oak trees and not very visible. But around it were red-and-white-coated cattle, grazing in between barbed wire fences.

"It is fenced!" Maxwell exclaimed.

"Fencing is what keeps the outlaws out and

my cattle in,'' John said, used to defending his fences. ''Many people dislike this new barbed wire, but it is the most economical way to contain my herds. And I don't have a great deal of capital to work with.''

''You are an honest man,'' Maxwell said. ''You did not have to admit such a thing to a stranger.''

''It is because you are a stranger that I can do it,'' John said amusedly. ''I would never admit to being poor around my own countrymen. A man has his pride. However, I intend to be the richest landowner hereabouts in a few years. So you must plan to come back to Texas. I can promise you will be very welcome as house-guests.''

''If I am able, I will,'' Maxwell agreed. ''So we must keep in touch.''

''Indeed we must. We will trade addresses before you leave town. But for now,'' John added, ''make a left turn at this next crossroads, and I will show you a mill, where we take our corn to be ground into meal.''

''We have mills at home, but I should like to see yours,'' Mrs. Maxwell enthused.

''And so you shall,'' John promised.

CHAPTER THREE

TWO HOURS LATER, TIRED AND thirsty, the tourists returned to the livery stable to return the horses and surrey.

"It has been a pleasure," John told the Maxwells, shaking hands.

"And for me, as well," Ellen added.

The older couple smiled indulgently. "We leave for New York in the morning," Maxwell said regretfully, "and then we sail to Scotland. It has been a pleasure to meet you both, although I wish we could have done so sooner."

"Yes," Mrs. Maxwell said solemnly. "How sad to make friends just as we must say goodbye to them."

"We will keep in touch," John said.

"Indeed we will. You must leave your address for us at the desk, and we will leave ours for you," Maxwell told John. "When you have made your fortune, I hope very much to return with my wife to visit you both."

Ellen flushed, because she had a sudden vivid

picture of herself with John and several children on a grand estate. John was seeing the same picture. He grinned broadly. "We will look forward to it," he said to them both.

The Maxwells went up to their rooms and John stopped with Ellen at the foot of the stairs, because it would have been unseemly for a gentleman to accompany a lady all the way to her bedroom.

He took her hand in his and held it firmly. "I enjoyed today," he said. "Even in company, you are unique."

"As you are." She smiled up at him from a radiant face surrounded by wisps of loose dark hair that had escaped her bun and the hatpins that held on her wide-brimmed hat.

"We must make sure that we build a proper empire," he teased, "so that the Maxwells can come back to visit."

"I shall do my utmost to assist you," she replied with teasing eyes.

He chuckled. "I have no doubt of that."

"I will see you tomorrow?" she fished.

"Indeed you will. It will be in the afternoon, though," he added regretfully. "I must help move cattle into a new pasture first. It is very dry and we must shift them closer to water."

"Good evening, then," she said gently.

"Good evening." He lifted her hand to his lips in a gesture he'd learned in polite company during his travels.

It had a giddy effect on Ellen. She blushed and laughed nervously and almost stumbled over her own feet going up the staircase.

"Oh, dear," she said, righting herself.

"Not to worry," John assured her, hat in hand, green eyes brimming with mirth. "See?" He looked around his feet and back up at her. "No mud puddles!"

She gave him an exasperated, but amused, look, and went quickly up the staircase. When she made the landing, he was still there, watching.

JOHN AND ELLEN SAW EACH other daily for a week, during which they grew closer. Ellen waited for John in the hotel dining room late the next Friday afternoon, but to her dismay, it was not John who walked directly to her table. It was her father, home unexpectedly early. Nor was he smiling.

He pulled out a chair and sat down, motioning imperiously to a waiter, from whom he ordered coffee and nothing else.

"You are home early," Ellen stammered.

"I am home to prevent a scandal!" he replied

curtly. "I've had word from an acquaintance of Sir Sydney's that you were seen flagrantly defying my instructions that you should stay in this hotel during my absence! You have been riding, in the country, alone, with Mr. Jacobs! How dare you create a scandal here!"

The Ellen of only a week ago would have bowed her head meekly and agreed never to disobey him again. But her association with John Jacobs had already stiffened her backbone. He had offered her a new life, a free life, away from the endless social conventions and rules of conduct that kept her father so occupied.

She lifted her eyebrows with hauteur. "And what business of Sir Sydney's friend is my behavior?" she wanted to know.

Her father's eyes widened in surprise. "I beg your pardon?"

"I have no intention of being coupled with Sir Sydney in any way whatsoever," she informed him. "In fact, the man is repulsive and ill-mannered."

It was a rare hint of rebellion, one of just a few he had ever seen in Ellen. He just stared at her, confused and amused, all at once.

"It would seem that your acquaintance with Mr. Jacobs is corrupting you."

"I intend to be further corrupted," she replied coolly. "He has asked me to marry him."

"Child, that is out of the question," he said sharply.

She held up a dainty hand. "I am no child," she informed him, blue eyes flashing. "I am a woman grown. Most of my friends are married with families of their own. I am a spinster, an encumbrance to hear you tell it, of a sort whom men do not rush to escort. I am neither pretty nor accomplished…"

"You are quite wealthy," he inserted bluntly. "Which is, no doubt, why Mr. Jacobs finds you so attractive."

In fact, it was a railroad spur, not money, that John wanted, but she wasn't ready to tell her father that. Let him think what he liked. She knew that John Jacobs found her attractive. It gave her confidence to stand up to her parent for the first time in memory.

"You may disinherit me whenever you like," she said easily, sipping coffee with a steady hand. Her eyes twinkled. "I promise you, it will make no difference to him. He is the sort of man who builds empires from nothing more than hard work and determination. In time, his fortune will rival yours, I daresay."

Terrance Colby was listening now, not blustering. "You are considering his proposal."

She nodded, smiling. "He has painted me a delightful picture of muddy roads, kitchen gardens, heavy labor, cooking over open fires and branding cattle." She chuckled. "In fact, he has offered to let me help him brand cattle in the fall when his second crop of calves drop."

Terrance caught his breath. He waited to speak until the waiter brought his coffee. He glowered after the retreating figure. "I should have asked for a teacup of whiskey instead," he muttered to himself. His eyes went back to his daughter's face. "Brand cattle?"

She nodded. "Ride horses, shoot a gun...he offered to teach me no end of disgusting and socially unacceptable forms of recreation."

He sat back with an expulsion of breath. "I could have him arrested."

"For what?" she replied.

He was disconcerted by the question. "I haven't decided yet. Corrupting a minor," he ventured.

"I am far beyond the age of consent, Father," she reminded him. She sipped coffee again. "You may disinherit me at will. I will not even need the elegant wardrobes you have purchased for me. I will wear dungarees and high-heeled boots.''

His look of horror was now all-consuming. ''You will not! Remember your place, Ellen!''

Her eyes narrowed. ''My place is what I say it is. I am not property, to be sold or bartered for material gain!''

He was formulating a reply when the sound of heavy footfalls disturbed him into looking up. John Jacobs was standing just to his side, wearing his working gear, including that sinister revolver slung low in a holster slanted across his lean hips.

''Ah,'' Colby said curtly. ''The villain of the piece!''

''I am no villain,'' John replied tersely. He glanced at Ellen with budding feelings of protectiveness. She looked flushed and angry. ''Certainly, I have never given Ellen such pain as that I see now on her face.'' He looked back at Colby with a cold glare.

Colby began to be impressed. This steely young man was not impressed by either his wealth or position when Ellen was distressed.

''Do you intend to call me out?'' he asked John.

The younger man glanced again at Ellen. ''It would be high folly to kill the father of my prospective bride,'' he said finally. ''Of course, I don't have to kill you,'' he added, pursing his lips and giving Colby's shoulder a quiet scrutiny. ''I could simply wing you.''

Colby's gaze went to that worn pistol butt. ''Do you know how to shoot that hog leg?''

''I could give you references,'' John drawled. ''Or a demonstration, if you prefer.''

Colby actually laughed. ''I imagine you could. Stop bristling like an angry dog and sit down, Mr. Jacobs. I have ridden hard to get here, thinking my daughter was about to be seduced by a bounder. And I find only an honest suitor who would fight even her own father to protect her. I am quite impressed. Do sit down,'' he emphasized. ''That gentleman by the window looks fit to jump through it. He has not taken his eyes off your gun since you approached me!''

John's hard face broke into a sheepish grin. He pulled out a chair and sat down close to Ellen, his green eyes soft now and possessive as they sketched her flushed, happy face. He smiled at her, tenderly.

Colby ordered coffee for John as well and then sat back to study the determined young man.

''She said you wish to teach her to shoot a gun and brand cattle,'' Colby began.

"If she wants to, yes," John replied. "I assume you would object…?"

Colby chuckled. "My grandmother shot a gun and once chased a would-be robber down the streets of a North Carolina town with it. She was a local legend."

"You never told me!" Ellen exclaimed.

He grimaced. "Your mother was very strait-laced, Ellen, like your grandmother Greene," he said. "She wanted no image of my unconventional mother to tempt you into indiscretion." He pursed his lips and chuckled. "Apparently blood will out, as they say." He looked at her with kind eyes. "You have been pampered all your life. Nothing that money could buy has ever been beyond your pocket. It will not be such a life with this man," he indicated John. "Not for a few years, at least," he added with a chuckle. "You remind me of myself, Mr. Jacobs. I did not inherit my wealth. I worked as a farm laborer in my youth," he added, shocking his daughter. "I mucked out stables and slopped hogs for a rich man in our small North Carolina town. There were eight of us children, and no money to be handed down. When I was twelve, I jumped on a freight train and was arrested in New York when I was found in a stock car. I was taken to the manager's office where the owner of the railroad had chanced to venture on a matter of business. I was rude and arrogant, but he must have seen something in me that impressed him. He had a wife, but no children. He took me home with him, had his wife clean me up and dress me properly, and I became his adoptive child. When he died, he left the business to me. By then, I was more than capable of running it."

"Father!" Ellen exclaimed. "You never spoke of your parents. I had no idea...!"

"My parents died of typhoid soon after I left the farm," he confessed. "My brothers and sisters were taken in by cousins. When I made my own fortune, I made sure that they were provided for."

"You wanted a son," she said sorrowfully, "to inherit what you had. And all you got was me."

"Your mother died giving birth to a stillborn son," he confessed. "You were told that she died of a fever, which is partially correct. I felt that you were too young for the whole truth. And your maternal grandmother was horrified when I thought to tell you. Grandmother Greene is very correct and formal." He sighed. "When she knows what you have done, I expect she will be here on the next train to save you, along with however many grandsons she can convince to accompany her.''

She nodded slowly, feeling nervous. ''She is formidable.''

''I wouldn't mind a son, but I do like little girls,'' John said with a warm smile. ''I won't mind if we have daughters.''

She flushed, embarrassed.

''Let us speak first of marriage, if you please,'' Colby said with a wry smile. ''What would you like for a wedding present, Mr. Jacobs?''

John was overwhelmed. He hesitated.

''*We* would like a spur line run down to *our* ranch,'' Ellen said for him, with a wicked grin. ''So that we don't have to drive our cattle all the way to Kansas to get them shipped to Chicago. We are going to raise extraordinary beef.''

John sighed. ''Indeed we are,'' he nodded, watching her with delight.

''That may take some little time,'' Colby mused. ''What would you like in the meantime?''

''A sidesaddle rig for Ellen, so that she can be comfortable in the saddle,'' John said surprisingly.

''I do not want a sidesaddle,'' she informed him curtly. ''I intend to ride astride, as I have seen other women do since I came here.''

"I have never seen a woman ride in such a manner!" Colby exploded.

"She's thinking of Tess Wallace," John confessed. "She's the wife of old man Tick Wallace, who owns the stagecoach line here. She drives the team and even rides shotgun sometimes. He's twenty years older than she is, but nobody doubts what they feel for each other. She's crazy for him."

"An unconventional woman," Colby muttered.

"As I intend to become. You may give me away at the wedding, and it must be a small, intimate one, and very soon," she added. "I do not wish my husband embarrassed by a gathering of snobby aristocrats."

Her father's jaw dropped. "But the suddenness of the wedding…!"

"I am sorry, Father, but it will be my wedding, and I feel I have a right to ask for what I wish," Ellen said stubbornly. "I have done nothing wrong, so I have nothing to fear. Besides," she added logically, "none of our friends live here, or are in attendance here at the Springs."

Her father sighed. "As you wish, my dear," he said finally, and his real affection for her was evident in the smile he gave her.

John was tremendously impressed, not only by

her show of spirit, but by her consideration for him. He was getting quite a bargain, he thought. Then he stopped to ask himself what she was getting, save for a hard life that would age her prematurely, maybe even kill her. He began to frown.

"It will be a harder life than you realize now," John said abruptly, and with a scowl. "We have no conveniences at all…."

"I am not afraid of hard work," Ellen interrupted.

John and Colby exchanged concerned glances. They both knew deprivation intimately. Ellen had never been without a maid or the most luxurious accommodations in her entire life.

"I'll spare you as much as I can," John said after a minute. "But most empires operate sparsely at first."

"I will learn to cook," Ellen said with a chuckle.

"Can you clean a game hen?" her father wanted to know.

She didn't waver. "I can learn."

"Can you haul water from the river and hoe in a garden?" her father persisted. "Because I have no doubt that you will have to do it."

"There will be men to do the lifting," John

promised him. "And we will take excellent care of her, sir."

Her father hesitated, but Ellen's face was stiff with determination. She wasn't backing down an inch.

"Very well," he said on a heavy breath. "But if it becomes too much for you, I want to know," he added firmly. "You must promise that, or I cannot sanction your wedding."

"I promise," she said at once, knowing that she would never go to him for help.

He relaxed a little. "Then I will give you a wedding present that will not make your prospective bridegroom chafe too much," he continued. "I'll open an account for you both at the mercantile store. You will need dry goods to furnish your home."

"Oh, Father, thank you!" Ellen exclaimed.

John chuckled. "Thank you, indeed. Ellen will be grateful, but I'll consider it a loan."

"Of course, my boy," Colby replied complacently.

John knew the man didn't believe him. But he was capable of building an empire, even if he was the only one at the table who knew it at that moment. He reached over to shake hands with the older man.

"Within ten years," he told Colby, "we will

entertain you in the style to which you are accustomed.''

Colby nodded, but he still had reservations. He only hoped he wasn't doing Ellen a disservice. And he still had to explain this to her maternal grandmother, who was going to have a heart attack when she knew what he'd let Ellen do.

But all he said to the couple was, ''We shall see.''

THEY WERE MARRIED by a justice of the peace, with Terrance Colby and the minister's wife as witnesses. Colby had found a logical reason for the haste of the wedding, pleading his forthcoming trip home and Ellen's refusal to leave Sutherland Springs. The minister, an easygoing, romantic man, was willing to defy convention for a good cause. Colby congratulated John, kissed Ellen, and led them to a buckboard which he'd already had filled with enough provisions to last a month. He'd even included a treadle sewing machine, cloth for dresses and the sewing notions that went with them. Nor had he forgotten Ellen's precious knitting needles and wool yarn, with which she whiled away quiet evenings.

''Father, thank you very much!'' Ellen exclaimed when she saw the rig.

''Thank you very much, indeed,'' John added

with a handshake. "I shall take excellent care of her," he promised.

"I'm sure you'll do your best," Colby replied, but he was worried, and it showed.

Ellen kissed him. "You must not be concerned for me," she said firmly, her blue eyes full of censure. "You think I am a lily, but I mean to prove to you that I am like a cactus flower, able to bloom in the most unlikely places."

He kissed her cheek. "If you ever need me…"

"I do know where to send a telegram," she interrupted, and chuckled. "Have a safe trip home."

"I will have your trunks sent out before I leave town," he added.

John helped Ellen into the buckboard in the lacy white dress and veil she'd worn for her wedding, and he climbed up beside her in the only good suit he owned. They were an odd couple, he thought. And considering the shock she was likely to get when she saw where she must live, it would only get worse. He felt guilty for what he was doing. He prayed that the ends would justify the means. He had promised little, and she had asked for nothing. But many couples had started with even less and made a go of their marriages. He meant to keep Ellen happy, whatever it took.

ELLEN JACOBS'S FIRST glimpse of her future home would have been enough to discourage many a young woman from getting out of the buckboard. The shade trees shaded a large, rough log cabin with only one door and a single window and a chimney. Nearby were cactus plants and brush. But there were tiny pink climbing roses in full bloom, and John confessed that he'd brought the bushes here from Georgia planted in a syrup can. The roses delighted her, and made the wilderness look less wild.

Outside the cabin stood a Mexican couple and a black couple, surrounded by children of all ages. They stared and looked very nervous as John helped Ellen down out of the buckboard.

She had rarely interacted with people of color, except as servants in the homes she had visited most of her life. It was new, and rather exciting, to live among them.

"I am Ellen Colby," she introduced herself, and then colored. "I do beg your pardon! I am Ellen Jacobs!"

She laughed, and then they laughed as well.

"We're pleased to meet you, *señora,*" the Mexican man said, holding his broad sombrero in front of him. He grinned as he introduced himself and his small family. "I am Luis Rodriguez.

This is my family—my wife Juana, my son Alvaro and my daughters Juanita, Elena and Lupita.'' They all nodded and smiled.

''And I am Mary Brown,'' the black woman said gently. ''My husband is Isaac. These are my boys, Ben, the oldest, and Joe, the youngest, and my little girl Libby, who is the middle child. We are glad to have you here.''

''I am glad to be here,'' Ellen said.

''But right now, you need to get into some comfortable clothing, Mrs. Jacobs,'' Mary said. ''Come along in. You men go to work and leave us to our own chores,'' she said, shooing them off.

''Mary, I can't work in these!'' John exclaimed defensively.

She reached into a box and pulled out a freshly ironed shirt and patched pants. ''You go off behind a tree and put those on, and I'll do my best to chase the moths out of this box so's I can put your suit in it. And mind you don't get red mud in this shirt!''

''Yes, ma'am,'' he said with a sheepish grin. ''See you later, Ellen.''

Mary shut the door on him, grinning widely at Ellen. ''He is a good man,'' she told Ellen in all seriousness as she produced the best dress she had and offered it to Ellen.

"No," Ellen said gently, smiling. "I thank you very much for the offer of your dress, but I not only brought a cotton dress of my own—I have brought bolts of fabric and a sewing machine."

There were looks of unadulterated pleasure on all the feminine faces. "New...fabric?" Mary asked haltingly.

"Sewing machine?" her daughter exclaimed.

"In the buckboard," Ellen assured them with a grin.

They vanished like summer mist, out the door. Ellen followed behind them, still laughing at their delight. She'd done the right thing, it seemed— rather, her father had. She might have thought of it first if she'd had the opportunity.

The women and girls went wild over the material, tearing it out of its brown paper wrapping without even bothering to cut the string that held it.

"Alvaro, you and Ben get this sewing machine and Mrs. Jacobs's suitcase into the house right this minute! Girls, bring the notions and the fabric! I'll get the coffee and sugar, but Ben will have to come back for the lard bucket and the flour sack."

"Yes, ma'am," they echoed, and burst out laughing.

THREE HOURS LATER, Ellen was wearing a simple
navy skirt with an indigo blouse, fastened high
at the neck. She had on lace-up shoes, but she
could see that she was going to have to have
boots if she was to be any help to John. The cabin
was very small, and all of the families would
sleep inside, because there were varmints out at
night. And not just crawly ones or four-legged
ones, she suspected. Mary had told her about the
Comanches John and Luis and Isaac had been
hunting when a calf was taken. She noted that a
loaded shotgun was kept in a corner of the room,
and she had no doubt that either of her companions could wield it if necessary. But she would
ask John to teach her to shoot it, as well.

"You will have very pretty dresses from this
material," Mary sighed as she touched the colored cottons of many prints and designs.

"*We* will have many pretty dresses," Ellen
said, busily filling a bobbin for the sewing machine. She looked up at stunned expressions.
"Surely you did not think I could use this much
fabric by myself? There is enough here for all of
us, I should imagine. And it will take less for the
girls," she added, with a warm smile at them.

Mary actually turned away, and Ellen was horrified that she'd hurt the other woman's feelings.

She jumped up from the makeshift chair John had cobbled together from tree limbs. "Mary, I'm sorry, I...!"

Mary turned back to her, tears running down her cheeks. "It's just, I haven't had a dress of my own, a new dress, in my whole life. Only hand-me-downs from my mistress, and they had to be torn up or used up first."

Ellen didn't know what to say. Her face was shocked.

Mary wiped away the tears. She looked at the other woman curiously. "You don't know about slaves, do you, Mrs. Ellen?"

"I know enough to be very sorry that some people think they can own other people," she replied carefully. "My family never did."

Mary forced a smile. "Mr. John brought us out here after the war. We been lucky. Two of our kids are lost forever, you know," she added matter-of-factly. "They got sold just before the war. And one of them got beat to death."

Ellen's eyes closed. She shuddered. It was overwhelming. Tears ran down her cheeks.

"Oh, now, Mrs., don't you...don't you do that!" Mary gathered her close and rocked her. "Don't you cry. Wherever my babies gone, they free now, don't you see. Alive or dead, they free."

The tears ran even harder.

"It was just as bad for Juana," Mary said through her own tears. "Two of her little boys got shot. This man got drunk and thought they was Indians. He just killed them right there in the road where they was playing, and he didn't even look back. He rode off laughing. Luis told the *federales,* but they couldn't find the man. That was years ago, before Mr. John's uncle hired Luis to work here, but Juana never forgot them little boys."

Ellen drew back and pulled a handkerchief out of her sleeve. She wiped Mary's eyes and smiled sadly. "We live in a bad world."

Mary smiled. "It's gonna get better," she said. "You wait and see."

"Better," Juana echoed, nodding, smiling. *"Mas bueno."*

"Mas…bueno?" Ellen repeated.

Juana chuckled. *"¡!Vaya! Muy bien!* Very good!"

Mary smiled. "You just spoke your first words of Spanish!"

"Perhaps you can teach me to speak Spanish," Ellen said to Juana.

"Señora, it will be my pleasure!" the woman answered, and smiled beautifully.

"I expect to learn a great deal, and very soon," Ellen replied.

THAT WAS AN UNDERSTATEMENT. During her first week of residence, she became an integral part of John's extended family. She learned quite a few words of Spanish, including some range language that shocked John when she repeated it to him with a wicked grin.

"You stop that," he chastised. "Your father will have me shot if he hears you!"

She only chuckled, helping Mary put bread on the table. She was learning to make bread that didn't bounce, but it was early days yet. "My father thinks I will be begging him to come and get me within two weeks. He is in for a surprise!"

"I got the surprise," John had to admit, smiling at her. "You fit right in that first day." He looked from her to the other women, all wearing new dresses that they'd pieced on Ellen's sewing machine. He shook his head. "You three ought to open a dress shop in town."

Ellen glanced at Mary and Juana with pursed lips and twinkling eyes. "You know, that's not really such a bad idea, John," she said after a minute. "It would make us a little extra money. We could buy more barbed wire and we might even be able to afford a milk cow!"

John started to speak, but Mary and Juana jumped right in, and before he ate the first piece of bread, the women were already making plans.

CHAPTER FOUR

ELLEN HAD JOHN DRIVE HER into town the following Saturday, to the dry goods store. She spoke with Mr. Alton, the owner.

"I know there must be a market for inexpensive dresses in town, Mr. Alton," she said, bright-eyed. "You order them and keep them in stock, but the ones you buy are very expensive, and most ranch women can't afford them. Suppose I could supply you with simple cotton dresses, ready-made, at half the price of the ones you special order for customers?"

He lifted both eyebrows. "But, Mrs. Jacobs, your father is a wealthy man...!"

"My husband is not," she replied simply. "I must help him as I can." She smiled. "I have a knack for sewing, Mr. Alton, and I think I do quite good work. I also have two helpers who are learning how to use the machine. Would you let me try?"

He hesitated, adding up figures in his head. "All right," he said finally. "You bring me about six dresses, two each of small, medium and large ones, and we will see how they sell."

She grinned. "Done!" She went to the bolts of fabric he kept. "You must allow me credit, so that I can buy the material to make them with, and I will pay you back from my first orders."

He hesitated again. Then he laughed. She was very shrewd. But, he noticed that the dress she was wearing was quite well-made. His women customers had complained about the lack of variety and simplicity in his ready-made dresses, which were mostly for evening and not everyday.

"I will give you credit," he said after a minute. He shook his head as he went to cut the cloth she wanted. "You are a shrewd businesswoman, Mrs. Jacobs," he said. "I'll have to watch myself, or I may end up working for you!"

Which amused her no end.

JOHN WAS DUBIOUS ABOUT HIS wife's enterprise, but Ellen knew what she was doing. Within three weeks, she and the women had earned enough money with their dressmaking to buy not one, but two Jersey milk cows with nursing calves. These John was careful to keep separate from his Hereford bull. But besides the milk, they made butter and buttermilk, which they took into town with their dresses and sold to the local restaurant.

"I told you it would work," Ellen said to John one afternoon when she'd walked out to the makeshift corral where he and the men were branding new calves.

He smiled down at her, wiping sweat from his face with the sleeve of his shirt. "You are a wonder," he murmured with pride. "We're almost finished here. Want to learn to ride?"

"Yes!" she exclaimed. But she looked down at her cotton dress with a sigh. "But not in this, I fear."

John's eyes twinkled. "Come with me."

He led her to the back of the cabin, where he pulled out a sack he'd hidden there. He offered it to her.

She opened it and looked inside. There was a man's cotton shirt, a pair of boots, and a pair of dungarees in it. She unfolded the dungarees and held them up to herself. "They'll just fit!" she exclaimed.

"I had Mr. Alton at the dry goods store measure one of your dresses for the size. He said they should fit even after shrinkage when you wash them."

"Oh, John, thank you!" she exclaimed. She stood on tiptoe and kissed him on the cheek.

He chuckled. "Get them on, then, and I'll

teach you to mount a horse. I've got a nice old one that Luis brought with him. He's gentle.''

''I won't be a minute!'' she promised, darting back into the cabin.

John was at the corral when she came back out. She'd borrowed one of John's old hats and it covered most of her face as well as her bundled-up hair. She looked like a young boy in the rig, and he chuckled.

''Do I look ridiculous?'' she worried.

''You look fine,'' he said diplomatically, his eyes twinkling. ''Come along and meet Jorge.''

He brought forward a gentle-looking old chestnut horse who lowered his head and nudged at her hand when she extended it. She stroked his forehead and smiled.

''Hello, old fellow,'' she said softly. ''We're going to be great friends, aren't we?''

John pulled the horse around by its bridle and taught Ellen how to mount like a cowboy. Then, holding the reins, he led her around the yard, scattering their new flock of chickens along the way.

''They won't lay if we frighten them,'' Ellen worried.

He looked up at her with a grin. ''How did you know that?''

''Mary taught me.''

"She and Juana are teaching you a lot of new skills," he mused. "I liked the biscuits this morning, by the way."

Her heart skipped. "How did you know that I made them?"

"Because you watched every bite I took."

"Oh, dear."

He only laughed. "I am constantly amazed by you," he confessed as they turned away from the cabin and went toward the path that led through the brush to a large oak tree. "Honestly, I never thought you'd be able to live in such deprivation. Especially after...Ellen?"

He'd heard a faint scraping sound, followed by a thud. When he turned around, Ellen was sitting up in the dirt, looking stunned.

He threw the reins over the horse's head and ran to where she was sitting, his heart in his throat. "Ellen, are you hurt?!"

She glared up at him. "Did you not notice the tree limb, John?" she asked with a meaningful glance in its direction.

"Obviously not," he murmured sheepishly. "Did you?" he added.

She burst out laughing. "Only when it hit me."

He chuckled as he reached down and lifted her up into his arms. It was the first time she'd been picked up in her adult life, and she gasped, locking her hands behind his neck so that she didn't fall.

His green eyes met her blue ones at point blank range. The laughter vanished as suddenly as it had come. He studied her pert little nose, her high cheekbones, her pretty bow of a mouth. She was looking, too, her gaze faintly possessive as she noted the hard, strong lines of his face and the faint scars she found there. His eyes were very green at the proximity, and his mouth looked hard and firm. He had high cheekbones, too, and a broad forehead. His hair was thick under the wide-brimmed hat he wore, and black. His ears were, like his nose, of imposing size. The hands supporting her were big, too, like his booted feet.

"I have never been carried since I was a child," she said in a hushed, fascinated tone.

"Well, I don't usually make a practice of carrying women, either," he confessed. His chiseled lips split in a smile. "You don't weigh much."

"I am far too busy becoming an entrepreneur to gain weight," she confessed.

"A what?"

She explained the word.

"You finished school, I reckon," he guessed.

She nodded. "I wanted to go to college, but

Father does not think a woman should be over-educated.''

''Bull,'' John said inelegantly. ''My mother educated herself and even learned Latin, which she taught me. If we have daughters, they'll go to college.''

She beamed, thinking of children. ''I should like to have children.''

He pursed his lips and lifted an eyebrow. His smile was sheer wickedness.

She laughed and buried her face in his throat, embarrassed. But he didn't draw back. His arms contracted around her and she felt his breath catch as he enveloped her soft breasts against the hard wall of his chest.

She felt unsettled. Her arms tightened around his strong neck and she shivered. She had never been held so close to a man's body. It was disconcerting. It was...delightful.

His cheek slid against hers so that he could find her soft lips with his mouth. He kissed her slowly, gently, with aching respect. When he pulled back, her lips followed. With a rough groan, he kissed her again. This time, there was less respect and more blatant hunger in the mouth that ravished hers.

She moaned softly, which brought him to his senses immediately. He drew back, his green eyes glittering with feeling. He wasn't breathing steadily anymore. Neither was she.

"We would have to climb a tree to find much privacy, and even then, the boys would probably be sitting in the branches," he said in a hunted tone.

She understood what he meant and flushed. But she laughed, too, because it was very obvious that he found her as attractive as she found him. She smiled into his eyes.

"One day, we will have a house as big as a barn, with doors that lock!" she assured him.

He chuckled softly. "Yes. But for now, we must be patient." He put her back on her feet with a long sigh. "Not that I feel patient," he added rakishly.

She laughed. "Nor I." She looked up at him demurely. "I suppose you have kissed a great many girls."

"Not so many," he replied. "And none as unique as you." His eyes were intent on her flushed face. "I made the best bargain of my life when I enticed you into marriage, Ellen Colby."

"Thank you," she said, stumbling over the words.

He pushed back a lock of disheveled dark hair that had escaped from under her hat. "It never occurred to me that a city woman, an aristocrat, would be able to survive living like this. I have felt guilty any number of times when I watched you carry water to the house, and wash clothes as the other women do. I know that you had maids to do such hard labor when you lived at home.''

"I am young and very strong," she pointed out. "Besides, I have never found a man whom I respected enough to marry, until now. I believe you will make an empire here, in these wilds. But even if I didn't believe it, I would still be proud to take your name. You are unique, also.''

His eyes narrowed. He bent again and kissed her eyelids shut, with breathless tenderness. "I will work hard to be worthy of your trust, Ellen. I will try never to disappoint you.''

She smiled. "And you will promise never to run me under oak limbs again?" she teased.

"You imp!" He laughed uproariously, hugging her to him like a big brother. "You scamp! What joy you bring to my days.''

"And you to mine," she replied, hugging him back.

"Daddy! Mr. John and Mrs. Ellen are spooning right here in the middle of the road!" one of Isaac and Mary's boys yelled.

"Scatter, you varmints, I'm kissing my wife!" John called in mock-rage.

There was amused laughter and the sound of brush rustling.

"So much for the illusion of privacy," Ellen said, pulling back from him with a wistful sigh. "Shall we get back to the business at hand? Where's my horse?"

John spied him in the brush, munching on some small green growth of grass he had found there. "He's found something nice to eat, I'll wager," he said.

"I'll fetch him," Ellen laughed, and started into the brush.

"Ellen, stop!"

John's voice, full of authority and fear, halted her with one foot in the act of rising. She stopped and stood very still. He was cursing, using words Ellen had never heard in her life. "Isaac!" he tacked onto the end, "fetch my shotgun! Hurry!"

Ellen closed her eyes. She didn't have to look down to know why he was so upset. She could hear a rustling sound, like crackling leaves, like softly frying bacon. She had never seen a rattlesnake, but during her visit to Texas with her father, she had heard plenty about them from local people. Apparently they liked to lie in wait and strike out at unsuspecting people who came near them. They could cause death with a bite, or extreme pain and sickness. Ellen was mortally afraid of snakes, in any event. But John would save her. She knew he would.

There were running feet. Crashing brush. The sound of something being thrown and caught, and then the unmistakable sound of a hammer being pulled back.

"Stand very still, darling," John told her huskily. "Don't move…a muscle!"

She swallowed, her eyes still closed. She held her breath. There was a horrifying report, like the sound of thunder and lightning striking, near her feet. Flying dirt hit her dungarees. She heard furious thrashing and opened her eyes. For the first time, she looked down. A huge rattlesnake lay dismembered nearby, still writhing in the hot sun.

"Ellen, it didn't strike you?" John asked at once, wrapping her up in the arm that wasn't supporting the shotgun. "You're all right?"

"I am, thanks to you," she whispered, almost collapsing against him. "What a scare!"

"For both of us," he said curtly. He bent and kissed the breath out of her, still shaken from the experience. "Don't ever march into the brush without looking first!"

She smiled under his lips. "You could have caught the brush on fire with that language," she murmured reproachfully. "Indeed, I think the snake was shocked to death by it!"

He laughed, and kissed her harder. She kissed him back, only belatedly aware of running feet and exclamations when the snake was spotted.

He linked his big hand into her small one. "Luis, bring the horse, if you please. I think we've had enough riding practice for one day!"

"Si, señor," Juan agreed with a chuckle.

THAT EVENING AROUND THE campfire all the talk was of the close call Ellen had with the snake.

"You're on your way to being a living legend," John told her as they roasted the victim of his shotgun over the darting orange and yellow tongues of flame. "Not to mention the provider of this delicious delicacy. Roasted rattler."

Ellen, game as ever, was soon nibbling on her own chunk of it. "It tastes surprisingly like chicken," she remarked.

John glowered at her. "It does not."

She grinned at him, and his heart soared. He grinned back.

"If you want another such treat, you will have to teach me how to shoot a gun," she proposed. "I am never walking into a rattler's mouth again, not even to provide you with supper!"

"Fair deal," he responded, while the others laughed uproariously.

IN THE DAYS THAT FOLLOWED, Ellen learned with hard work and sore muscles the rudiments of staying on a horse through the long days of watching over John's growing herd of cattle.

She also learned how not to shoot a shotgun. Her first acquaintance with the heavy double-barreled gun was a calamity. Having shouldered it too lightly, the report slammed the butt back into her shoulder and gave her a large, uncomfortable bruise. They had to wait until it healed before she could try again. The one good thing was that it made churning butter almost impossible, and she grinned as she watched Mary shoulder that chore.

"You hurt your shoulder on purpose," Mary chided with laughing dark eyes. "So you wouldn't have to push this dasher up and down in the churn."

"You can always get Isaac to teach you how to shoot, and use the same excuse," Ellen pointed out.

Mary grinned. "Not me. I am not going near a shotgun, not even to get out of such chores!"

Juana agreed wholeheartedly. "Too much bang!"

"I'll amen that," Mary agreed.

"I like it," Ellen mused. She liked even more knowing that John was afraid for her, that he

cared about her. He'd even called her "darling"
when he'd shot the snake. He wasn't a man to
use endearments normally, which made the ver-
bal slip even more pleasurable. She'd been walking around in a fog of pleasure ever since the
rattler almost bit her. She was in love. She hoped
that he was feeling something similar, but he'd
been much too busy with work to hang around
her, except at night. And then there was a very
large audience. She sighed, thinking that privacy
must be the most valuable commodity on earth.
Although she was growing every day fonder of
her companions, she often wished them a hundred miles away, so that she had even an hour
alone with her husband. But patience was golden,
she reminded herself. She must wait and hope for
that to happen. Right now, survival itself was a
struggle.

So was the shotgun. Her shoulder was well
enough for a second try a week later. Two new
complications, unbeknownst to Ellen, had just
presented themselves. There were new mud puddles in the front yard, and her father had come
to town and rented a buggy to ride out to visit
his only child.

Ellen aimed the shotgun at a tree. The resulting
kick made the barrel fly up. A wild turkey, which
had been sitting on a limb, suddenly fell to the

ground in a limp heap. And Ellen went backward right into the deepest mud puddle the saturated yard could boast.

At that particular moment, her father pulled up in front of the cabin.

Her father looked from Ellen to the turkey to the mud puddle to John. "I see that you are teaching my daughter to bathe and hunt at the same time," he remarked.

Ellen scrambled to her feet, wiping her hair back with a muddy hand. She was so disheveled, and so dirty, that it was hard for her immaculate father to find her face at all.

He grimaced. "Ellen, darling, I think it might not be a bad idea if you came home with me," he began uneasily.

She tossed her head, slinging mud onto John, who was standing next to her looking concerned. "I'm only just learning to shoot, Father," she remarked proudly. "No one is proficient at first. Isn't that so, John?"

"Uh, yes," John replied, but without his usual confidence.

Her father looked from one to the other and then to the turkey. "I suppose buying meat from the market in town is too expensive?" he asked.

"I like variety. We had rattlesnake last week, in fact," Ellen informed him. "It was delicious."

Her father shook his head. "Your grandmother is going to have heart failure if I tell her what I've seen here. And young man, this house of yours...!" He spread an expansive hand helplessly.

"The sooner we get *our* spur line," Ellen told her father, "the quicker we will have a real house instead of merely a cabin."

John nodded hopefully.

Terrance Colby sighed heavily. "I'll see what I can do," he promised.

They both smiled. "Will you stay for dinner?" Ellen invited, glancing behind her. She grinned. "We're having turkey!"

Her father declined, unwilling to share the sad surroundings that his daughter seemed to find so exciting. There were three families living in that one cabin, he noted, and he wasn't certain that he was democratic enough to appreciate such close quarters. It didn't take a mind reader to note that Ellen and John had no privacy. That might be an advantage, he mused, if Ellen decided to come home. There would be no complications. But she seemed happy as a lark, and unless he was badly mistaken, that young man John Jacobs was delighted with her company. His wife's mother was not going to be happy when he got up enough nerve to tell her what had happened to Ellen. She was just on her way home from a vacation in Italy. Perhaps the ship would be blown off course and she would not get home for several months, he mused. Otherwise, Ellen was going to have a very unhappy visitor in the near future.

He did make time to see John's growing herd of cattle, and he noticed that the young man had a fine lot of very healthy steers. He'd already seen how enterprising Ellen was with her dress-making and dairy sales. Now he saw a way to help John become quickly self-sufficient.

WORD CAME THE FOLLOWING WEEK that Ellen's father was busy buying up right of way for the spur that would run to John's ranch. Not only that, he had become a customer for John's yearling steers, which he planned to feed to the laborers who were already hard at work on another stretch of his railroad. The only difficulty was that John was going to have to drive the steers north to San Antonio for Terrance Colby. Colby would be there waiting for him in a week. That wasn't a long cattle drive, certainly not as far as Kansas, but south Texas was still untamed and dangerous country. It would be risky. But John knew it would be worth the risk if he could deliver the beef.

So John and his men left, reluctantly on John's part, to drive the steers north. He and his fellow cowhands went around to all the other ranches, gathering up their steers, making sure they appropriated only the cattle that bore their 3J brand for the drive.

"I don't want to go," John told Ellen as they stood together, briefly alone, at the corral. "But I must protect our investment. There will be six of us to drive the herd, and we are all armed and well able to handle any trouble. Isaac and the older boys are going with me, but Luis will stay here to look after the livestock and all of you."

She sighed, smoothing her arms over the sleeves of his shirt, enjoying the feel of the smooth muscles under it. "I do not like the idea of you going away. But I know that it is necessary, so I'll be brave."

"I don't like leaving you, either," he said bluntly. He bent and kissed her hungrily. "When I return, perhaps we can afford a single night away from here," he whispered roughly. "I am going mad to have you in my arms without a potential audience!"

"As I am," she choked, kissing him back hungrily.

He lifted her clear of the ground in his embrace, flying as they kissed without restraint. Finally, he forced himself to put her back down and he stepped away. There was a ruddy flush on his high cheekbones, and his green eyes were fierce. Her face was equally flushed, but her eyes were soft and dreamy, and her mouth was swollen.

She smiled up at him bravely, despite her concern. "Don't get shot."

He grimaced. "I'll do my best. You stay within sight of the cabin and Luis, even when you're milking those infernal cows. And don't go to town without him."

She didn't mention that it would be suicide to take Luis away from guarding the cattle, even for that long. She and the women would have to work something out, so that they could sell their dresses and butter and milk in town. But she would spare him the worry.

"We'll be very careful," she promised.

He sighed, his hand resting on the worn butt of his .45 caliber pistol. "We'll be back as soon as humanly possible. Your father…"

"If he comes to town, I'll go there to wait for you," she promised, a lie, because she'd never leave Mary and Juana by themselves, even with Luis and a shotgun around.

"Possibly that's what you should do, anyway," he murmured thoughtfully.

"I can't leave here now," she replied. "There's too much at stake. I'll help take care of our ranch. You take care of our profit margin."

He chuckled, surprised out of his worries. "I'll be back before you miss me too much," he said, bending to kiss her again, briefly. "Stay close to the cabin."

"I will. Have a safe trip."

He swung into the saddle, shouting for Isaac and the boys. The women watched them ride away. The cattle had already been pooled in a nearby valley, and the drovers were ready to get underway. As Ellen watched her tall husband ride away, she realized why he'd wanted his railroad spur so badly. Not only was it dangerous to drive cattle a long way to a railhead, but the potential risk to the men and animals was great. Not only was there a constant threat from thieves, there were floods and thunderstorms that could decimate herds. She prayed that John and Isaac and the men going with them would be safe. It was just as well that Luis was staying at the ranch to help safeguard the breeding bulls and cows, and the calves that were too young for market. Not that she was going to shirk her own responsibilities, Ellen thought stubbornly.

Nobody was stealing anything around here while she could get her hands on a gun!

THE THREAT CAME UNEXPECTEDLY just two days after John and the others had left south Texas for San Antonio on the cattle drive.

Ellen had just carried a bucketful of milk to the kitchen when she peered out the open, glassless window at two figures on horseback, watching the cabin. She called softly to Juana and Mary.

Juana crossed herself. "It is Comanches!" she exclaimed. "They come to raid the cattle!"

"Well, they're not raiding them today," Ellen said angrily. "I'll have to ride out and get Luis and the boys," she said. "There's nothing else for it, and I'll have to go bareback. I'll never have time to saddle a horse with them sitting out there."

"It is too dangerous," Juana exclaimed. "You can hardly ride a saddled horse, and those men are Comanches. They are the finest riders of any men, even my Luis. You will never outrun them!"

Ellen muttered under her breath. They had so few cattle that even the loss of one or two could mean the difference between bankruptcy and survival. Well, she decided, there was only one thing to do. She grabbed up the shotgun, loaded it, and started out the back door, still in her dress and apron.

"No!" Mary almost screamed. "Are you crazy? Do you know what they do to white women?!"

Ellen didn't say a word. She kept walking, her steps firm and sure.

She heard frantic calls behind her, but she didn't listen. She and John had a ranch. These were her cattle as much as his. She wasn't about to let any thieves come and carry off her precious livestock!

The two Comanches saw her coming and gaped. They didn't speak. They sat on their horses with their eyes fixed, wide, at the young woman lugging a shotgun toward them.

One of them said something to the other one, who laughed and nodded.

She stopped right in front of them, lifted the shotgun, sighted along it and cocked it.

"This is my ranch," she said in a firm, stubborn tone. "You aren't stealing my cattle!"

There was pure admiration in their eyes. They didn't reach for the rifles lying across their buckskinned laps. They didn't try to ride her down. They simply watched her.

The younger of the two Indians had long pigtails and a lean, handsome face. His eyes, she noted curiously, were light.

"We have not come to steal cattle," the young one said in passable English. "We have come to ask Big John for work."

"Work?" she stammered.

He nodded. "We felt guilty that we butchered one of his calves. We had come far and were very hungry. We will work to pay for the calf. We hear from the Mexican people that he is also fair," he added surprisingly. "We know that he looks only at a man's work. He does not consider himself better than men of other colors. This is very strange. We do not understand it. Your people have just fought a terrible war because you wanted to own other people who had dark skin. Yet Big John lives with these people. Even with the Mexicans. He treats them as family."

"Yes," she said. She slowly uncocked the shotgun and lowered it to her side. "That is true."

The younger one smiled at her. "We know more about horses than even his vaquero, who knows much," he said without conceit. "We will work hard. When we pay back the cost of the calf, he can pay us what he thinks is fair."

She chuckled. "It's not really a big cabin, and it has three families living in it," she began.

They laughed. "We can make a teepee," the older one said, his English only a little less accented than the younger one's.

"I say," she exclaimed, "can you teach me to shoot a bow?!"

The younger one threw back his head and laughed uproariously. "Even his woman is brave," he told the older one. "Now do you believe me? This man is not as others with white skin."

"I believe you."

"Come along, then," Ellen said, turning. "I'll introduce you to…Luis! Put that gun down!" she exclaimed angrily when she saw the smaller man coming toward them with two pistols leveled. "These are our two new horse wranglers," she began. She stopped. "What are your names?" she asked.

"I am called Thunder," the young one said. "He is Red Wing."

"I am Ellen Jacobs," she said, "and that is Luis. Say hello, Luis."

The Mexican lowered his pistols and reholstered them with a blank stare at Ellen.

"Say hello," she repeated.

"Hello," he obliged, and he nodded.

The Comanches nodded back. They rode up to

the cabin and dismounted. The women in the cabin peered out nervously.

"Luis will show you where to put your horses," Ellen told them. "We have a lean-to. Someday, we will have a barn!"

"Need bigger teepee first," Red Wing murmured, eyeing the cabin. "Bad place to live. Can't move house when floor get dirty."

"Yes, well, it's warm," Ellen said helplessly.

The young Comanche, Thunder, turned to look at her. "You are brave," he said with narrow light eyes. "Like my woman."

"She doesn't live with you?" she asked hesitantly.

He smiled gently. "She is stubborn, and wants to live in a cabin far away," he replied. "But I will bring her back here one day." He nodded and followed after Luis with his friend.

Juana and Mary came out of the cabin with worried expressions. "You going to let Indians live with us?" Juana exclaimed. "They kill us all!"

"No, they won't," Ellen assured them. "You'll see. They're going to be an asset!"

CHAPTER FIVE

THE COMANCHES DID KNOW more about horses than even Luis did, and they were handy around the place. They hunted game, taught Luis how to tan hides, and set about building a teepee out behind the cabin.

"Very nice," Ellen remarked when it was finished. "It's much roomier than the cabin."

"Easy to keep clean," Red Wing agreed. "Floor get dirty, move teepee."

She laughed. He smiled, going off to help Thunder with a new corral Juan was building.

JOHN RODE BACK IN WITH ISAAC and stopped short at the sight of a towering teepee next to the cabin he'd left two weeks earlier.

His hand went to his pistol as he thought of terrible possibilities that would explain its presence.

But Ellen came running out of the cabin, followed by Mary and Juana, laughing and waving.

John kicked his foot out of the stirrup of his

new saddle and held his arm down to welcome Ellen as she leaped up into his arms. He kissed her hungrily, feeling as if he'd come home for the first time in his life.

He didn't realize how long that kiss lasted until he felt eyes all around him. He lifted his head to find two tall Comanches standing shoulder to shoulder with Juan and the younger boys and girls of the group, along with Juana and Mary.

"Bad habit," Thunder remarked disapprovingly.

"Bound to upset horse," Red Wing agreed, nodding.

"What the hell…!" John exclaimed.

"They're our new horse wranglers," Ellen said quickly. "That's Thunder, and that's Red Wing."

"They taught us how to make parfleche bags," Juana's eldest daughter exclaimed, showing one with beautiful beadwork.

"And how to make bows and arrows!" the next youngest of Isaac's sons seconded, showing his.

"And quivers," Luis said, resigned to being fired for what John would surely consider bad judgment in letting two Comanches near the women. He stood with his sombrero against his chest. "You may fire me if you wish."

"If you fire me, I'm going with them," Isaac's second son replied, pointing toward the Indians.

John shook his head, laughing uproariously. "I expect there'll be a lynch mob out here any day now," he sighed.

Everybody grinned.

Ellen beamed up at him. "Well, they certainly do know how to train horses, John," she said.

"Your woman meet us with loaded shotgun," Red Wing informed him. "She has strong spirit."

"And great heart," Thunder added. "She says we can work for you. We stay?"

John sighed. "By all means. All we need now is an Eskimo," he murmured to Ellen under his breath.

She looped her arms around his neck and kissed him. "Babies would be nice," she whispered.

He went scarlet, and everyone laughed.

"I GOT ENOUGH FOR THE STEERS to buy a new bull," John told her. "Saddles for the horses we have, and four new horses," he added. "They're coming in with the rest of the drovers. I rode ahead to make sure you were all right."

She cuddled close to him as they stood out behind the cabin in a rare moment alone. "We had no trouble at all. Well, except for the Comanches, but they turned out to be friends anyway.''

''You could have blown me over when I saw that teepee,'' he confessed. ''We've had some hard battles with Comanches in the past, over stolen livestock. And I know for a fact that two Comanches ate one of my calves…''

''They explained that,'' she told him contentedly. ''They were hungry, but they didn't want to steal. They came here to work out the cost of the calf, and then to stay on, if you'll keep them. I think they decided that it's better to join a strong foe than oppose him. That was the reason they gave me, at least.''

''Well, I must admit, these two Comanches are unusual.''

''The younger one has light eyes.''

''I noticed.'' He didn't add what he was certain of—that these two Comanches were the fugitives that the deputy marshal in Sutherland Springs had been looking for. Fortunately for them, James Graham had headed up beyond San Antonio to pursue them, acting on what now seemed to be a very bad tip.

She lifted her head and looked up at him. ''They rode up and just sat there. I loaded my shotgun and went out to see what they wanted.''

"You could have been killed," he pointed out.

"It's what you would have done, in my place," she reminded him, smiling gently. "I'm not afraid of much. And I've learned from you that appearances can be deceptive."

"You take chances."

"So do you."

He sighed. "You're learning bad habits from me."

She smiled and snuggled close. "Red Wing is going to make us a teepee of our own very soon." She kissed him, and was kissed back hungrily.

"Yesterday not be soon enough for that teepee," came a droll accented voice from nearby.

Red Wing was on the receiving end of two pairs of glaring eyes. He shrugged and walked off noiselessly, chuckling to himself.

John laughed. "Amen," he murmured.

"John, there's just one other little thing," Ellen murmured as she stood close to him.

"What now? You hired a gunslinger to feed the chickens?"

"I don't know any gunslingers. Be serious."

"All right. What?"

"My grandmother sent me a telegram. She's coming out here to save me from a life of misery and poverty."

He lifted his head. "Really!"

She drew in a soft breath. "I suppose she'll faint dead away when she sees this place, but I'm not going to be dragged back East by her or an army. I belong here."

"Yes, you do," John replied. "Although you certainly deserve better than this, Ellen," he said softly. He touched her disheveled hair. "I promise you, it's only going to get better."

She smiled. "I know that. We're going to have an empire, all our own."

"You bet we are."

"Built with our own two hands," she murmured, reaching up to kiss him, "and the help of our friends. All we need is each other."

"Need teepee worse," came Red Wing's voice again.

"Listen here," John began.

"Your horse got colic," the elder of the Comanches stood his ground. "What you feed him?"

"He ate corn," John said belligerently. "I gave him a feed bucket full!"

The older man scoffed. "No wonder he got colic. I fix."

"Corn is good for horses, and I know what to do for colic!"

"Sure. Not feed horse corn. Feed him grass. We build teepee tomorrow."

John still had his mouth open when the older man stalked off again.

"Indian ponies only eat grass," Ellen informed him brightly. "They think grain is bad for horses."

"You've learned a lot," he remarked.

"More than you might realize," she said dryly. She reached up to John's ear. "These two Comanches are running from the army. But I don't think they did anything bad, and I told Mr. Alton that I saw two Comanches heading north at a dead run. He told the…"

"…deputy marshal," he finished for her, exasperated.

"When you get to know them, you'll think they're good people, too," she assured him. "Besides, they're teaching me things I can't learn anywhere else. I can track a deer," she counted off her new skills, "weave a mat, make a bed out of pine straw, do beadwork, shoot a bow and arrow, and tan a hide."

"Good Lord, woman!" he exclaimed, impressed.

She grinned. "And I'm going to learn to hunt just as soon as you take me out with my shotgun."

He sighed. This was going to become difficult if any of her people stopped by to check on her. He didn't want to alienate them, but this couldn't continue.

"Ellen, what do you think about schooling?" he asked gently.

She blinked. "Excuse me?"

"Well, do any of the children know how to read and write?"

She hadn't considered that. "I haven't asked, but I don't expect they can. It was not legal for slaves to be taught such things, and I know that Juana can't even read Spanish, although it is her native tongue."

"The world we build will need educated people," he said thoughtfully. "It must start with the children, with this new generation. Don't you agree?"

"Yes," she said, warming quickly to the idea. "Educated people will no longer have to work at menial jobs, where they are at the mercy of others."

"That is exactly what I think. So, why don't you start giving the children a little book learning, in the evenings, after supper?" he suggested.

She smiled brightly. "You know, that's a very good idea. But, I have no experience as a teacher."

"All you will need are some elementary books and determination," he said. "I believe there is a retired schoolteacher in Victoria, living near the blacksmith. Shall I take you to see him?"

She beamed. "Would you?"

"Indeed I would. We'll go up there tomorrow," he replied, watching her consider the idea. If nothing else, it would spare her the astonished surprise of her people if they ever came to visit and found Ellen in dungarees and muddy boots skinning out a deer.

He drove her to Victoria the next morning in the small, dilapidated buggy he'd managed to afford from his cattle sales, hitched to one of the good horses he'd also acquired. Fortunately it took to pulling a buggy right away. Some horses didn't, and people died in accidents when they panicked and ran away.

The schoolteacher was long retired, but he taught Ellen the fundamentals she would need to educate small children. He also had a basic reader, a grammar book and a spelling book, which he gave to Ellen with his blessing. She clutched them like priceless treasure all the way back down the dusty road to the 3J Ranch.

"Do you think the Brown and the Rodriguez families will let me teach the children?" she wondered, a little worried after the fact. "They might not believe in education."

"Luis and Isaac can't even sign a paper," he told her. "They have to make an 'x' on a piece of paper and have me witness it. If they ever leave the ranch, they need to know how to read and write so that nobody will take advantage of them."

She looked at him with even more admiration than usual. He was very handsome to her, very capable and strong. She counted her blessings every single day that he'd thought her marriageable.

"You really care for them, don't you?" she asked softly.

"When the Union Army came through Atlanta, they burned everything in sight," he recalled, his face hardening. "Not just the big plantations where slaves were kept. They burned poor white people's houses, because they thought we all had slaves down south." He laughed coldly. "Sharecroppers don't own anything. Even the house we lived in belonged to the plantation owner. They set it ablaze and my sister and mother were trapped inside. They burned to death while my other sister and I stood outside and watched." He touched his lean cheek, where the old scars were still noticeable. "I tried to kill the cavalry officer responsible, but his men saved him. They gave me these,'' he touched his cheek. ''I never kept slaves. I hid Isaac and Mary in the root cellar when they ran away from the overseer. I couldn't save their oldest son, but Mary was pregnant. She and Isaac saved me from the Union Army,'' he said with a sigh. ''They pleaded for my life. Shocked the cavalry into sparing me and my oldest sister. Isaac helped me bury my mother and my younger sister.'' He looked down at her soft, compassionate expression. ''My sister went to North Carolina to live with a cousin, but I wanted to go to my uncle in Texas. Isaac and Mary had no place else to go, so they traveled with me. They said they wanted to start over, but they didn't fool me. They came with me to save me from the Union Army if I got in trouble. Those two never forget a debt. I owe them everything. My life. That's why they're partners with me.''

''And how did you meet Luis and Juana?'' she asked.

''Luis was the only cowboy my uncle had who wasn't robbing him blind. Luis told me what the others had done, and I fired the lot. I took care of my uncle, with their help, and rounded up stray calves to start my herd.'' He chuckled. ''The cabin was the only structure on the place.

It got real crowded when Isaac and Mary moved in with me. Juana and Luis were going to live in the brush, but I insisted that we could all manage. We have. But it hasn't been easy.''

"And now the Comanches are building tee-pees for us," she told him. "They've been hunting constantly to get enough skins. We're going to have privacy for the very first time. I mean..." She flushed at her own forwardness.

He reached for her small hand and held it tight. His eyes burned into hers. "I want nothing more in the world than to be alone with you, Camellia Ellen Jacobs," he said huskily. "The finest thing I ever did in my life was have the good sense to marry you!"

"Do you really think so?" she asked happily. "I am no beauty..."

"You have a heart as big as all outdoors and the courage of a wolf. I wouldn't trade you for a debutante."

She beamed, leaning against his broad shoulder. "And I would not trade you for the grandest gentleman who ever lived. Although I expect you will make a fine gentleman, when we have made our fortune."

He kissed her forehead tenderly. "You are my fortune," he said huskily.

"You mean, because my father is giving us a

railroad spur for a wedding present,'' she said, confused.

He shook his head. ''Because you are my most prized treasure,'' he whispered, and bent to kiss her mouth tenderly.

She kissed him back, shyly. ''I had never kissed anyone until you came along,'' she whispered.

He chuckled. ''You improve with practice!''

''John!'' she chided.

He only laughed, letting her go to pay attention to the road. ''We must get on down the road. It looks like rain.'' He gave her a roguish glance. ''We would not want you to tumble into a mud puddle, Mrs. Jacobs.''

''Are you ever going to forget that?'' she moaned.

''In twenty years or so, perhaps,'' he said. ''But I cannot promise. That is one of my most delightful memories. You were so game, and Sir Sydney was such a boor!''

''Indeed he was. I hope he marries for money and discovers that she has none.''

''Evil girl,'' he teased.

She laughed. ''Well, you will never be able to accuse ME of marrying you for your money,'' she said contentedly. ''In twenty years or so,'' she added, repeating his own phrase, ''you will be exceedingly rich. I just know it.''

''I hope to break even, at least, and be able to pay my debts,'' he said. ''But I would love to have a ranch as big as a state, Ellen, and the money to breed fine cattle, and even fine horses.'' He glanced at her. ''Now that we have two extra horse wranglers, we can start building up our herd.''

She only smiled. She was glad that she'd stood up to the Comanches. She wondered if they'd ever have wanted to work for them if she'd run away and hid.

THE TEEPEE THE COMANCHES built for the couple was remarkably warm and clean. No sooner was it up than Ellen built a small cooking fire near its center and put on a black iron pot of stew to cook. Red Wing had already taught her how to turn the pole in the center to work the flap for letting smoke out while she cooked. She also learned that she was born to be a rancher's wife. Every chore came easily to her. She wasn't afraid of hard work, and she fell more in love with her roguish, unconventional husband every day. She did still worry about her grandmother coming down to rescue her. She had no intention of being carted off back East, where she would have to dress and act with decorum.

She sat the children down in the cabin one evening after she and the other women and older girls had cleared away the precious iron cookware and swished the tin plates and few utensils in a basin of soapy water and wiped them with a dishrag.

"What are we going to do?" one of Juana's daughters asked.

Ellen produced the books that the retired Victoria schoolteacher had given her, handling them like treasure.

"I'm going to teach you children to read and write," she told them.

Mary and Juana stood quietly by, so still that Ellen was made uneasy.

"Is it all right?" she asked the adults, concerned, because she'd worried that they might think education superfluous.

"Nobody ever taught me to write my name," Mary said. "Nor Isaac, either. We can only make an x. Could you teach me to write? And read?"

"Me, too!" Juana exclaimed.

Their husbands looked as if they might bite their tongues off trying not to ask if they could learn, too, but they managed.

"You can all gather around and we'll let the

older folk help show the young ones how to do it,'' she said, managing a way to spare the pride of the men in the process of teaching them as well.

''Yes, we can show them, *señora*,'' Luis said brightly.

''Sure we can,'' Isaac added with a big grin.

''Gather around, then.'' She opened the book with a huge smile and began the first lesson.

SHE LOOKED DOWN AT THE dungarees she was wearing with boots that John had bought her. She had on one of his big checked long-sleeved shirts, with the sleeves rolled up, and her hair was caught in a ponytail down her back. She checked the stew in her black cooking pot and wiped sweat from her brow with a weary hand. The Comanches had gathered pine straw from under the short-leafed pines in the thicket to make beds, which Ellen covered with quilts she and the other women had made in their precious free time. It wasn't a mansion, but she and John would have privacy for the first time that night. She thought of the prospect with joy and a certain amount of trepidation. Like most young women of her generation, her upbringing had been very strict and moral. She knew almost nothing of what happened between married people in the dark. What she didn't know made her nervous.

The sudden noise outside penetrated her thoughts. She heard voices, one raised and strident, and she ran out of the teepee and to the cabin to discover a well-dressed, elderly woman with two young men in immaculate suits exchanging heated words with Juana, who couldn't follow a thing they were saying. Mary was out with the others collecting more wood for the fireplace in the small cabin.

"Do you understand me?" the old woman was shouting. "I am looking for Ellen Colby!"

"Grandmother!" Ellen exclaimed when she recognized the woman.

Her grandmother Amelia Greene was standing beside the buggy beside two tall young men whom Ellen recognized as her cousins.

Amelia turned stiffly, her whole expression one of utter disapproval when she saw the way her granddaughter was dressed.

"Camellia Ellen Colby!" she exclaimed. "What has become of you!"

"Now, Grandmother," Ellen said gently, "you can't expect a pioneer wife to dress and act as a lady in a drawing room."

The older woman was not convinced. She was bristling with indignation. "You will get your things together and come home with me right away!'' she demanded. ''I am not leaving you here in the dirt with these peasants!''

Ellen's demeanor changed at once from one of welcome and uneasiness to one of pure outrage. She stuck both hands on her slender hips and glared at her grandmother.

''How dare you call my friends peasants!'' she exclaimed furiously. She went to stand beside Juana. ''Juana's husband Luis, and Mary's husband Isaac, are our partners in this ranching enterprise. They are no one's servants!''

Mary came to stand beside her as well, and the children gathered around them. While the old woman and her companions were getting over that shock, John came striding up, with his gunbelt on, accompanied by Luis and Isaac and the two Comanche men.

Amelia Greene screeched loudly and jumped behind the tallest of her grandchildren.

''How much you want for old woman?'' Red Wing asked deliberately, pointing at Amelia.

Amelia looked near to fainting.

Ellen laughed helplessly. ''He's not serious,'' she assured her grandmother.

''I should hope not!'' the tallest of her cousins muttered, glaring at him. ''The very idea! Why do you allow Indians here?''

"These are our horse wranglers," Ellen said pointedly. "Red Wing and Thunder. And those are our partners, Luis Rodriguez and Isaac Brown. Gentlemen, my grandmother, Amelia Greene of New York City."

Nobody spoke.

John came forward to slide his arm around Ellen's waist. He was furious at the way her relatives were treating the people nearby.

"Hospitality is almost a religion to us out here in Texas," John drawled, although his green eyes were flashing like green diamonds. "But as you may notice, we have no facilities to accommodate visitors yet."

"You cannot expect that we would want to stay?" the shorter cousin asked indignantly. "Come, Grandmother, let us go back to town. Ellen is lost to us. Surely you can see that?"

Ellen glared at him. "Five years from now, cousin, you will not recognize this place. A lot of hard work is going to turn it into a show-place...."

"Of mongrels!" her grandmother said haughtily.

"I'm sorry you feel that way, but I find your company equally taxing," Ellen shot back. "Now will you all please leave? I have chores, as do the others. Unlike you, I do not sit in the parlor waiting for other people to fetch and carry at my instructions.''

The old woman glowered. ''Very well, then, live out here in the wilds with savages! I only came to try and save you from a life of drudgery!''

''Pickles and bread,'' Ellen retorted haughtily. ''You came hoping to entice me back into household slavery. Until I escaped you and came west with my father, I was your unpaid maidservant for most of my life.''

''What else are you fit for?'' her grandmother demanded. ''You have no looks, no talent, no…!''

''She is lovely,'' John interrupted. ''Gentle and kind and brave. She is no one's servant here, and she has freedom of a sort you will never know.''

The old woman's eyes were poisonously intent. ''She will die of hard work here, for certain!''

''On her own land, making her own empire,'' John replied tersely. ''The road is that way,'' he added, pointing.

She tossed her head and sashayed back to the buggy, to be helped in by her grandsons, one of whom gave Ellen a wicked grin before he climbed in and took the reins.

"Drive on," Amelia said curtly. "We have no kinfolk here!"

"Truer words were never spoken," Ellen said sweetly. "Do have a safe trip back to town. Except for cattle thieves from Mexico and the bordering counties of Texas, and bank robbers, there should be nothing dangerous in your path. But I would drive very fast, if I were you!"

There were muttered, excited exchanges of conversation in the buggy before the tallest grandson used the buggy whip and the small vehicle raced forward down the dusty dirt road in the general direction of town.

"You wicked girl!" John exclaimed on a burst of laughter, hugging her close.

"So much for my rescuers," she murmured contentedly, hugging him back. "Now we can get back to work!"

THAT NIGHT, ELLEN AND JOHN spent their first night alone, without prying eyes or ears, in the teepee the Comanches had provided for them.

"I am a little nervous," she confessed when John had put out the small fire and they were together in the darkness.

"That will not last," he promised, drawing her close. "We are both young, and we have all the years ahead to become more accustomed to each other. All you must remember is that I care more for you than for any woman I have ever known. You are my most prized treasure. I love you. I will spend my life trying to make you happy.''

"John!" She pressed close to him and raised her face. "I will do the same. I adore you!"

He bent and kissed her softly, and then not so softly. Tender caresses gave way to stormy, devouring kisses. They sank to the makeshift mattress and there, locked tight in each others' arms, they gave way to the smoldering passion that had grown between them for long weeks. At first she was inhibited, but he was skillful and slow and tender. Very soon, her passion rose to meet his. The sharpness of passion was new between them, and as it grew, they became playful together. They laughed, and then the laughing stopped as they tasted the first sweet sting of mutual delight in the soft, enveloping darkness.

When Ellen finally fell asleep in John's arms, she thought that there had never been a happier bride in the history of Texas.

CHAPTER SIX

ELLEN'S GRANDMOTHER AND cousins went back East. Her father came regularly to visit them in their teepee, finding it touching and amusing at once that they were happy with so little. He even offered to loan them enough to build a bigger cabin, but they refused politely. All they wanted, Ellen reminded him, was a spur of the railroad.

That, too, was finally finished. John loaded his beef cattle into the cattle cars bound for the stockyards of the Midwest. The residents of the ranch settled into hard work and camaraderie, and all their efforts eventually resulted in increasing prosperity.

The first thing they did with their newfound funds was to add to the cattle herd. The second was to build individual cabins for the Rodriguez and Brown clans, replacing the teepees the Comanches had built for them. The Comanches, offered a handsome log cabin of their own, declined abruptly, although politely. They could never understand the white man's interest in a stationary house that had to be cleaned constantly, when it was so much easier to move the teepee to a clean spot! However, John and Ellen continued to live in their own teepee for the time being, as well, to save money.

A barn was the next project. As in all young communities, a barbecue and a quilting bee were arranged along with a barnraising. All the strong young men of the area turned out and the resulting barn and corral were quick fruit of their efforts. Other ranches were springing up around the 3J Ranch, although not as large and certainly not with the number of cattle and horses that John's now boasted.

The railroad spur, when it came, brought instant prosperity to the area it served. It grew and prospered even as some smaller towns in the area became ghost towns. Local citizens decided that they needed a name for their small town, which had actually grown up around the ranch itself even before the railroad came. They decided to call it Jacobsville, for John Jacobs, despite his protests. His hard work and lack of prejudice had made him good friends and dangerous enemies in the surrounding area. But when cattle were rustled and houses robbed, his was never among them. Bandits from over the border made a wide route around the ranch.

As the cattle herd grew and its refinement continued, the demand for Jacobs's beef grew as well. John bought other properties to go along with his own, along with barbed wire to fence in his ranges. He hired on new men as well, black drovers as well as Mexican and white. There was even a Chinese drover who had heard of the Jacobs ranch far away in Arizona and had come to it looking for a job. Each new addition to the ranch workforce was placed under the orders of either Luis or Isaac, and the number of outbuildings and line camps grew steadily.

Ellen worked right alongside the other women, adding new women to her dressmaking enterprise, until she had enough workers and enough stock to open a dress shop in their new town of Jacobsville. Mary and Juana took turns as proprietors while Ellen confined herself to sewing chair and sofa covers for the furniture in the new white clapboard house John had built her. She and her handsome husband grew closer by the day, but one thing was still missing from her happiness. Their marriage was entering into its second year with no hope of a child.

John never spoke of it, but Ellen knew he wanted children. So did she. It was a curious thing that their passion for each other was ever growing, but bore no fruit. Still, they had a good

marriage and Ellen was happier than she ever
dreamed of being.

In the second year of their marriage, his sister
Jeanette came west on the train with her husband
and four children to visit. Only then did Ellen
learn the extent of the tragedy that had sent John
west in the first place. The attack by the Union
troops had mistakenly been aimed at the sharecroppers' cabin John and his mother and sisters
occupied, instead of the house where the owner's
vicious overseer lived. The house had caught fire
and John's mother and elder sister had burned to
death. John had not been able to save them. The
attack had been meant for the overseer who had
beaten Isaac and Mary's son to death, along with
many other slaves. John was told, afterward, but
his grief was so sweeping that he hardly understood what was said to him. His sister made sure
that he did know. The cavalry officer had apologized to her, and given her money for the trip
to North Carolina, unbeknownst to John. His sister obviously adored him, and he was a doting
uncle to her children.

She understood John's dark moods better after
that, the times when he wanted to be alone, when
he went hunting and never brought any wild
game home with him. Ellen and Jeanette became
close almost at once, and wrote to each other

regularly even when Jeanette and her family went home to North Carolina.

Deputy Marshal James Graham had come by unexpectedly and mentioned to John that he hadn't been able to find the two Comanche fugitives who were supposed to have shot a white man over a horse. It turned out that the white man had cheated the Comanches and had later been accused of cheating several army officers in horse trading deals. He was arrested, tried and sent to prison. So, Graham told John, the Comanches weren't in trouble anymore. Just in case John ever came across them.

Thunder and Red Wing, told of the white man's arrest, worked a few months longer for John and then headed north with their wages. Ellen was sad to see them go, but Thunder had promised that they would meet again one day.

The Maxwells came to visit often from Scotland, staying in the beautiful white Victorian house John later built for his beloved wife. They gave the couple the benefit of their extensive experience of horses, and John branched out into raising thoroughbreds. Eventually a thoroughbred of the lineage from his ranch would win the Triple Crown.

YEARS PASSED WITH EACH YEAR bringing new

prosperity to the 3J Ranch. One May morning, Ellen unexpectedly fainted at a church social. John carried her to the office of their new doctor, who had moved in just down the boardwalk from the new restaurant and hotel.

The doctor examined her and, when John had been invited into the examination room, grinned at him. "You are to be a father, young man," he said. "Congratulations!"

John looked at Ellen as if she'd just solved the great mystery of life. He lifted her clear of the floor and kissed her with aching tenderness. His happiness was complete, now.

Almost immediately, he began to worry about labor. He remembered when Luis's and Isaac's wives had given birth, and he turned pale.

The doctor patted him on the back. "You'll survive the birth of your children, Mr. Jacobs, we all do. Yes, even me. I have had to deliver mine. Something, I daresay, you will be spared!"

John laughed with relief, thanked the doctor for his perception, and kissed Ellen again.

She bore him three sons and two daughters in the years that followed, although only two of their children, their son Bass and their daughter Rose Ellen, lived to adulthood. The family grew and prospered in Jacobsville. Later, the entire county, Jacobs, was named for John as well. He diversified his holdings into mining and real estate and banking. He was the first in south Texas to try new techniques in cattle ranching and to use mechanization to improve his land.

The Brown family produced six children in all. Their youngest, Caleb, would move to Chicago and become a famous trial lawyer. His son would be elected to the United States Senate.

The Rodriguez family produced ten children. One of their sons became a Texas Ranger, beginning a family tradition that lived on through subsequent generations.

John Jacobs founded the first bank in Jacobs County, along with the first dry goods store. He worked hard at breeding good cattle, but he made his fortune in the terrible blizzard of 1885-86 in which so many cattlemen lost their shirts. He endowed a college and an orphanage, and, always active in local politics, he was elected to the U.S. Senate at the age of fifty. He and Ellen never parted for fifty years.

His son, Bass Jacobs, married twice. By his young second wife, he had a son, Bass, Jr., and a daughter, Violet Ellen. Bass Jacobs, Jr., was the last of the Jacobs family to own land in Jacobs County. The 3J Ranch was sold after his death. His son, Ty, born in 1955, eventually moved to Arizona and married and settled there. His daughter, Shelby, born in 1961, stayed in Jacobsville and married a local man, Justin Ballenger. They produced three sons. One of them was named John Jackson Jacobs Ballenger, so that the founding father of Shelby's family name would live on in memory.

A bronze statue of Big John Jacobs, mounted on one of the Arabian stallions his ranch became famous for, was erected in the town square of Jacobsville just after the first world war.

Portraits of the Rodriguez family and the Brown family are prominently displayed in the Jacobs County Museum, alongside a portrait of Camellia Ellen Jacobs, dressed in an elegant blue gown, but with a shotgun in a fringed sheath at her feet and a twinkle in her blue eyes. All three portraits, which had belonged to Bass Jacobs, Jr., were donated to the museum by Shelby Jacobs Ballenger. In a glass case nearby are a bow and arrow in a beaded rawhide quiver, in which also resides a black-and-white photograph of a Comanche warrior with a blond woman and five children, two of whom are also blond. But that is another story…

Dear Reader,

Growing up in rural Virginia, my family was among the first in our community to have a television set. It was a black-and-white Philco—complete with rabbit ears. My dad watched boxing and Mother adored Perry Mason, but the Westerns that dominated the airwaves belonged to me.

What young girl wouldn't lose her heart to the rugged Rowdy Yates, played by Clint Eastwood? Or the brooding Josh Randall that Steve McQueen portrayed in *Wanted: Dead or Alive*? And what about those dashing Maverick brothers?

When I wrote "Wild West Wager" I tried to include many of these same qualities in Jack Delaney, Marlow, Colorado's only saloon owner with a conscience, a man who's presented with a moral dilemma that leaves him speechless. And who puts him in this position but Rebecca Merriweather, the refined beauty from the East? She intends to make Jack live up to their bargain—regardless.

But the troubles in the little town of Marlow don't end with Jack and Rebecca. I hope you'll watch for *Maggie and the Law*, a March 2004 Harlequin Historical release, to find out what becomes of the lonely mountain man Seth Grissom and Lucy Hubbard, a woman who must choose between her marriage vows and the man she loves.

Happy reading!

Judith Stacy

WILD WEST WAGER

Judith Stacy

To David—after thirty years you're still the one.

To Judy and Stacy—you always make me proud.

CHAPTER ONE

Colorado, 1888

SO MANY WOMEN. Which one to pick?

Jack Delaney leaned his elbow atop the batwing doors of the Lucky Streak Saloon and gazed outside at the skirts swishing down Main Street. Midafternoon and the women of Marlow were going about their business, doing whatever it was women did all day.

Jack sighed. Lots of women.

But he needed only one—didn't *want* one, just needed one.

Glancing back over his shoulder he saw Roy Hanover, his bartender, and a couple of cowboys standing at the bar. Not a lot of customers, especially for a warm afternoon.

Jack grumbled under his breath and once more turned his attention outside. For a moment, a vision of New York—his home—swam before his eyes. He'd left there and come west several years ago. Jack's gut twisted into a quick knot at the memory of his decision to leave home—and what he'd left behind.

After rambling around for several years, he'd had a lucky run at a poker table, and two months ago, he'd bought the Lucky Streak Saloon. Jack thought his luck had changed.

He'd been wrong about that, too.

"Something going on?" Roy appeared at Jack's side and rose on his toes to see over the door. Jack had no such trouble. At over six feet tall, he towered over most everything and everybody.

"Looking." Jack pushed his fingers through his black hair, forcing aside the old memories. "Looking for a woman."

Roy's thick mustache bobbed and Jack guessed a grin lurked beneath it. "The girls down at Miss Dora's parlor house can take care of you."

Jack rubbed his chin. He needed a woman, all right. But not just any woman. One with particular…skills.

"I was thinking more along the lines of Rebecca Merriweather," he said.

"Miss Merriweather?" Roy's eyes narrowed. "Are you sure you know who Miss Merriweather is?"

At the mention of her name, Jack's gut tightened again, but for a different reason. He knew exactly who she was. He'd seen her around town. How could he miss her? Dark hair, brown eyes, always dressed in the fashionable gowns of a fine Eastern lady rather than the simple gingham and calico most of the local women wore.

Roy shook his head. "Miss Merriweather is a respectable woman. Hell, they don't come more respectable than her."

That was true. The first time Jack had spotted her on the street he'd seen her stiff back, her level chin, her moderate steps. She'd practiced for hours walking with a book balanced on her head, surely, as his sisters had done.

Rebecca Merriweather was a tight little package, all right—that no one had opened.

Jack knew her type. He'd learned the hard way.

"Now, I know you're still kinda new in town, and all," Roy said, "and you already had that run-in with Mrs. Frazier. But Miss Merriweather isn't the kind of woman—"

"Yes, she is." Jack fetched his black Stetson from the peg beside the door. "Miss Merriweather is just the woman I need."

"You're not going over to her place, are you?" Roy asked, horror and panic causing his voice to rise.

Jack settled his hat on his head. "That woman has got something I need. And I intend to have it."

He walked outside, leaving his stunned bartender, his two lone customers, the saloon and all its problems behind.

Marlow's main street was a long line of wooden buildings fronted by boardwalks, hitching rails and water troughs. Horses, carriages and wagons filled the dirt street.

The town had pushed outward with the promise of the railroad expected next spring. East Street and West Street bracketed the town, adding more shops, stores and houses to Marlow's already burgeoning economy. Business was increasing in anticipation of the arrival of the railroad. That's why Jack had chosen to invest his money here.

It had seemed like a good idea at the time, anyway.

Jack greeted the men he passed on the boardwalk. He smiled and tipped his hat to the women who crossed his path, but as usual, got little more than a cold stare in return.

Thanks to that ol' battle-ax Mrs. Frazier.

Shortly after he'd arrived in town, the woman had barged into his saloon making demands on how he should run his business. He'd sent her packing, but made himself an enemy. Aside from being the wife of the richest rancher in the area, she also headed up Marlow's social and church functions.

Along with Miss Prim and Proper herself, Rebecca Merriweather.

Jack stopped on the boardwalk and gazed at the unmistakable storefront owned by Rebecca and her aunt. He saw the Marlow Tearoom and Gift Emporium every day from the door of his saloon, just across the street and down the block. Nobody could miss the place.

Pink. She'd painted it pink.

Jack had heard the story many times about Rebecca and the ''discussion'' she'd had in the middle of the boardwalk with Seth Grissom, the local carpenter—and probably the scariest-looking man Jack had ever laid eyes on—over the choice of color. Rebecca had gotten her way, a fact that hadn't surprised Jack in the least, and Griss was still getting grief over it.

Jack pulled his hat a little lower on his forehead. He didn't think for a minute that Miss Merriweather would eagerly go along with what he wanted. He knew it would take some work on his part to gain her cooperation. And once she agreed, he'd have to proceed cautiously.

A man always had to be careful around a woman like Rebecca Merriweather.

"WHAT ELSE, LADIES?"

Rebecca Merriweather gazed across the table at the two women, ready to add another item to her long list should Doris Tidwell or Nelly Walker come up with anything. Neither, she feared, had noticed the gaping hole in their list of preparations for this Sunday's church social.

Mrs. Tidwell and Mrs. Walker exchanged a troubled look. Rebecca had seen the same expression on the students' faces in Miss Whitney's classroom when she helped at the school.

While the women pondered the social's missing ingredient, Rebecca let her own mind rush on to other matters requiring her attention this afternoon.

The first, of course, was the room in which she and the ladies now sat. Rebecca looked around with pride at what she'd accomplished with the— if at first reluctant—blessing of her aunt Virginia Kent.

When Rebecca had moved here from Maryland to join her aunt six months ago, she'd been stunned by the little restaurant Aunt Virginia had owned. Dismal and unappealing, it drew only a few guests despite her aunt's excellent cooking.

Years spent working at her father's side in his Baltimore department store had sent dozens of ideas exploding in Rebecca's mind. A walk through town and a chat with the mayor confirmed that her initial thoughts were correct.

At first, Aunt Virginia was less than excited about Rebecca's idea to close the restaurant and start over with a new business. She'd opened the little eatery with her husband, now dead, and was getting by well enough.

But Rebecca had sold her on the idea, and within two months the Marlow Tearoom and Gift Emporium had opened. She'd had the interior painted a creamy yellow, put delicate linens and fresh flowers on the tables, and served tea and elegant foods from the china service Rebecca had ordered from her father's store. Everything in the tearoom was meant to appeal to feminine tastes.

At Rebecca's request, her father had also sent some of the unique items he carried in his own establishment, and Rebecca had used a portion of the tearoom's space to sell embroidered handkerchiefs, hair accessories and other items the ladies of Marlow couldn't buy elsewhere.

The town's women had warmed up to the tearoom. Now it was a place where mothers brought their daughters for a special afternoon, ladies planned the town's social and civic functions, chatted, shared news and, of course, gossip.

There was always plenty of gossip.

"Oh, I know!" Mrs. Tidwell sat up straighter, her eyes bright with the sure knowledge that she'd figured out the one thing Sunday's church social still needed. "Games!"

Mrs. Walker's lips turned down, disappointed that she hadn't thought of it first.

"Yes, games for the children," Rebecca said and made a note on her tablet. "What sort should we have?"

Mrs. Walker rushed ahead with a half-dozen suggestions before Mrs. Tidwell could respond. Rebecca wrote them all down, nodding in agreement. When she finished, she studied the tablet, then announced, "That's everything. We're sure to have another successful social."

Mrs. Tidwell and Mrs. Walker smiled with pride and helped themselves to their tea and the remaining tiny sandwiches artfully arranged on the pink-flowered platter on the table before them.

"How's the wedding coming?" Mrs. Walker asked.

Mrs. Tidwell, whose niece was getting married soon, proceeded to update them with the details.

Rebecca cringed at the mere mention of a wedding—an old habit, one she'd not completely rid herself of, even after living in Marlow for so long.

Since her mother's death nine years ago, Rebecca had cared for her younger brothers and sisters and helped with her father's business. The years slipped by somehow, and at age twenty-six, staring head-on into the prospect of being labeled a spinster, she was bombarded by her well-intentioned friends and family with "advice" and helpful "suggestions" on how she might improve herself and find a husband.

Rebecca hadn't objected to the idea of being married. In fact, she was all for it. But her age had made her too old to be appealing—except to men whom she found completely unappealing.

Moving to Marlow, Rebecca had made a fresh start. After spurning the advances of the town's older gentlemen—every single one of them, in short order—she'd settled into a comfortable life, one without a constant barrage of suggestions on how to catch a man. The people of Marlow had come to accept her as she was, and that suited Rebecca just fine.

After all, she had everything she could ever want. A pleasant aunt, friends, enough social and civic functions to keep her occupied.

And her business, of course. Rebecca adored

her restaurant and shop. She'd discovered she had a gift for running a business, tackling the problems, making all the decisions—and she loved doing it. So much so that at times she thought that having a husband would be a distraction from the things she truly loved.

Really, the last thing she needed was a man in her life.

"Oh yes, the wedding," Mrs. Tidwell said. "My niece—"

The door burst open, the little bell above it clanging madly.

Mrs. Tidwell gasped. Mrs. Walker's eyes widened to the size of saucers.

Rebecca turned in her chair.

A man. A man had entered her tearoom.

There wasn't a No Men Allowed sign on the door, but there may as well have been. Never in all the months since the place had opened had a man set foot in the Marlow Tearoom and Gift Emporium. Not once.

Heat coiled deep in Rebecca's stomach, then surged outward. Good gracious, this wasn't simply a *man*. It was that awful Jack Delaney.

She'd never been properly introduced, but she knew who he was. Everyone in Marlow knew who he was.

The saloon owner who'd insulted Mrs. Frazier,

and had yet to set foot in church. The man who could ruin a woman's reputation by simply speaking to her on the street.

And he was in her tearoom.

Rebecca got to her feet, her knees quivering, unsure if it was anger, outrage, fear—or something different—that threatened to take her breath away.

"I believe, Mr. Delaney," she said, struggling to keep her voice from shaking, "that you've entered this building by mistake."

He didn't bother to look around. His gaze locked on Rebecca and held there.

"I'm in the right place," he said. "I'm here to see you, Miss Merriweather."

"*Me?*"

He nodded. "I've got a proposition for you."

CHAPTER TWO

MRS. WALKER'S EYES had yet to blink, and Mrs. Tidwell had recoiled so far that Rebecca feared she might topple out of her chair.

Then, as one, they both turned to Rebecca, their shock at seeing Jack Delaney walk into the tearoom changing from surprise to suspicion. What had Rebecca done to bring on this visit by the town's most notorious saloon owner? their expressions seemed to ask.

Rebecca's stomach knotted. What *had* she done? Her mind whirled, but she came up with nothing—except to worry what would happen to her business when word of this got out.

Jack pulled off his Stetson and glanced toward the door, looking for a peg on which to hang it. There was none, of course, since only ladies visited the tearoom. He pressed his hat to his chest.

''I'd like a few minutes of your time, Miss Merriweather,'' he said, his voice as smooth as the amber liquid that flowed so freely in his saloon.

Rebecca just looked at him, her mind spinning. What could he possibly want to talk to her about? What could they have to discuss?

And why had she never noticed how handsome he was?

The thought startled her, but she couldn't let it go.

Black hair. Blue eyes with lashes so long he might have been thought pretty, were it not for his crooked nose and square jaw. Tall. Wide, straight shoulders, full chest, lean waist—

Rebecca stifled another gasp, stunned to realize that she was openly staring at the man, and horrified to think that Mrs. Walker and Mrs. Tidwell may have noticed it. But when she dared glance their way, she realized they blatantly ogled him as well.

Curiosity. Rebecca seized upon the notion that they all were simply curious about the man so often the topic of the town's unsavory gossip.

What else could it be?

"Miss Merriweather?" he prompted.

Rebecca blushed, realizing she was still staring and hadn't answered his question.

"I—I can't imagine that we'd have anything to discuss," she said, trying to sound aloof, but managing nothing more than a breathy whisper.

"We do," Jack assured her. Then a little grin

pulled at the corner of his mouth and he leaned toward her ever so slightly. "I'm here to extend you an offer."

A warmth, a strength—something—radiated from him, pulling at Rebecca, urging her to lean toward him. She glanced at the other women. They swayed forward in their chairs, their eyes glazed, answering that same unspoken call.

Rebecca clamped her lips together, catching a whimper before it slipped through. Good gracious, did she have that same expression on *her* face?

She came to her senses, ready to invite Jack Delaney to leave her tearoom before she humiliated herself completely. But he spoke first.

"Ladies, would you excuse us, please?" he asked, favoring Mrs. Tidwell and Mrs. Walker with a full smile.

"Well…" Mrs. Tidwell hesitated, unwilling, it seemed, to give up her front-row seat on the juicy bit of gossip unfolding before her.

"Thank you," Jack said, though the ladies had agreed to nothing. He backed up, opened the door wide and smiled graciously as the two women passed in front of him. Mrs. Walker turned backward as he closed the door, craning her neck for one final glimpse of the goings-on inside.

Rebecca cringed. Those women would make her tearoom the talk of the town before nightfall.

Thanks to Jack Delaney.

"I don't appreciate you barging into my place of business and running off my customers," Rebecca said, unable now to keep the anger from her voice.

"I thought you'd rather discuss my proposition in private." He gestured toward the door. "If you'd like me to ask those ladies back inside, I'm sure they'll be glad—"

"No!" Rebecca forced herself to calm down. "I mean, no. The damage is done now, anyway. What do you want?"

"I have a business proposal for you, Miss Merriweather."

"Forgive me, Mr. Delaney, but I can't imagine what sort of business you and I might have in common."

"I think we have more in common than you realize."

Rebecca couldn't fathom how that might be true, by any stretch of the imagination. He was completely out of place in her tearoom. Big, rugged, masculine. Whiskers shadowed his chin. A sharp contrast to her delicate china service, the lace curtains, the ruffled linens. And she certainly had no interest in anything remotely related to his saloon.

"May I sit down and explain?" Jack asked, waving his hand toward the table the other ladies had just vacated.

Rebecca hesitated. She wished he'd leave. She wished he'd never showed up in her tearoom in the first place. He'd thrown her into a very awkward position.

But he was here now, and if her reputation had to suffer because of it, she should at least hear him out. She was just the tiniest bit curious.

"Very well," she said, trying to sound inhospitable so he wouldn't linger.

Jack pulled out a chair for her. She hadn't expected a modicum of good manners from him, and was surprised.

She almost asked if he cared for a cup of tea, then realized how ridiculous he'd look holding one of her tiny cups in his huge hand.

Rebecca lowered herself into the chair and Jack pushed it beneath her, then he circled the table and sat down opposite her, tossing his hat aside.

He hesitated, as if gathering his thoughts, then looked across the table at her and said, "I need a woman."

Rebecca gasped.

Jack held up his palm, a silent plea for another moment. "What I mean is, I want you." He shifted in his chair. "Actually, what I'm trying to say is that you have some feminine qualities which I'm in need of, and—"

Jack muttered a curse and plowed his fingers through his hair. He looked across the table at her, his cheeks slightly pink.

"This seemed a hell of a lot easier on the walk over here," he said.

Rebecca smiled. She couldn't help it. The infamous Jack Delaney looked sweet and endearing and flustered, a man in need of rescuing if ever she'd seen one.

In a gesture so natural Rebecca thought nothing of it, she reached across the table and patted his hand. Warm. Rough. Hairy. She'd meant it as a gesture of comfort, but a peculiar sensation raced up her arm, making her decidedly *uncomfortable*. She withdrew her hand quickly.

"Perhaps you should just start at the beginning," she suggested.

Jack nodded. "I own the Lucky Streak Saloon."

"Yes, I know," Rebecca said. "You moved here two months ago and you're building yourself a house on West Street."

His brows drew together, wondering, she was

sure, how she knew so much about him. Apparently, he was willing to let it go because he continued without asking her, and that suited Rebecca fine. If Jack didn't already know he was the topic of gossip among the ladies in town, she didn't want to be the one to tell him.

"The house is finished now," Jack said.

"It is?" Rebecca didn't know how that bit of news had escaped the town's rumor mill. Mrs. Tidwell and Mrs. Walker had been here for nearly an hour and hadn't mentioned it. "Are you certain?"

He raised an eyebrow. "Yes, I'm certain. Anyway, I've purchased furnishings for the house from New York—"

"Furniture?" Speculation on what was in the many crates Jack received had run rampant among the ladies in the tearoom for weeks.

He nodded. "Now it's time to fix up the place. Make it liveable. That's what I want you for. I want you to turn the house into a home."

"Me?" Rebecca sat back in her chair. "Mr. Delaney, there are many women in Marlow who could—"

"I want you for the job." Jack waved his hand toward her. "You're a fine, upstanding Eastern woman. You know the way things should be done. I want this house done properly."

"But—"

"I've got company coming from back East," Jack said. "Important company. I want the house to…"

"Be warm and welcoming in the tradition to which your guests are accustomed?" Rebecca asked.

Jack grinned. "I knew I had the right woman for the job."

Flattered by his words, Rebecca smiled along with him. It pleased her to know he thought highly of her, that he'd noticed the way she carried herself. Her mother, God rest her soul, would be infinitely pleased.

Yet she couldn't allow herself to be swept into agreeing to something simply because of flattery.

"I understand your situation, Mr. Delaney," Rebecca said. "But I'm not sure I should accept your offer."

"Why not?"

"I have my own business to run," she said, waving her hands to encompass the tearoom.

"You do," Jack agreed. "But you've got things running smooth. Your aunt is here to help. A few hours a day away from this place won't do it any harm."

Rebecca couldn't disagree. In fact, she often took time away from the tearoom to attend to charitable causes in Marlow, do a little shopping or visit friends.

"I'm not sure it would be…decent…for me to be in your home, among your personal things," Rebecca said.

"It's not my home yet. I've got a room over the saloon. Nothing of mine is in the house." Jack's expression hardened. "Let's get something straight right now, Miss Merriweather. This is a business deal I'm talking about. You're being hired to do a job. That's all."

"But still…"

"I assumed you understood the business world," Jack said, his tone almost a challenge. "Was I wrong about that?"

Rebecca sat straighter in her chair, his words causing her spine to stiffen. Yes, she knew a great deal about the workings of businesses. She'd learned it from listening to her father and working at his side. She'd have taken over his store, eventually, if she'd been born male.

"I assure you, Mr. Delaney," Rebecca said, "that I'm well aware of the workings of a business."

"Good," he said. "Then you'll understand how important this project is to me when I tell you to name your price for the job."

She stifled a gasp. She'd heard he was wealthy, but never imagined *this*.

"Name it," he told her. "Whatever you want. It's yours."

"Your offer is extremely generous," Rebecca said. "But I'll have to think it over."

"There're some nice things in those crates, Miss Merriweather. I'd like to see them put where they belong by somebody who knows how." Jack rose from the chair. "But if you won't do it, I'll find somebody who will."

He gave her a nod, took his hat and walked to the door. He opened it, then looked back. "You've got until noon tomorrow to give me your answer. After that, I'll offer the work to someone else."

Rebecca watched him walk out, saw the door close, looked at him as he moved past her window and disappeared across the street. But she couldn't force herself out of her chair. Her legs wouldn't hold her up.

She'd been a party to business deals before, when she worked with her father, when she got the tearoom up and running. But no matter what Jack said, the things she felt at the moment had nothing to do with business.

CHAPTER THREE

JACK NEVER LIKED doing the paperwork necessary to run a business. He liked it even less when
the profits went down instead of up.

As he sat at the desk in his room over the
Lucky Streak, golden light from the lantern cast
a dull glow over the ledger before him. Neat columns detailed the saloon's income and each of
its expenses.

Neat columns that told him he was on his way
to losing his shirt over this place.

"Damn…" Jack tossed his pencil aside and
sat back in his chair.

He'd thought long and hard before deciding to
buy the saloon. Opening a new business had its
risks, of course. But he hadn't expected things to
be this bad.

The saloon had been closed for some time before Jack bought it. From the stories he'd heard,
the place had been pretty wild back in those days.
Fistfights and gunplay were routine. The former
owner had caught a bullet during a disagreement

over a card game and sold out to Jack in the midst of a long, slow recovery.

Jack had figured that once he opened the doors and offered a little competition to Marlow's two other saloons, customers would flock in, as they had before. They hadn't.

Of course, Jack didn't allow fights and shoot-outs, though the customers found them entertaining. Even before that old heifer Mrs. Frazier had burst into his place demanding civilized behavior from his clients, he'd decided not to put up with that sort of thing. Not that he particularly cared if two men duked it out or shot each other. He just didn't want his place damaged, or to be stuck with the repair bills.

Rising from the chair, Jack stretched, nearly scraping his knuckles on the low ceiling. He looked around the room, thinking it was simply that: a room. Nothing warm or welcoming about it.

That brought Rebecca Merriweather to mind.

Jack walked to the window that overlooked Main Street and pressed his forehead against the glass, angling for a view of the Marlow Tearoom and Gift Emporium just down the street. The sun had dipped toward the horizon shining its last rays on the pink storefront.

From this distance, he couldn't tell if anyone

was inside, but he suspected there was. Women always flowed in and out of the place. He'd been lucky this afternoon to catch only two of them in there, besides Rebecca.

Jack's stomach twisted a little, thinking of what a fool he'd made of himself in front of her. Talking to people—even women—had never been a problem for him. But, somehow, sitting across the table from Rebecca had rattled him.

But that was her fault, in a way. She'd caught him off guard.

He'd expected her to be uppity, which she was. He'd expected her to be aloof, and she was that, too.

But he hadn't expected her to be pretty. He'd seen her on the streets, but like most of the other women in town, she'd never allowed herself to come close enough that he could get a good look.

So he had no idea that her brown eyes were so large and liquid, hadn't suspected she'd have lips that pink, or that the tip of her nose turned up ever so slightly.

Yet there she'd sat looking nice, smelling nicer, done up in dozens of petticoats and carefully coiffed hair. For a moment or two while he'd sat across from her, she'd actually seemed warm and a little friendly. Those things he'd found more surprising than her good looks.

What hadn't surprised him was that she didn't leap at his offer to decorate his house.

Jack looked around the little room he'd been living in for the past few months. He'd never liked it in the first place, and with each day that passed it grew more confining.

He'd been telling himself for weeks now that once the house was finished, once his company arrived from New York, things would be better. He still believed that was true.

All he needed was Miss Rebecca Merriweather's help to make it happen.

Help from Rebecca…a woman. Jack's gut knotted at the realization of what he was opening himself up to by offering her the work. Memories surfaced, stirring his anger.

A woman in his new house. Having the run of the place. Taking over.

Drawing in a slow breath, Jack pushed the idea away, determination hardening in his belly.

He'd accept her help with the house—but he'd make damn sure she remembered her place.

Jack stalked out of the room and down to the saloon.

About a half-dozen men occupied the room, several playing cards, others standing at the bar. Among them was Ian Caldwell, one of Marlow's deputy sheriffs.

Since the saloon opened, Sheriff Harding himself had been by often, but that was to get a bead on Jack and the saloon, see what was going on, make sure no trouble was brewing. Harding was a lawman who brooked no nonsense from anyone, certainly not a drunken cowboy. Ian came by just to socialize.

"How's it going?" Jack said, easing up next to Ian at the bar.

He smiled easily. In his thirties, Ian was tall and slender with neat brown hair, always dressed in pressed clothes, even though he had no wife to look after him.

"Just making the rounds," Ian said, and saluted him with his mug of beer before taking another swallow.

"Things quiet?" Jack asked, nodding toward the street.

"Quiet enough," Ian said. He wore a pistol on each hip and looked as if he knew how to handle them. "There's talk around town about you."

Jack grunted. "More talk?"

"Talk that you've got more guts than any other man in Marlow." Ian shook his head in disbelief. "Did you really go inside the ladies' tearoom today?"

"Yeah, I did," Jack admitted. "I had a little business to discuss with Miss Merriweather."

"Damn…"

Ian finished his beer and headed for the door. Jack walked along with him, and when they reached the boardwalk, both turned toward the tearoom.

"Maybe I'll go over there myself," Ian said. "Have me a cup of that tea the women are all so excited about."

"Just remember to keep your pinkie finger sticking out when you drink," Jack said.

Ian laughed and walked away. Jack stood there for a while, gazing at the tearoom. He considered going back over there, talking to Rebecca again. The notion he'd awakened with this morning to have her decorate his house had gotten stronger as the day went on. Even more so now that he'd gone to her place and talked to her. Having that house fixed up—properly—clawed at his gut. Worth the risk of having a woman like Rebecca involved.

But he decided not to push her. He'd given her until noon tomorrow to make a decision. And if she turned him down…well, maybe it was for the best.

"SO, WHAT DO YOU THINK?" Rebecca asked.

Across the table from her in the tearoom sat her closest friend Lucy Hubbard. A few years younger than Rebecca, Lucy had been married for about four months. She and her husband had moved to Marlow shortly after their wedding. Lucy stopped by the tearoom most every day now that her husband was out of town.

Lucy touched her dark hair. "What does your aunt think?"

She'd told Aunt Virginia about Jack's proposition as soon as she'd composed herself. Virginia hadn't looked up from the dough she was kneading. A simple woman, Virginia wasn't crazy about all the gossip that went on in the tearoom—even where Jack Delaney was concerned.

"She didn't see anything wrong with me working for Mr. Delaney," Rebecca said.

Lucy drew in a sharp breath. "Can you imagine what Mrs. Frazier will say when she finds out?"

"I've thought about it," Rebecca admitted. "But this is a business arrangement. There's nothing personal in it. Mr. Delaney intends to pay me for the work."

"Really?" Lucy leaned closer. "How much?"

Rebecca didn't mind her friend's personal question. Images of Jack's rumored wealth would intrigue Lucy; money was tight for her and her husband.

"We haven't settled on payment yet," Rebecca said, then got back to the more worrisome issue. "But Mrs. Frazier would respect a business arrangement. Don't you think?"

"Your reputation is solid gold in this town. You sing in the church choir, organize all the socials, help at the schoolhouse. No one would dare say anything against you."

When she'd arrived in Marlow, Rebecca had set about contributing her time and energy to the betterment of the town, just as she'd done in Baltimore. That was simply what one *did.*

"And you know what else?" Lucy proposed. "If you got better acquainted with Mr. Delaney, perhaps you could get him to apologize to Mrs. Frazier."

Rebecca's eyes widened. After sitting across the table from Jack this afternoon, seeing the determination on his face, she couldn't imagine anyone talking him into anything.

"It's worth a try," Lucy said. "Wouldn't it be nice not to have to hear Mrs. Frazier complain about him and the Lucky Streak at every meeting?"

"Yes, it would," Rebecca conceded.

A little smile crept over Lucy's face. "Besides, he's awfully handsome."

"Lucy!"

"Well, he is. Don't tell me you hadn't noticed."

"Well, yes. But that has no bearing on my decision."

"Then how about plain old curiosity?" Lucy asked. "Aren't you just dying to know what sort of furniture he had shipped all the way from New York? And just *who* his company is? People so important he'd go to all this trouble?"

"Probably business investors," Rebecca said. "Lots of people are interested in Marlow now that the train is coming through next year."

"Aren't you just the least bit interested in finding out for sure?" Lucy asked.

Rebecca couldn't deny that she was. From the moment Jack had left the tearoom this afternoon—and as soon as she'd composed herself again—the idea of decorating his house had taken root in her mind.

She loved her new home in Marlow, but it was different from the life she'd led in Baltimore. She missed the grand home her family lived in, the extravagant gowns her father treated her to, and the many occasions on which to wear them— even if the conversation at most of those events had turned to speculation on why Rebecca still wasn't married.

"Don't tell me you wouldn't enjoy the challenge," Lucy said, giving her a knowing look.

"That's true," she admitted. Since work on the tearoom had been completed, Rebecca had found herself a little bored with simply running the place. She'd caught herself eyeing the wall connecting her tearoom to Mrs. Wagner's millinery shop next door. Rumor had it that Mrs. Wagner was considering moving to Keaton with her daughter. Rebecca had envisioned purchasing the shop, knocking out the walls, expanding and redecorating her tearoom. On her walks through town she'd often speculated on what other sort of shop or store she might open in Marlow. Since coming here, the business portion of her mind had flourished.

"Mr. Delaney gave me until noon tomorrow to decide."

"So think about it tonight," Lucy said, as she rose from her chair. "Then tomorrow morning tell him you'll accept his offer. After all, it's a business arrangement. Right?"

"Yes, a business arrangement," Rebecca said as they moved toward the door. "Oh, by the way. Several ladies have asked about the scented soaps you made. Can you bring more?"

Lucy looked pleased, and relieved. "Of course."

With her husband out of town for so long now, Lucy had started taking in wash and mending, and baking pies for the Pink Blossom Restaurant to make ends meet. She'd come up with the idea of making scented soaps wrapped in colorful fabric and fancy bows, and asked Rebecca to sell them in her store. They'd gone over well with the ladies.

"Have you heard from Raymond lately?" Rebecca asked, though she wasn't sure if she should since he'd been gone for over a month now.

Lucy's smile faded. "No, not lately. But I'm sure he's terribly busy looking for investments, and things."

"Yes, I'm sure he is," Rebecca agreed.

They stepped out onto the boardwalk as the sun touched the horizon, sending long shadows across the street. "I'll get those soaps over to you as soon—"

Lucy stopped, the words dying on her lips, her attention riveted to Ian Caldwell as he stepped out of the shadows. He stopped as well. But neither spoke. Neither moved. They just stood there face-to-face on the boardwalk.

"Good evening, Deputy," Rebecca finally said.

Ian hurriedly touched the brim of his hat. "Oh,

ah, evening, Miss Merriweather...Mrs. Hubbard.''

''G-good evening,'' Lucy managed to say.

''Making your rounds?'' Rebecca asked when it became apparent that no one else would—or could—speak.

''Yes, ma'am,'' Ian said, pulling his gaze from Lucy. He shifted. ''Well, I'd better get going.''

He nodded to both women, then reluctantly stepped off the boardwalk and crossed the street.

''Lucy—'' Rebecca began.

''I'm a married woman,'' she insisted harshly, turning to Rebecca, ''and it's sinful to even think about Ian Caldwell.''

''I know,'' she replied softly. ''I was only going to thank you for listening to my problem with Mr. Delaney.''

''Oh...'' Lucy's face softened. ''I'm sorry. I shouldn't have snapped at you. It's just that—''

Rebecca touched her friend's arm. ''I understand,'' she said, because really, she did.

''Well, good night,'' Lucy said, and headed up the boardwalk toward her little house on East Street.

Rebecca watched her for a moment before her gaze drifted to the Lucky Streak Saloon down the block. Images of Jack Delaney floated through her mind. What was he doing inside his saloon?

She couldn't even imagine. She'd never been inside that sort of establishment.

For a moment, Rebecca envied men their lack of concern for their reputation. When faced with a business decision, men only troubled themselves with the merits of the transaction, never how they'd look in the eyes of others should they decide to proceed.

Things were never that simple for women.

In Rebecca's mind she pictured the dozens of crates she'd seen carted down Main Street from the express office to Jack's house these past weeks. Furnishings all the way from New York. Her fingers itched to pry the tops from the wooden boxes in search of the hidden treasures.

And she could name her price for the job. Rebecca eyed the stores on Main Street. Her tearoom generated a nice profit, and she still had most of the money she'd brought from Baltimore. With the cash from Mr. Delaney's job, might she open yet another business in Marlow?

Rebecca paused, suddenly unsure if it was the idea of another business venture that caused her stomach to tingle with delight—or thoughts of Jack.

CHAPTER FOUR

NO SENSE IN WAITING until noon, Rebecca told herself as she slipped out of her bedroom in back of the tearoom. In the adjoining kitchen, past the big cookstove, the worktables and cupboards, she saw that Aunt Virginia's door was still closed, as she'd expected at this early hour.

Rebecca had hardly slept at all last night, tossing and turning, thinking over Jack's proposal.

And Jack.

But while some in Marlow might raise an eyebrow at her decision, Rebecca knew that business was business. This, definitely, was not an opportunity she wanted to let pass her by.

Rebecca quietly opened the kitchen door and glanced up and down the alley. Seeing no one, she stepped outside and closed the door with a soft thud.

She'd decided to go to the saloon early and inform Jack of her decision. She didn't want him in her tearoom again. Rebecca didn't relish the idea of being the topic of gossip for a second day in a row—business deal or not.

With the sun only just now rising above the horizon, Rebecca crossed Main Street and followed the alley to the rear of the Lucky Streak Saloon.

Like most of the other businesses in town, outbuildings, a small barn and paddock and a woodpile were situated across the narrow alley. Yet for all its sameness, Rebecca shivered at the thought of knocking on the rear door of the Lucky Streak. It was, after all, a saloon. Jack's saloon.

Glancing around one final time, Rebecca climbed the wooden steps onto the small porch. She'd chosen a dark green skirt and blouse, thinking the color would make her appear more businesslike. Men always dressed in dark colors, giving them an aura of seriousness. She wondered how much real business would be conducted if men wore pink suits.

Rebecca rapped on the door, waited, and waited. She knocked again, again and again, a little harder each time. Backing up a step, she gazed at the second-floor windows. No movement. She edged closer to the door, but heard nothing. Jack must be up and gone already.

Her heart sank. She'd wanted to get the meeting concluded with as little an audience as possible, but apparently that would not be possible. She raised her arm to give the door a final knock, and it flew open.

Jack glared out at her, his eyes squinted against the sunlight, his hair sticking up on one side. He wore dark trousers, but the top button was unfastened. One suspender crossed his shoulder atop a white shirt that hung open.

Rebecca gasped, horrified at confronting a half-dressed man. She knew she should leave— run, actually. But all she could do was stand there and look at his bare chest.

How could she not? Dark, coarse curls met in the center of his taut belly and arrowed downward among hard, rippling muscles. She'd never seen such a sight in her life. Never.

And now that she had, she couldn't drag her gaze away.

"Oh, Miss Merriweather."

Hearing her name jolted Rebecca. She broke eye contact with his belly and lifted her gaze to his face. Heat swamped her cheeks and she knew they must be red.

Jack didn't seem to notice, though, as he rubbed the sleep from his eyes and stepped back from the door.

"Come on in," he said and disappeared from the doorway.

Rebecca hesitated a moment, unsure of what to do. How unseemly to be in a saloon, of all places, with Jack, of all people—half-dressed. Yet how silly would she look if she bolted to the safety of her tearoom, only to have him follow later and remind her once again that this was *business?*

Rebecca didn't want to appear silly. Especially not to Jack. She stepped inside the large kitchen.

Sunlight beaming through the grimy windows cast the room in a dim pallor. A layer of dust covered the rickety table, mismatched chairs and cupboards. Spiderwebs clung to high corners. A desolate feel chilled the morning air.

Rebecca shuddered to think of this as someone's home. No wonder Jack had built himself a house. At once she was overwhelmed with the desire to rush to his new house, rip open the crates, turn it into a warm and welcoming home.

"Be right with you," Jack called.

She saw him at the sideboard where he leaned over a bowl of water he'd just pumped, and was splashing his face. He straightened, water sliding down his cheeks, dripping onto the hair of his chest. He groped for a towel nearby and dragged it down his face.

"Didn't expect you this early," Jack said, as he threaded his fingers through his hair, slicking it in place.

Rebecca gulped, trying desperately to keep her gaze on the room and not him. "I shouldn't have come by so early. I…"

"It's okay," Jack said with a shrug.

Indeed, he didn't seem to mind at all that she'd roused him from his bed just after dawn. Nor did he seem to mind that she was standing only feet away as he went through the personal details of dressing.

He closed the buttons on his shirt, shoved the tail into his trousers and fastened the top button, then hiked both suspenders into place.

If they continued to conduct business under these conditions, Rebecca didn't know if she could bear it.

"Can I get you some coffee?" Jack gazed around the kitchen. "I've got some here. Somewhere. Probably."

"No," Rebecca said, anxious to focus on something other than the droplets of water glistening in the dark hair that curled above the top button of his shirt. "I came to discuss your business proposal."

"Sit down," he invited, gesturing to the table and chairs in the corner.

"No, thank you," Rebecca said, not because the furnishings were covered with dust, but because she was suddenly anxious to get this over with and return to the safety of her tearoom.

Jack leaned his hip against the sideboard and crossed his arms over his chest, then nodded for her to proceed.

"Well," she began, "after giving it a good deal of thought, I've decided to accept your proposal."

Caution clouded his expression, as if he'd expected her to reject his offer, and a moment passed before he straightened away from the sideboard.

"Okay, then," he finally said. "The job is yours."

"I can start this afternoon," she told him. Her words sounded hollow in the chilly room. Another awkward moment passed while she waited for him to say something. When he didn't, she went on. "So, I suppose that's that."

"What about your payment?" he asked.

"Oh, yes…" She silently chastised herself for not having thought of that already. How very unbusinesslike of her. Then an idea occurred to her.

"I can't set a price without knowing exactly what the job will entail."

"I'll give you until the work is done to let me

know," Jack said. His expression hardened. "But no longer. I won't have a debt hanging over my head indefinitely."

"Of course not," Rebecca agreed.

His gaze remained harsh and he took a step closer. "You understand, Miss Merriweather, that I expect you to follow through with our agreement. I can't have you getting halfway into this thing, then losing interest, or quitting."

"I know how the business world works," Rebecca assured him. "I'll see the project through."

He watched her for a while, as if judging her words—or maybe just her. His expression grew more stern. "And you understand you're the hired help. You do what I tell you to do. I have the final say-so."

"Well, of course," Rebecca said, thinking it a little odd he'd even mention those things.

For a few more moments Jack continued to look hard at her, then he nodded briskly, as if satisfied with their deal.

"I've made arrangements for someone to help you with the heavy lifting, moving the furniture and such," he told her.

"Fine," Rebecca said, then desperate for a diversion, changed the subject. She waved her hand, taking in the room. "I've never actually been in a saloon before."

He grinned, the intensity he'd exhibited a moment ago suddenly gone. "No, I don't suppose you have."

She gave him a small smile in return.

"Would you like to see inside?" He nodded toward the swinging door that led to the saloon.

Such a question. Women—decent women—never went into a saloon. Rebecca couldn't imagine stepping one foot inside the place. Yet, until this morning, she couldn't have imagined standing in the kitchen of a saloon either, entering into a business deal with the most talked-about man in town.

Her gaze bounced from Jack to the door, then back to him again. "There's no one in there, is there?"

"It's a little early for saloon patrons," he said, and she could see he was making an effort not to smile.

"Well, yes, of course it is." She hesitated for another moment. "I—I suppose it would be all right to take a *peek*."

"Peek all you want," Jack said, pushing the door open.

Rebecca squeezed past him, feeling the heat from his body as he held the door for her.

"Or," he said, freezing her in front of him, "get up on the bar and sing, if you're so inclined."

She raised an eyebrow. "How kind of you to offer."

Jack grinned and followed her inside.

The saloon was larger than Rebecca had imagined. A piano and stool sat on the opposite wall. Round tables covered with green baize filled most of the room. A long bar with a brass footrail ran the width of the place, backed by shelves of glasses and dozens of liquor bottles. A large, empty space was centered behind the bar, as if a picture of some sort had once occupied the spot.

"There used to be a painting of a grizzly bear," Jack said, as if reading her thoughts. "I understand it got shot up and the old owner threw it out."

"Are you going to replace it?"

Jack shrugged. "It's one of the items on a long list of things I've got to do."

Rebecca nodded her understanding.

"Disappointed?" Jack asked, and moved a little closer.

She glanced up at him. "I didn't really know what to expect, but is this all men do here? Drink and play cards? No activities? Special events?"

"The men just like to drink and gamble."

"Well, all right," Rebecca said, thinking that surely there must be more to drinking and gambling than she realized, if it kept men entertained for hours. She also wondered if it was worth the fuss Mrs. Frazier made over it.

Thinking of that particular woman spurred Rebecca's conscience. "I'd better go," she said.

To her surprise, Jack followed her outside and walked with her through the alley to the rear corner of the saloon.

At a moment such as this, the conclusion of a business deal, Rebecca had seen her father shake hands with his new associate, clasp his shoulder, offer words of confident praise for their mutual success.

But what of her business arrangement with Jack Delaney? What gesture was appropriate to seal their arrangement?

A handshake? That would be acceptable. But the thought of touching Jack made her stomach quiver, for some reason.

She tried to come up with something to say, but no words formed, just the new, strange feeling that accompanied her quivering stomach. Gazing at Jack, she realized he didn't seem to know what to say either.

Yet words didn't seem to be necessary. Jack leaned down and kissed her.

Stunned, Rebecca froze. Jack didn't seem to notice as he moved his lips smoothly over hers and settled his hands on her shoulders.

Then, without wanting to, Rebecca sighed, giving in to the warmth that spun between them. Delightful. Simply delightful.

Jack lifted his head, ending their kiss. Rebecca hung where she was for a few seconds, raised slightly on her toes, her face tilted up to meet his.

With a slow smile, Jack stepped back. He didn't speak, but really, what was there to say?

Rebecca turned and walked away. When she reached the boardwalk she looked back and saw that Jack still stood in the alley. He waved. She waved back, then turned and ran straight into Mrs. Frazier.

CHAPTER FIVE

WHEN SHE'D ENCOUNTERED Mrs. Frazier on the street outside the Lucky Streak this morning, Rebecca had fought off the guilty look that had crept over her face, greeted the woman, then simply walked away, allowing no time for the questions sure to come. If pressed, how would she explain her business deal with Jack—without blushing red remembering his kiss? Rebecca didn't understand it herself.

Now, as she headed toward West Street, Mrs. Frazier was the furthest thing from her mind, though Jack's kiss still lurked in a cozy corner. Threading her way through the crowd, Rebecca noticed the young married women on the boardwalk, some with babies bundled in their arms, some with a duckline of children following, others with both.

A sense of freedom stirred in her stomach. If burdened with a husband and children, she wouldn't have been available to accept Jack's business proposal. As it was, all she had to do was ask Aunt Virginia to watch over the tearoom this afternoon, and off she went.

Rebecca smiled to herself. Yes, her life was going just the way she wanted it.

Turning the corner onto West Street, she spotted Jack's new house. Everyone in town knew about it. Not the biggest house—Mrs. Frazier held that distinction—but certainly one of the nicest.

A two-story home painted gleaming white with dark-green shutters, it sported a large covered front porch, a picket fence and twin maples in the front yard. A lovely home.

Rebecca opened the gate and walked up the path and onto the porch. The door stood open. The scent of sawdust, fresh paint and wallpaper glue drifted out.

She paused before crossing the threshold, a new sense of pride filling her. After today, would she be known in town for her business sense as well as her charity work? The idea thrilled her. Rebecca squared her shoulders and stepped into the house.

In the large entryway, a staircase rose to the second floor. To the right through an open doorway was a sizeable parlor. On the left was a smaller room, suitable for a bedroom or perhaps Jack intended to use it as an office. She'd have to ask him. Both of the rooms were crammed full of wooden crates.

"Hello?" she called, gazing down the central hallway.

She heard a muffled commotion from the back of the house, but no answer. Apparently, whoever Jack had hired to help her with the heavy work was already on the job. She followed the sound to a room where a large table, chairs, sideboard and cupboard were shoved into one corner. The dining room, of course. Here, too, rows of large and small wooden crates—some of them open already—filled almost all the available space.

Rebecca said a prayer of thanks that Jack had hired someone to help with the crates and move the furnishings. She'd never be able to handle it alone—and what sort of business person would she be if she had to ask for help immediately?

She stepped into the kitchen which adjoined the dining room. Beyond the massive cookstove, she saw the man Jack had hired to build the house. Had she not already known him, she would have run screaming into the street.

Seth Grissom was the most frightening-looking man she had ever laid eyes on. He was huge. If a bear suddenly reared up on its hind legs in front of her, Rebecca was sure it would be *smaller* than Seth Grissom. Not more than thirty years old, he had a full beard and mustache that reached halfway down his chest, and hair that hung to his shoulders, all a golden blond. His clothing was clean, but poorly mended since he had no wife to handle such things.

She'd employed Seth to do the renovations on her tearoom. He'd quietly gone about his work, talking with her rarely. Yet Rebecca had come to realize that beneath his rough exterior lay a gentle, artistic soul. Not only was Seth an excellent carpenter, but also a painter, woodcarver and cabinetmaker. They'd worked well together on the tearoom's renovations until suddenly—she'd never known why—Seth had simply stopped speaking to her.

"Good afternoon, Mr. Grissom," Rebecca said, making an effort to sound friendly. "I understand we'll be working together to finish up the house."

Seth looked up at her from the cabinet door he'd been studying. His eyes narrowed. "Delaney hired *you?*"

"Yes," she said, keeping her smile in place. "He said that you'd help with moving the boxes and—"

"I quit."

"You—what? Mr. Grissom?"

He shouldered his way past her without another word.

"Wait!" Rebecca hurried after him. "Mr.

Grissom, wait! You're supposed to help with—I can't possibly—Mr. Grissom?''

Rebecca stopped at the front door and watched helplessly as he trudged away, taking her business reputation along with him. For an instant, she considered running after him, but sensed it would do no good. Seth Grissom would not easily be swayed once his mind was made up, as it obviously was.

Slowly, she turned and faced the wooden crates. Dozens of them. Many, undoubtedly, filled with heavy pieces of furniture that she couldn't possibly lift—even if she could figure how to get the lids off.

Her shoulders slumped. How would she ever fulfill her end of the business deal now?

JACK PUSHED HIS WAY through the crowded boardwalk outside the Lucky Streak and headed toward his new house, mumbling one curse after another. Just when things were looking up, when everything seemed to finally be falling into place, *this* had to happen.

Five minutes ago, Seth Grissom had walked into the saloon and told Jack that he quit. Quit. Just like that. No explanation, no apology, no nothing.

Turning the corner onto West Street, Jack grumbled another curse, this one at himself. He hadn't bothered to ask Griss the reason; he already knew.

Jack took the front porch steps two at a time and strode down the hallway of his new house. In what was to become his dining room, he jerked to a stop.

Rebecca's bottom was in the air.

He drew in a sharp breath, frozen in midstride, all thoughts of Seth Grissom and the unfinished house flying out of his head.

There it was, right in front of him, draped in the folds of her dark-green skirt, her little bustle perched atop it.

She was bent over the side of a large crate, struggling to reach something in the very bottom, and all he could see was her bottom. And her legs, of course. Long legs. Calves and silk stockings visible where her skirt had hiked up. Leather slippers. Her ankles.

A familiar warmth slammed low in his gut. His mouth went dry. He knew he should say something, make his presence known—he wasn't the kind of man to ogle a woman caught in a compromising situation—but he couldn't seem to form any real words. Nor could he get his feet to move. Only one part of him was working at the moment—and working well.

Just then, one of Rebecca's feet left the floor as she reached deeper inside the crate. She struggled for a moment, then pushed off with the other foot.

"No...don't..." Jack saw that she'd pushed too hard, knew what was coming. She teetered on the edge of the crate for a second, then toppled inside headfirst.

Jack rushed to the crate. "Rebecca? Are you all right?"

Slumped in the bottom of the crate, packing straw in her hair and stuck to her dress, she gazed up at him and her eyes widened.

"Mr. Delaney, your organ!" she declared.

"Huh?"

"Your organ," she said again, tugging her skirt down over her ankles.

Jack shifted uncomfortably. "My...?"

"It's so impressive!"

"Well..."

She struggled to her feet. "I had no idea it was an Alister Penworthy."

"What?"

"See? Right here." Rebecca pushed the brochure toward him that she'd retrieved from the floor of the crate. "Alister Penworthy and Sons is a very old, very well-respected company. Perhaps the most prestigious maker of musical instruments on the East coast."

Jack frowned at the brochure depicting several models of musical organs on its cover. *"Oh..."*

"It's in one of these crates somewhere," Rebecca said, waving her arm around the room. "I had no idea you played."

"Come on out of there," Jack said, suddenly anxious to change the subject. He looped one arm around her shoulders, the other behind her knees and hefted her out of the crate.

Her breast settled comfortably against his chest and the sweet scent of her hair tickled his nose. The temptation to lean closer and kiss her nearly overcame him. Instead, Jack clamped his lips together to stifle a groan, and set her on her feet.

"I suppose you're here about Mr. Grissom?" Rebecca asked.

"Who?"

"Seth Grissom."

"Oh, yeah. Right," Jack said, forcing his mind from the packing straw clinging to her bodice. "What did you do to him?" he asked, a little more harshly than he'd intended.

"Nothing," she said.

"Then what did you *say?*"

"All I did was greet him—pleasantly, I might add."

"You didn't fire him? Run him off on purpose?" Jack demanded.

Rebecca looked at him as if he'd lost his senses. "No, of course not. Why would I do such a thing?"

Jack ignored her question, unwilling to give her an answer. "You must have done or said *something*."

Rebecca pressed her lips together, then leaned a little closer looking slightly distressed. "I don't think Mr. Grissom likes me very much."

That was sure as hell true. Jack knew that Griss had taken a ribbing from the men in town about painting Rebecca's tearoom pink, but Jack had thought that was all over with now. Obviously, it wasn't—for Griss, anyway.

"Perhaps if I spoke to Mr. Grissom about the situation?" Rebecca offered.

Jack stifled another curse. One visit from Rebecca and Griss would probably come to the saloon and shoot him in the leg.

"That's not a good idea," Jack told her.

Rebecca drew herself up straighter and announced, "Don't give the situation another thought, Mr. Delaney, I have everything under control."

He raised both brows at her. "You do?"

"Yes," she said briskly. "You needn't worry about a thing. You hired me to do this job and I intend to see it done. So just run along and leave everything to me."

He squared his shoulders. "Look, Miss Merriweather, I've already told you that I'm in charge of the work here. Not you."

Rebecca huffed impatiently. The last thing she wanted was for Jack to think she couldn't handle the job. Yet his interference was irritating—and unnecessary.

"Fine then," she told him and waved her hand toward the front door. "Go out and find a replacement for Mr. Grissom. And hurry up. I have a work schedule and you're slowing things down considerably."

Jack's eyes narrowed as he glared down at her.

For a moment, Rebecca feared he might fire her on the spot. She rushed on. "There. You see how silly that sounds? You have too many important things to concern yourself with. Let me handle the house—you're paying me to do just that."

Jack hesitated. It went against his grain to walk out and leave her in this situation, but she had a point. He had hired her to do the job. He'd made a fuss of insisting it was a business deal.

He'd also told her he wouldn't allow her to run roughshod over him either.

"As soon as I find a replacement for Mr. Grissom," Rebecca promised, "I'll let you know, and if you don't like him, I'll find someone else."

He certainly couldn't argue with that. "Well, all right."

"Good day, Mr. Delaney." With a firm nod she returned to the opened crates.

Jack headed down the hallway. Halfway to the front door, he stopped and looked back.

He'd known all along that Rebecca was independent-minded. Any woman who could come from a big city like Baltimore, make a home in Colorado and build a successful business on tea and funny-looking sandwiches had to be strong. And he should be relieved that Rebecca had taken over preparations at the house, freeing him for other, more important matters.

But he wouldn't stand for a woman—any woman—to jump in and take things over. He'd made that decision years ago.

Still, the idea of Rebecca being alone in the house bothered him on a very different level. The familiar, pleasurable ache presented itself again as he watched her bend over one of the smaller crates. He felt territorial all of a sudden, thinking of some other man in his house. Working. Helping Rebecca.

Watching her bend over.

Damn if he was going anywhere. Jack stalked back into the dining room.

CHAPTER SIX

"I'M HELPING YOU," Jack announced, striding into the room.

Rebecca whirled around. "You blame me for Mr. Grissom's resignation, don't you. That's why you're here."

"I don't blame you."

"Then what is it?" she demanded.

What could he tell her? That he couldn't stand the thought of another man in his house working alongside her? Ogling her fanny when she bent over? Hell no.

"Look, Miss Merriweather," Jack said. "I've got a lot of problems to deal with right now—this place, the saloon—"

"What's wrong with your saloon?" She walked closer.

Jack pulled off his hat and dragged his sleeve across his brow. It wasn't that hot, but he was sweating.

"Business is a little slow. That's all."

"It is? Perhaps if you—" She stopped and

flushed slightly. "Sorry, it's not my place to say anything."

"What were you going to say?"

"Nothing. Never mind." She spared him a quick, apologetic glance. "I tend to be too outspoken."

"Who told you that?"

"My father. Friends."

Jack shrugged. "I like outspokenness."

"Even in women?"

He grinned. "Especially in women."

She smiled then, the first genuine smile he'd seen. Her face lit up, and for some reason, he lit up, too.

"What were you going to say about the saloon?" he asked.

"Well, when I opened the tearoom, no one really knew what it was about. I had to lure women inside. The men in town are content spending their time at the other saloons. You need to draw them into the Lucky Streak."

Jack sat on one of the low crates. "Got any ideas?"

She thought for a moment. "I provided my customers with all the things ladies find appealing. The table linens, the china. I have framed drawings of current fashions hanging on the walls. Mr. Grissom made them for me."

"Griss drew pictures of ladies' clothing?" Jack asked. Thank God word of that hadn't gotten out. He'd have left town, for sure.

"He copied them from one of my catalogs. He's quite an accomplished artist," she said. "I also schedule special events. We have poetry readings and sing-alongs."

Jack rubbed his chin. "I don't think the men in Marlow are going to take too well to poetry readings in the saloon."

"No, but there are activities men enjoy," she pointed out. "If you provide them, they'll come."

He thought for a minute, then slapped his palms on his thighs and rose. "I'll think about it. Let's get to work."

He headed for the kitchen, found a hammer among the tools Grissom had left behind, returned to the dining room and started prying lids off the crates.

"This is quite lovely," Rebecca said as she lifted a lead crystal pickle server from the packing straw. "Which catalog did you order from?"

"I didn't order anything." Jack paused, hammer in hand. "I sent the floor plan of the house to my sisters. They picked out everything, shipped it here."

"They have excellent taste," Rebecca said.

"Please tell them how much I admire your organ."

"Yeah...I'll do that," he mumbled and went back to work.

"When is your company arriving?" Rebecca asked.

"Can't say for sure, since the train doesn't come all the way to Marlow yet, and the stagecoach line is so unreliable."

"Your family is all back East?" she asked.

"In New York." He tossed the lid into the corner with the others, then glanced back over his shoulder, and there she was again, bent over a crate, her bottom in the air. Once again, he had the same reaction, swift and strong.

Jack pressed his lips together. How the hell was he ever going to get the house finished like this?

"Yes, New York," he said, focusing his thoughts on their conversation. "My family owns a shipyard."

"*Those* Delaneys?" she asked, turning to him with wide eyes. "Why don't you work in the family business?"

For a moment, Jack was tempted to tell her the truth, tell her what had gone on. Something about this woman made him want to confide in her, trust her.

But he couldn't bring himself to do it. "I don't like ships," he said, and went back to work.

AFTER OVER A WEEK of spending his afternoons with Rebecca, Jack found himself looking forward to seeing her each day. The realization surprised him as he climbed onto the porch of the house. He'd finally relented and given her a key; it pleased him knowing that she was already inside, waiting for him.

Today he found her in the kitchen. He stood in the doorway and watched her at the cookstove. Even in her apron with wisps of her hair loose about her face, she looked like an elegant woman.

In his years of rambling around the West, he'd tried hard to forget what it was like to be around a well-bred woman, the type of women he knew in New York. Glimpses of crisp petticoats, graceful movements, attention to detail in dress and appearance. Rebecca displayed all of those things. And suddenly, after all these years, it pleased him to see them.

She must have sensed his presence because she looked up at him. To his pleasure, she smiled.

"Arm wrestling," Jack said.

"Is that how you propose we decide which of

us will move the parlor furniture today?'' She gave him a saucy grin.

Jack hung his hat on the peg beside the door and ambled over to the stove. ''What are you cooking? Smells good.''

''I thought it was time we gave this stove a try.'' She pulled a pan of cookies from the oven. ''Oatmeal.''

''My favorite.'' He breathed in the delicious aroma.

''I made coffee, too. Get some cups down, will you?''

Rebecca had insisted on getting the kitchen in order first. Blue curtains hung on the windows, a matching cloth covered the little table in the corner. A cupboard displayed dishes that Rebecca had said were for everyday; the china set still waited to be arranged in the dining room cabinet.

Jack fetched cups, saucers and a serving plate and put them on the table.

''I've been thinking about what you said the other day about drawing men into the saloon,'' he said. ''It came to me last night—arm wrestling.''

''Hmm…'' Rebecca sank into thought for a moment and, had he not known her so well, it might have irked him that she hadn't immediately pronounced his idea brilliant. One thing he'd learned about her as they'd decorated the house, Rebecca didn't come to any decision without a great deal of deliberate thought.

"I like it," she finally said, filling their coffee cups. "You're intending to stage a tournament?"

"That's what I'm thinking." Jack seated her, then took the chair across from her and helped himself to two cookies.

"Cash prize to the winner?" she asked. When he shook his head, she nodded in agreement. "A bottle of whiskey should suffice—along with bragging rights. Have you thought of having a singer in to perform? You have the piano."

"A singer costs money," he pointed out.

"Pass a hat after the performance. Let the crowd pay."

"What woman in town would sing at a saloon?" he asked, helping himself to another cookie.

She sipped her coffee. "There are some women in Marlow who might appreciate…alternate…employment."

Jack's gaze came up quickly as the meaning of her suggestion dawned on him. Miss Prim and Proper thought he might get some of the girls from Miss Dora's parlor house to sing at his saloon?

Rebecca rushed ahead. "And you might serve

food in the evenings, after the restaurants close. Perhaps some fried chicken, boiled eggs, pickles, that sort of thing. I know someone who might do the cooking, if you're interested.''

''Who's that?'' he asked, anxious to get thoughts of the parlor-house girls out of his head at the same moment he was looking across the table at Rebecca.

''Lucy Hubbard. She's an excellent cook.''

''Is she willing to cook for a saloon?''

''I doubt she'd like the fact advertised, but I'm sure she'd do it.'' Rebecca lowered her voice. ''She needs money.''

Jack grumbled. ''Is that bastard she's married to ever coming back home?''

''He's looking for work, investments,'' Rebecca said.

''Hubbard ought to be shot for going off leaving his wife to fend for herself,'' Jack said. ''Worthless bastard.''

''He tried two different businesses here in Marlow.''

''Damn near impossible to make a go of it when he was spending nearly every night gambling away the day's profits.''

Rebecca gasped. ''He was? Oh, dear. I wonder if Lucy knew?''

"She knew," Jack said sourly. "But she's too good a wife to say so in public."

They finished their coffee and Jack ate the last cookie, then they rose from the table.

"You've got a little something on your lip," Jack said, gesturing toward her.

"Oh." Rebecca reached for a napkin, but Jack stepped closer and tilted her face up.

"It's just a little oatmeal crumb," he said, gazing into her eyes. "Be a shame to let a good bite of cookie go to waste."

She wasn't sure what he meant until he eased closer and kissed her. He blended their mouths together comfortably, yet with an excitement that made Rebecca's heart thud harder in her chest. Jack slid his arms around her and drew her against him. Warmth seeped into her, drawing her closer.

After a long, languid moment, Jack lifted his head. A grin tugged at his lips. "I could have sworn there was a crumb on your mouth."

Rebecca just looked at him, locked in his embrace. Would he kiss her again? She thought—hoped—he would.

But he didn't. Instead, Jack released her and backed up a step.

"You're sure you don't want to arm wrestle

to see which of us is going to move the parlor furniture?'' he asked, grinning.

''I'd hate to embarrass you,'' she said as she cleared the table.

They spent hours working in the parlor, centering the rug, placing the furniture, putting up curtains, hanging pictures. Jack did all of the real work. Rebecca pointed.

He didn't kiss her again.

Darkness settled into the room as he pushed the settee two inches down the wall, then pulled it back another three at Rebecca's request.

''Perfect,'' she declared.

He blew out a heavy breath. ''You're sure? You don't think it needs another half-inch? Quarter-inch, maybe?''

''Well…'' she mused, pretending she hadn't noticed his sarcasm. ''Perhaps we should move everything out into the entryway and start over.''

Jack rounded on her, a playful grin pulling at his lips. ''Maybe I'll just move *you* out into the entryway and fix this room myself.''

He charged toward her. Stunned, Rebecca managed nothing more than a weak squeal as he swept her into his arms.

''Maybe I'll toss you out back with the trash instead,'' he declared, striding out of the room.

''No! Don't!'' Rebecca threw her arms around

his neck, giggling so hard she barely got the words out.

He stopped, but didn't say anything for a moment. They gazed into each other's eyes. A long moment dragged by while some unnamed expectation hung between them. Finally, Jack broke the spell.

"I guess I'll keep you," he said softly, then grinned. "At least until the work is finished."

Jack eased her to the floor. "Get your things. I'll walk you home."

Rebecca got her handbag and hat while Jack fetched his Stetson and made certain the back door was locked. They walked out the front together. She hadn't realized it had gotten so late. Most of the businesses had closed already. Jack hooked her elbow and led her down the alley behind the stores. They stopped at the rear of the tearoom.

Faint light glowed in the kitchen window casting the deserted alley in pale shadows. In the dim light, Rebecca gazed up at Jack.

"I'll finish up the parlor tomorrow and we can..."

Her thoughts evaporated as Jack stepped closer. His gaze seemed to sap her strength. His body gave off a heat, a heat so warming that it caused the same to rise in her. A tingle rushed through her. Never in her life had she been so *aware*. Of another person. Of herself.

He kissed her. Rebecca gasped as his arms circled her, pulled her close. She leaned her head back—unable not to—as his lips covered hers completely. His mouth moved across hers, its warmth somehow chilling her to the bone.

He broke their kiss but his lips hovered near hers. After a long moment, he released her, then reached behind her and opened the kitchen door.

Rebecca's mind reeled with indecision. Should she run inside? Launch herself into his arms again? At once, she wanted to do *both*. Ached to do both.

"Good night," he whispered.

"Good night," she answered, and slipped into the kitchen.

WHEN REBECCA AWOKE the next morning, the world seemed different—even the little room she slept in.

When she'd moved in, she'd taken great pride and pleasure in selecting just the right bed linens. She'd had a friend from church hook the perfect rug. The rocking chair had come from her father's store, selected by him personally. Seth Grissom had built a bookcase for the spot beneath the window, before he'd stopped speaking to her.

The room had been a comfortable retreat. Until this morning.

Rebecca turned away from the mirror, tucking a stray lock of hair into place. The room seemed small. Smaller than she'd noticed before.

The morning passed quickly enough, as it usually did, with she and Aunt Virginia having breakfast, then preparing for their customers. Aunt Virginia barely spoke. But that wasn't unusual, Rebecca realized. Yet, somehow, it bothered her this morning.

She went about serving her customers through the noon hour. Business was brisk. As she moved between the tables serving tea and the delicacies Aunt Virginia had prepared, snippets of gossip reached her ears. Normal gossip. But it held no interest to Rebecca today.

She was almost relieved to leave the tearoom behind and head for Jack's house. Gray clouds gathered overhead, promising rain. But as Rebecca walked along Main Street, it wasn't the potential business investment that drew her attention the way they usually did. It was the women.

Women on the arms of their husbands. Women clutching babies. Women holding tiny hands, shepherding children safely across the street.

She'd seen these things dozens of times. But today, for some reason, everything seemed different.

By the time Rebecca unlocked the front door of Jack's house and let herself inside, the notion occurred to her that perhaps the world hadn't changed. Perhaps *she* had.

Raindrops tapped gently against the windowpanes as she made her way to the kitchen and left her hat and handbag on the table. Jack wasn't there yet.

A heaviness settled around Rebecca's heart as she tied on her apron and strolled slowly to the parlor. Her work here was almost done. In a few days, she'd leave and never return. Jack would have his home and she'd have—

What?

Rebecca stopped, her gaze drifting across the parlor. With pride she admitted that she'd made the most of the lovely furnishings. The house would be a comfortable home.

For Jack.

Her bedroom behind the tearoom seemed suddenly smaller still. Uninviting, compared to this house.

Her spirits lifted as Rebecca realized that she, too, could have a house this nice. Her tearoom was doing well. She had cash. Her father would help her, if needed. The idea grew quickly, causing her stomach to warm at the notion.

A home, a lovely home. She'd have it built, send to Baltimore—New York, perhaps—for the furnishings. She would fix it up, then live in it—

All alone.

A sadness jolted Rebecca and her gaze flew to the window. Jack? Through the drizzling rain, she'd expected to see him, she realized, but he wasn't there.

No one was there.

No one would ever be there.

What had brought on these thoughts? Rebecca wondered. His kiss last night? By far the most delightful. Had it caused her to rethink her entire life?

No, she realized. These feelings had been inside her for a long time—back in Baltimore, even—but she'd refused to acknowledge them.

The lonely ache stabbed her heart. Rebecca eased onto the settee as the vision of her future flashed in her mind.

The large, lovely home she would build.

Who would live in it with her? A husband? A child?

No. Only herself.

Rebecca bounced from the settee and threaded

her way between the marble-topped table and the crates still waiting to be unpacked.

Intolerable. The vision of her future was completely intolerable. This was why she'd refused to accept the thoughts that had lurked in the back of her mind for so long. They were simply intolerable.

But did it have to be that way?

She didn't want to grow old alone. She couldn't—wouldn't—allow that to happen. One hand on her hip, she paced, forcing herself to think.

In order to have a family, one needed a husband. Rebecca cringed at the very thought. She'd already shunned every older gentleman in Marlow who'd expressed the slightest interest in her. She hadn't been able to bear the thought of being courted by any of them.

Should she give them another try?

Mr. Harrison at the bank, with his long nose hairs. Mr. Kessler at the feed store, whose buttons strained across his wobbly belly. And that rancher just outside of town, the one who smelled like cows.

Rebecca shuddered at the thought of marriage to any of them. She couldn't, simply could not, do it. Even if one of the men would actually court her again, which she doubted, after the way she'd already turned them all down. And the younger men in town all had eyes for the younger women, just as they'd had in Baltimore.

So where did that leave her?

She started pacing again. If she couldn't find a husband, she'd never have a child. Unless...

Rebecca gasped in the silent room and stopped still in her tracks. Perhaps she *could* have a child without saddling herself with an unwanted husband.

She looked around at the house she'd spent weeks decorating, the result of the business arrangement she'd entered into with Jack.

He'd given her until the job was done to name her price. He'd never said it had to be *cash*.

Rebecca shivered at the thought racing through her head.

Jack could give her a baby.

CHAPTER SEVEN

GOOD HEAVENS, what was she thinking?

The notion that had come to her in Jack's parlor yesterday had haunted Rebecca all night. She'd left him a note saying she couldn't work on the house—she couldn't possibly look at him, with what was on her mind. Now, with the midday customers expected at the tearoom, Rebecca couldn't face the afternoon at Jack's place.

Not until she decided once and for all what to do.

Rebecca swept the boardwalk in front of the tearoom, absently going about the chore. Over and over her gaze crept down Main Street to the Lucky Streak. No sign of Jack, but that wasn't unusual this time of day. Besides, she had her eye out for a different man. Finally, Deputy Ian Caldwell rounded the corner. Rebecca set the broom aside.

"Morning, Miss Merriweather," he said.

"Good morning." She prattled on with what she hoped was sufficient small talk, then pulled the envelope from her pocket that she'd prepared earlier this morning.

"Would you be kind enough to take this to Mr. Delaney?" she asked, discreetly passing it to the deputy.

He slipped it into his pocket. "Sure," he said.

He hadn't asked for an explanation, but Rebecca felt compelled to provide one; perhaps it was the lawman in him that demanded it.

"I'm sure you know I've been helping Jack with his house," she said. "I wanted him to know I can't be there today."

"I'll take care of it," he promised, then craned his neck for a view through the open door of the tearoom.

"Lucy's not here," Rebecca said.

Disappointment clouded his features. Ian touched his hat brim and moved on.

The ache of loneliness that had crowded Rebecca's heart expanded a bit to include Ian. They were alike, she thought, both wanting something that seemed impossible to acquire.

By noon, the tearoom buzzed with conversation and the clink of bone china and silverware. Since Rebecca had begun working for Jack, it seemed her tearoom was busier than ever. Each day she faced a barrage of questions about Jack and his house. It hardly seemed right to dole out the details of his home that the women craved, so Rebecca kept her comments as vague as possible.

"Lovely furnishings," she reported, "of the utmost quality." She included tidbits of Jack's wealthy family, the shipyard, details that left the ladies in awe. Even Mrs. Frazier hadn't said anything nasty about Jack in days.

She wondered how that would change if word ever got out about what she was contemplating—with Jack's cooperation.

After another day of mulling over the idea, Rebecca still thought that having a child without benefit of a husband seemed like a good idea—it was a business arrangement, after all—but she wanted another opinion. There was only one person with whom she could freely consult.

Rebecca clutched her shawl around her shoulders as she hurried through the alley toward East Street. Rain showers had blown through town for several days bringing a damp and chilly wind, yet Rebecca's belly burned as if on fire.

She rounded the corner onto East Street. A few yards from where the boardwalk ended sat the little house that Lucy and her husband rented. She rapped briskly on the door and Lucy appeared a moment later wearing an apron.

"Rebecca, what a nice surprise. Come in."

The house was one room, the bed partitioned off from the living area with a dark curtain. The meager furnishings attested to the Hubbards' financial difficulties. They also displayed Lucy's determination to overcome those problems.

A basket of other peoples' clothing sat beside the rocker, mending that Lucy had taken in. The sideboard was crowded with baking ingredients for the pies she made and sold to the Pink Blossom Restaurant.

Despite her own problems, Rebecca thought of what Jack had told her about Raymond Hubbard. The man was worthless as a provider. Her overriding thought was that Lucy deserved so much more—in a home and a husband.

Rebecca dropped her shawl and handbag on the table. "I need to talk to you."

Lucy turned, hearing the desperation in Rebecca's voice. "What's wrong?"

"I need some advice."

Lucy pointed to the kitchen chairs and they sat. The house was silent except for the gusts of winds that moaned in around the windows.

"I had a vision of my future," Rebecca said, "and I didn't like what I saw. I don't want to end up alone. I'm wondering if I should marry...even if it's to someone I don't love."

"Oh, Rebecca, no..." Lucy gripped Rebecca's

hand with a strength she hadn't expected. "No, you mustn't do that."

"But isn't it better to be married to someone I don't really love, and have children, than to be alone?"

"There is nothing worse than marriage to a man you don't love," Lucy said, her expression pained.

A quiet moment passed, then Rebecca asked, "You and Raymond...?"

Lucy withdrew her hand. "Raymond came into my life like a godsend. An answer to prayer. Everyone believed everything he said. He insisted we marry quickly. Raymond is...not exactly what he portrayed himself to be."

"Yet you stay with him," Rebecca said.

"I married him before God. It's my duty to make my marriage work, somehow," Lucy said. "But don't put yourself in the position of regretting the biggest decision of your life, Rebecca. Don't do it."

Rebecca nodded. In her heart, she'd known she could never marry a man simply out of desperation. Hearing Lucy say the same thing sealed her decision.

"There's a man out there somewhere who'll be perfect for you," Lucy offered with a hopeful smile. "I just know it."

"I'm sure you're right." Rebecca slipped her shawl around her shoulders and picked up her handbag, her thoughts moving on. "By the way, I told Mr. Delaney you might be willing to cook for his saloon customers. He'll pay you."

"Wonderful." Her smile quickly faded. "But—"

"I know," Rebecca said, understanding her friend's concern. "We'll figure some way for you to deliver the food without ruining your reputation."

Lucy laughed gently and called her thanks as Rebecca left the house.

Storm clouds rumbled overhead as she stepped up onto the boardwalk. Her heart ached a little knowing that Lucy was mired in a loveless marriage. Her own stomach hardened with the determination not to put herself in the same predicament.

So where did that leave her? Rebecca turned the corner onto Main Street, considering her options. Briefly, she thought of adopting a child. Surely, there was an orphans' asylum somewhere eager to find good homes for destitute children. Yet Rebecca was also sure that an unmarried woman didn't constitute a "good home" in anyone's eyes.

That left her once again with the business-

arrangement idea she'd had in Jack's parlor. A
bold step. But no suitors were knocking on her
door—certainly none in Marlow, after the way
she'd treated them all—and she wasn't getting
any younger. If she wanted her future to change,
she'd have to take charge of it herself—just as
she had when she'd left Baltimore, when she'd
opened her tearoom.

Reaching Jack's house, Rebecca went to the
kitchen. Vaguely, the house smelled like him.
She realized she'd missed seeing him these past
few days.

Rebecca returned to the parlor, tying on her
apron. As she dug through the straw, it occurred
to her that since she was going to change her life
so drastically, it was prudent to do it logically.
Selecting the right man to father her child was
of the utmost importance. Jack had been the obvious choice—he owed her, after all—but perhaps she should give the matter further thought.

She wanted an intelligent man, Rebecca decided, standing beside one of the crates. A man
of good breeding. Someone with good looks, and
who understood business. Jack fit all those requirements.

A little smile came to Rebecca's lips. Yes,
Jack met all her requirements. And…

Heat wafted through her at the memory of

Jack's kisses. The touch of his lips had brought her to life in places she'd never imagined. Rebecca's stomach quivered at the thought. He'd lifted her into his arms effortlessly, swept her up, held her against him. His body was strong and hard, all male. Being in his bed—

"Are you all right?"

Jack's voice boomed from behind her. She hadn't heard him come into the house. Rebecca spun around, heat flooding her face. Good gracious, did he have any idea what she'd just been thinking—imagining? Her whole body sprang to life at the sight of him.

"Y-yes," Rebecca stammered. "I'm—I'm fine."

He came closer, scrutinizing her, concern in his expression. "When you didn't come to work on the house these past few days, I thought maybe you were sick."

"Oh, no," she said, giving him a quick smile, hoping it would cover the lie she intended to tell. "I had some things to do at the tearoom. Didn't Ian give you my note?"

"Yes," he told her, still looking closely at her. "I just wanted to be sure."

Kindness. Another wonderful quality he might pass on to her child. Rebecca struggled to keep from smiling.

"Sorry I'm late," Jack said. "I had to oversee the liquor delivery."

Commitment to duty. Excellent.

Rebecca forced her thoughts back to the task at hand.

"I only got here myself," she said. "And I was just—"

What? Imagining herself in bed with him?

She gulped and whirled around.

"Do you need my help in here?" Jack asked.

"No," she answered, making a show of pawing through the packing straw so she wouldn't have to face him.

"Okay. I'll go on up to the bedroom."

"Where?" Rebecca whipped around, her heart banging in her chest. Her gaze swept him from head to toe before she could stop herself. Big, strong. Oh, the babies he could provide…

Jack's brows pulled together. He looked down at his legs. "Have I got something on my pants?"

"No," she croaked. Flames raced up her cheeks. She whirled to the crate and leaned into it. "You run on upstairs. I'll finish here."

She rummaged through the straw until she heard Jack's footsteps on the staircase, then collapsed onto the settee.

Good gracious, she had to get control of herself. This was a business arrangement. She had to remember that.

Rebecca sat up and gave herself a little shake. While Jack—physically—was the perfect man to father her child, she really knew very little about him. Prudence demanded she learn more.

She climbed the stairs and found Jack in the bedroom on the left side of the hallway. Crammed with furniture and crates, it was the largest of the three rooms on the second floor. The window stood open letting in the cool, damp breeze and the dim afternoon light. Outside, the gray sky threatened rain again. Jack busied himself prying the lids from the crates.

Rebecca lingered in the doorway. How intimate the setting. A *bedroom*. Her heart beat a little faster at the thought of stepping into the room with Jack in it.

She pushed her chin higher and drew in a determined breath. She needed information from him to make her final decision about selecting the father of her child, and she was going to get it.

"So," she said airily as she came into the room, "your family all live in New York?"

"Yeah," he said, prying another nail from the lid.

"Where are they from, originally?" She sidled closer.

"England."

"Nobles?" Rebecca asked, trying to make her question sound casual. "Gentry? Country squires?"

Jack uttered a soft laugh. "My mama claimed there was royalty somewhere in the family line, but I don't know for sure."

"Royalty?" Rebecca struggled to suppress a smile. "How nice."

Jack just grunted as he set aside the lid of the final crate.

"I couldn't help but notice that your nose is a bit crooked," she said, waving her fingers at her own nose when he looked up. "Is that from a disagreement, or were you...born that way."

"You could say it was a disagreement." Jack smiled faintly at the memory. "By the time we were done, the other fella had come around to my way of thinking."

She laughed politely, then went on.

"You have a large family?" she asked, following him across the room to where the bed frame rested against the wall.

"Pretty big."

"Not a lot of illness? Hereditary diseases?"

Jack shook his head. "No. The family's pretty healthy."

"How many *boys?*"

"My pa's got six brothers. I've got five."

"Do they all still have their hair?"

Jack turned slowly to her. "Are you trying to get at something?"

"Oh, no." Rebecca plastered on a big smile, struggling to look innocent. "Just making conversation."

"Oh. Okay," he said and turned back to his work.

"So do they?" Rebecca asked, leaning closer. "Have all their hair?"

His brows pulled together. "Everybody's still got all their hair—and their teeth, in case you're interested in that, too."

Rebecca struggled to keep her smile in place. "I'm going to unload the crates now."

She busied herself dragging the straw from the boxes, lifting out the items buried beneath it, satisfied that she'd gotten all the information she could about Jack's past. Everything she'd learned so far made him the perfect candidate to father her child.

So why wait?

Rebecca straightened, a quilt clutched in her hands. Why not do it now while she had her nerve up?

She glanced over her shoulder. Jack had assembled the bed frame, fitted the springs and mattress in place.

Jack, her, the bed, all in the same place. A perfect opportunity.

Doubt crossed her mind. What would he think if she hopped onto the bed without warning or explanation and invited him to join her? Would he think ill of her? Think she'd lost her mind? Both were possible. Rebecca couldn't bear the thought that he'd refuse her. Could she lure him into her arms using her feminine wiles? Probably not, since she wasn't sure exactly what feminine wiles were.

No, she decided, better to stick to her original plan. A business agreement. Plain and simple.

She gulped in several deep breaths, readying herself to present her proposal. She thought hard, desperate to come up with the best way to make her presentation. Nothing came to her. Finally, she simply turned to him.

"Jack," she announced, "I've decided what I want for decorating your house."

He didn't bother to glance up from what he was doing. "Yeah? What?"

Rebecca straightened her shoulders. "I want you to give me a baby."

CHAPTER EIGHT

"A BABY?" Jack turned to her, confused. "A *baby?*"

She gave him a brisk nod. "Yes. A baby."

He spread his arms. "Where in the hell am I supposed to find you a baby?"

Rebecca willed herself not to blush. "I don't want you to *find* me a baby. I want you to…give me one."

"*Give* you one? What are you talking about?"

Rebecca didn't answer. She didn't have to. Realization dawned on Jack's face. His jaw sagged. His face paled.

"Are you saying what I think you're saying?" he asked cautiously.

She cringed at having to speak the words aloud. "I want you to…get me…with child."

He narrowed his eyes. "If this is some sort of joke, I don't think it's funny."

"I'm deadly serious." Rebecca took a step closer. "Will you do it? Will you get me…pregnant?"

"Hell no." He drew back looking as prudish as a spinster schoolmarm.

"But Jack—"

He backed away, as if he expected her to attack him and take what she wanted.

"Jack, it's a business—"

"Get the hell away from me." He strode out of the room.

"Wait!" Rebecca clattered down the stairs after him. "Jack, wait. If you'll just listen—"

He grabbed his hat from where he'd left it in the parlor, and pushed past her toward the front door.

"Jack! You *owe* me!"

He froze, his hand on the doorknob.

"You said I could name my price," Rebecca told him. "Is this what your word means? Are you welshing on your debt?"

Slowly, he turned to face her. "Have you taken leave of your senses?"

"No," she told him, standing straighter. "I know exactly what I'm doing."

He stepped closer, crowding her. "You want me to get you pregnant—as part of a business deal?"

"Yes," she said, refusing to back away. "I've given it a great deal of thought. It's what I want."

"And how are you going to explain it to everybody when you turn up pregnant?" he challenged.

"Once I'm…with child…I'll go back to Baltimore, tell everyone I married briefly and that my husband died."

"And you think people are going to believe—"

"You needn't worry about the details beyond your limited role," Rebecca insisted. "This is a business arrangement."

"Like hell it is," he growled.

"You can do it, can't you?" she asked, and looked him up and down. "You can provide me with a child?"

Jack shifted closer, his expression so fierce Rebecca thought she might conceive simply by maintaining eye contact. She backed up a step.

"You're making too much of this," Rebecca said softly.

He leaned down and lowered his voice. "Do you have any idea—any idea—what you're asking?"

She pushed her chin up and met his gaze. "I know exactly what I want. The only question is whether or not you intend to honor your word and live up to our agreement."

He straightened, eyeing her harshly. "So that's

what all those questions were about upstairs. Checking out my pedigree, like I'm some sort of stud service?''

Rebecca blushed. ''It's business. The questions were reasonable, under the…circumstances.''

Another long moment dragged by while Jack glared at her. She couldn't read his thoughts, but an odd expression—disgust, hurt, perhaps?—crossed his face, and he latched onto her arm.

''All right,'' he barked. ''Fine. Let's go do it.''

Rebecca gasped and pulled against him. *''Now?''*

He held fast to her arm. ''Yeah. Now. For starters.''

Her eyes rounded. ''For starters?''

''It doesn't always work the first time,'' he told her, none too politely. ''So you'd better let your aunt know she'll have to run the tearoom all afternoon.''

''*All* afternoon?''

''For the next couple of weeks.''

''Weeks?''

''Let's get at it,'' he declared, pulling on her arm.

Rebecca dug in her heels. ''Wait—''

''Come on. I don't want this debt hanging over my head any longer,'' he insisted.

''No!'' Rebecca jerked her arm from his grasp.

Her cheeks flamed and her heart pounded wildly. "This is *my* payment and *I'll* decide when I'm ready to collect it."

Jack leaned down until his breath puffed hot against her cheek. She thought he was about to say something more, but didn't. He spun around and bounded up the stairs.

Rebecca braced her arm against the wall, so light-headed she thought she might actually swoon. She gulped in great breaths of air. Good gracious, had her brilliant business plan turned into the worst nightmare of her life?

HE SHOULD HAVE *KNOWN*. Should have known better than to trust a woman—even Rebecca.

Jack stood in the corner of the saloon, ignoring the crowd, his own thoughts holding all his attention.

For years now, since leaving New York, he'd held back his feelings for a woman—any woman. After what he'd been through, the last thing he'd ever intended to do was put his trust in another female.

But with Rebecca he'd done just that. Slowly, she'd won him over. And then she pulls *this* on him? Wanting him to give her a baby?

Anger deepened in his gut. She'd easily agreed to decorate his house—too easily, he'd thought at the time. Did she have this in mind all along? Was Rebecca just another cunning, calculating female?

Visions of her surfaced among his angry thoughts. Baking cookies, helping with his saloon, smiling, making him laugh. Jack didn't want to believe she was truly the type of woman he'd left behind in New York. But still…

The full gamut of thoughts and feelings had plagued him since she'd presented her *business proposal* three days ago. And still, he didn't know what to make of it.

The only constant was that the idea of bedding down with Rebecca had taken over his life.

Jack shifted uncomfortably as he took in the dozens of men at the bar, the packed gaming tables. The crowd was lively in anticipation of tonight's singer. He'd made an agreement with Miss Dora to allow some of her girls to sing at the Lucky Streak, and Jonah Walker, the blacksmith who played the piano in church, was more than anxious to provide accompaniment. This was the third night, and the crowd grew larger each time.

The chalkboard Jack had hung near the swinging doors bore the names of the men who'd signed up for next week's arm wrestling tournament. The flyers he'd hung around town had brought surprising results. Fifteen men, so far, were anxious to take on all comers.

Customers rolled in, bringing money with them. Jack drummed his fingers on the edge of the bar, annoyed to no end that he couldn't enjoy any of it.

All he could think of was Rebecca.

When she'd presented her proposal, he'd been so angry that he insisted they get down to *business* immediately. He'd wanted to shock her, make her realize what she was asking. He'd thought she'd call the whole thing off. She hadn't.

So here he was thinking of her. Thinking of getting into bed with her.

True, the idea had often crept into his mind. Before they'd officially met, when he'd seen her on the street. After she'd agreed to help with his house. The days they'd spent together. When he'd kissed her. Looking at her, being close to her, talking with her, almost always the notion of rolling around under the sheets with her danced in his mind.

But then she'd gone and *asked* him to do just that. Bed down with her. Make love. Insinuate herself into his life. Take over.

And as if that weren't enough, she'd decided to take her own sweet time about when and where, while his body simmered and seethed almost constantly. Plus, he hadn't seen her in days. Since the afternoon when she'd made her so-called business proposal, he'd gone to the house to work, as usual, but he'd never found her there. He could see that she'd been unpacking things, putting them in place. It irked him that she seemed determined to avoid him—which, somehow, just made him want her more...even though he didn't want to.

Jack grumbled under his breath, pushed through the swinging door into the kitchen and went out back into the dark alley. Since Lucy Hubbard had started cooking for his customers he'd made a point to meet her on Main Street and bring the food to the saloon himself. Tonight, when he turned the corner, he spotted Lucy standing in the shadows and, as usual, Ian Caldwell was with her.

Jack watched them for a moment. Nothing untoward was going on, they stood a respectable distance apart, neither touched. Yet something passed between them. Even in the dim moonlight, Jack could see it. Rebecca came into his mind, bringing on a familiar ache.

They exchanged pleasantries and Jack told Lucy once again how much his customers enjoyed her cooking. She blushed modestly when

Jack paid her. He took her basket and headed back to the saloon, waiting in the shadows long enough to see Ian walk with her toward her home on East Street before going into the kitchen again.

A short while later, after Roy had the food and was selling it at the bar, Ian entered the saloon. He got a beer and joined Jack near the kitchen door.

"Good crowd tonight," Ian commented, gesturing with his foamy glass.

"Things are picking up," Jack said, determined to put his problems behind him. "You seen Seth Grissom lately?"

Ian shook his head. "No, can't say that I have."

"I thought maybe he was at one of the other saloons."

"I make the rounds every night," Ian said. "I haven't seen him anywhere, now that you mention it."

"You reckon he's sick?"

"I'll check," Ian said. "More likely he's just tired of getting kidded about Miss Merriweather's pink storefront."

They stood side by side for a while looking out over the barroom. Finally, Jack said, "She's a married woman."

Ian studied the contents of his glass, then sighed heavily. "Yeah, I know."

"Her husband is about as worthless as they come," Jack said. "He ought to be shot."

"I've considered it."

"You'd be better off keeping your distance," Jack said.

"Yeah, I know that, too," Ian agreed. "I can't stop thinking that maybe her husband won't ever come back."

"You intend to step in?"

"I intend to marry her. All she has to do is say the word." Ian finished his beer and left the saloon.

Jack followed him to the door and gazed down Main Street. No lights burned in the windows of the Marlow Tearoom and Gift Emporium. The place had closed hours ago.

But where was Rebecca? Jack wondered. In the kitchen? Reading? Sewing? Working on her plan to take over his life? Plotting how to drive him even crazier by making him continue to wait?

Maybe he'd just go over there tonight and insist they commence their business deal immediately. That would show her who was running things. And he was sure as hell ready—he'd been ready for days now. If he got any more ready he wouldn't be fit to be seen in public.

Jack grumbled under his breath and went back to the bar.

"Rebecca, what's happening at Mr. Delaney's house?"

Rebecca, serving tray in hand, paused beside the table where Mrs. Tidwell and two other ladies sat. Midafternoon now, and the other tearoom customers had moved along. Only these three lingered.

"Almost finished," Rebecca reported, as she placed a selection of Aunt Virginia's sandwiches on the table.

"I'd love to see the house," Nelly Walker confided, and the other women nodded in agreement.

"Do you think he'll have a party in the new house?" Mrs. Tidwell asked. The other women looked anxious as well.

"Perhaps when his company arrives," Rebecca speculated. For some reason, it pleased her that the ladies of Marlow had changed their opinion of Jack drastically in only a few short weeks. The last time Mrs. Frazier had said something against him, the other ladies had come to his defense.

"I wonder when that will be?" Mrs. Tidwell mused.

Inez Becker drew herself up. "My Stanley knows," she proclaimed with a triumphant lift of her chin.

Rebecca's interest piqued along with the other ladies'. Stanley Becker ran Marlow's express office. He knew everything that went on in town.

"Well, tell us," Mrs. Walker insisted.

Mrs. Becker took a moment to savor the spotlight, then announced, "My Stanley told me that Mr. Delaney received a telegram this morning. His company will arrive *tomorrow*."

"Tomorrow?" Rebecca exclaimed.

"Who was the telegram from?" Mrs. Tidwell asked.

Mrs. Becker let the drama build before answering. "It wasn't signed."

Mrs. Tidwell and Mrs. Walker gasped at the significance. Rebecca gasped at the anxiety that shot though her.

Tomorrow? Jack's company was arriving tomorrow?

Her heart thumped harder in her chest. That meant only one thing: she'd have to get Jack into bed *tonight*.

CHAPTER NINE

MAYBE SHE'D CHANGED her mind.

Jack threaded through the crowd at the Lucky Streak, blocking out the conversation, laughter, the clink of glasses. At the bat-wing door he gazed down the street. Dark. No lights on at the Marlow Tearoom and Gift Emporium.

Not for the first time, he wondered if she'd changed her mind about the business proposal that had turned his life upside down.

Part of him—the part centered in the portion of his brain that still functioned logically—hoped that she had. He hoped, too, that he'd been wrong in thinking the worst of her. He wished that he still didn't feel angry.

Jack turned away from the door. His neck was sore from gazing down the street at the tearoom so many times. He ought to be thinking about tomorrow and the stage from the East he would meet. Things would change for him then. He should have been looking forward to it.

But all he could think of was Rebecca.

A part of him wondered if he should honor his word and give her the payment she wanted for decorating his house—despite the lifelong ramifications? Should he give in to the desire that had driven him to distraction, and go along with what she wanted?

The swinging doors parted and Ian walked into the saloon. Jack greeted him, grateful for the interruption.

"Miss Merriweather stopped me just now," Ian said, and pulled an envelope from his shirt pocket.

Jack hesitated a moment before accepting the pink envelope decorated with Rebecca's curly writing. Would her note state that she'd come to her senses and canceled her business proposal? A flash of unexpected disappointment tightened his gut, along with a thread of anger. She'd kept him tied in knots thinking of sleeping with her, and now she was changing her mind? Just like that?

Logic sifted into Jack's thoughts. Of course, it would be for the best if, in fact, that was what the note said. But still…

Jack ripped open the envelope. On a pink-flowered sheet of stationery was written one word: *Now*.

He grabbed his hat and left the saloon.

WHAT HAD SHE DONE?

Rebecca paced fitfully in the bedroom on the second floor of Jack's house, twisting her fingers together and questioning her own sanity.

Was it too late to change her mind? She hurried to the window and peered out at the dark street. No sign of Jack. Yet. So she could leave, if she wanted. Leave and tell him she'd rethought the whole proposal. And then—

And then what? Turn her back on her only viable chance to have a child, and a rich, full future?

She curled her hands into fists. No. No, she couldn't back away now. The stakes were too high. She had to get through this evening—somehow.

Pacing across the room, Rebecca stopped in front of the large mirror she'd uncrated and Jack had placed in the corner of the room. She eyed her reflection. Pale-yellow nightgown and wrapper covering her from throat to wrist to ankle. Bare feet. Hair caught in a simple ribbon at her nape.

A wave of anxiety crashed over her. The color—was it wrong for her? Would Jack even *care* about the color? Should she have dressed in her nightwear *before* he arrived? And her hair—

should she have left it up? Was taking it down herself too presumptuous? Would Jack prefer to do it himself?

Rebecca's knees shook so severely she had to sit down on the chair beside the fireplace. She waved her hands, fanning her face. Good gracious, she was about to perspire. What would Jack think if he walked in and found her sweating?

And what was taking him so long? Rebecca sprang from the chair, pacing again. She'd given the envelope to Ian before rushing over here, and he'd promised to deliver it to Jack immediately. Did he think she had all evening to wait around? She had to start work early in the morning, for goodness' sake.

Another thought flashed in her mind, Jack's warning that these things didn't always work the first time.

All afternoon.

Weeks.

"Oh…"

She stopped and pressed her palm to her forehead. Her mother had died when Rebecca was young—too young to learn advice crucial to this occasion. What was expected of her? Would Jack think her a harlot if she met his advances with wanton abandonment? Should she simply allow him to proceed as he chose while she contemplated the wallpaper pattern?

Lucy. She should have asked Lucy. Rebecca cringed at realizing she should have thought of her friend sooner.

A noise came from outside. Rebecca rushed to the window and pressed her face to the glass. Her stomach welled with fear, then knotted when she saw no sign of Jack.

An unwanted thought barged into her already churning mind. She'd insisted to Jack that this arrangement was a business deal. She'd told herself over and over that's all it was.

So why, at the moment, did it seem like so much more?

She'd missed Jack, she realized, backing away from the window. These past few days when she'd made a point to come to the house when she knew he wouldn't be there, she'd missed the sound of his heavy footsteps on the floor, his masculine scent, his deep voice echoing through the house. She'd missed talking with him. Jack always seemed to understand her problems—and he wasn't offended when she offered help with his.

Another thought flashed in Rebecca's mind, stilling her pacing. If this weren't simply a business deal, then that must mean—

Rebecca fought off the idea. She wouldn't allow herself to contemplate the notion that Jack meant more to her than an opportunity to have a child.

"Good gracious..." Rebecca mumbled. She had to get a grip on herself. Somehow, she must get through this evening.

With another quick look out the window, Rebecca dashed down the staircase, her wrapper billowing behind her, and raced into the kitchen. Jack had stocked the cupboards already so she went directly to the cabinet beneath the sideboard and withdrew the bottle of whiskey he'd left there.

Without another thought, Rebecca pulled out the stopper and took a swig. Fire ignited in her throat and pooled in her stomach. She coughed, wheezed. Tears blurred her eyes. A moment passed and she was surprised to realize that as dreadful as the stuff tasted, it steadied her nerves. She sipped again and again as she made her way upstairs.

The bedroom seemed warmer as she eased into the chair and tipped up the bottle. The whiskey didn't taste quite so sharp. She drank more, thinking the stuff seemed almost mellow running down her throat.

She settled back in the chair. Why had she

been so upset about this evening? She couldn't quite remember.

The sound of the front door closing and heavy footsteps on the stairs reached her ears, and briefly, she wondered who might be coming to visit at this time of night. A large figure filled the doorway. She squinted in the dim light.

"Jack...how nice of you to...stop by," she said, and giggled.

He was in front of her then, towering over her. Gracious, he was handsome. And so tall, so sturdy. Rebecca couldn't recall just why she'd been afraid of his arrival. All she knew was that some unnamed, unseen force drew her to him— the only place in the world she wanted to be.

Jack took her hands and helped her from the chair. She collapsed into his waiting arms.

REBECCA WOKE with a start. An irrational fear stole though her, then surged nearly uncontrollably as she lay on her side looking at a strange room.

Where was she?

She remained perfectly still on the bed. A lantern burned low on the bureau. Vague recollection filled her head. A mirror, a chair beside the fireplace. Why, they looked exactly like the furnishings she'd placed in—

Jack's room.

Horror whipped through Rebecca. She slapped her hand over her lips to keep from crying out. She was in Jack's room! Jack's bed!

Cautiously, she rolled over.

Jack.

He lay on the mattress next to her, on his side, his back to her. The flesh of his bare shoulder gleamed in the lantern light.

Rebecca nearly cried out. Good gracious, he was *naked.*

Visions of the evening zinged through her mind. Waiting for him in the bedroom, the whiskey, then finally, his arrival. Her heart beat faster remembering how he'd come straight to her, taken her into his arms and—

Cautiously, Rebecca lifted the quilt and peeked under. She wore her yellow nightgown, but it was bunched up around her knees.

Good Lord, what had she done?

Humiliation boiled in her churning stomach. What had she been thinking? How could she have put herself into this compromising position? How could she have imagined *this* could in any way be construed as a business deal?

Rebecca's stomach lurched as she slipped from under the covers, desperate to leave, to get away before Jack woke.

She shoved her arms through the sleeves of her wrapper, grabbed her clothing and dashed for the door.

REBECCA DRAGGED HERSELF from the bed—her own, this time—then fell back onto it. Her head pounded. Her stomach rolled.

Yet those weren't the worst of her problems.

After she'd run though the streets of Marlow in her wrapper, trailing an armload of her clothing in the dead of night, she'd reached the safety of her room. Climbing into bed she'd slept fitfully, then claimed illness when Aunt Virginia had come to check on her sometime after dawn.

Now sunlight streamed in around the edges of the window curtains. The mantel clock told her it was midafternoon.

She rose from the bed but another wave of nausea washed over her, causing her head to pound harder. She felt awful. But worse, she couldn't remember a thing that had happened last night. After Jack's arrival, anyway.

But how could that be? How could she have been deflowered and not recall any of it?

The liquor had wiped out her memory, she realized, sinking onto the bed again. And just because she couldn't remember the details didn't mean it hadn't happened.

Jack had taken her into his arms, she knew that. She'd awakened in his bed. He'd been naked. Her gown was bunched up. Jack certainly was not the type of man to have a woman in his bed and *not* have something happen.

But wouldn't there be some evidence? Sitting on the bed, Rebecca mentally took inventory of her state of wellness. Other than her headache and upset stomach, everything else seemed exactly as it always was. Surely *something* about her ought to be different. Shouldn't it?

Rebecca dragged herself from the bed, washed, slipped into a gray dress and twisted her hair into a simple knot atop her head. In the kitchen cooking odors greeted her. Ordinarily, Aunt Virginia's food caused her mouth to water. Now it turned her stomach.

Carefully, she peeked through the curtain that separated the kitchen from the tearoom and saw about a half-dozen women seated at the tables, and her aunt—an empty serving tray braced against her hip—chatting with them.

The quiet comfort of the tearoom washed over Rebecca and she wanted to go inside, savor the sameness of the day, the food, the conversation. But she hesitated. With one look at her, could the women see what she'd done last night? If, in fact, anything at all had happened?

A feeble flicker of hope rose in Rebecca as she fetched the teapot. Perhaps nothing had happened. Perhaps Jack—

The back door swung open. Jack stood in the doorway. Rebecca dropped the teapot.

A slow, lazy grin spread across his face as he leaned one shoulder against the door. His gaze slid to her feet and rose leisurely—knowingly—to her face.

Rebecca's stomach dropped. Any doubt about what had—or hadn't—happened last night evaporated with one look at Jack's expression.

"Sleep late?" he asked, his voice rich and deep. His brows rose slightly. "After last night, you need your rest."

Rebecca's face flamed.

"You surprised me," he admitted. "I didn't think you'd be so wild in bed."

Her knees weakened. Wild? She'd been wild last night?

His grin widened. "A real hellcat."

Rebecca turned away, her cheeks throbbing with embarrassment. She gripped the sideboard for support.

"I—I'd like you to leave now," she said, straining to keep her voice steady.

Jack's footsteps thudded on the bare floor as he walked closer. "I brought you something."

He'd brought her something? A gift? Her mind raced. Was a gift appropriate after such an occasion? She couldn't imagine how she'd word the thank-you note.

Rebecca turned slowly. Jack stood close. Heat wafted from his body, warming her, threatening to rob what little strength she had left.

"You left these behind," Jack said. He pulled a garment from his pocket and dangled it in front of her.

Her drawers. The pink ones with the lace around the legs and the little bows sewn at the seams. She must have missed them when she'd gathered her clothing and raced from his room. Mortified, Rebecca recoiled at the sight.

Jack shrugged. "If you don't want them, I can hang them behind the bar where that picture used to be, like a flag—"

Rebecca snatched them from his hand. "That's disgusting."

He leaned in and lowered his voice. "Don't worry. I won't tell anybody about your lacy underwear—or that little mole you've got, either."

Rebecca winced and squeezed her eyes shut momentarily, attempting to ward off her embarrassment. It didn't help.

"I figured you'd be ready to go another round this afternoon," Jack said and hitched up his trousers. "We can slip into your room right now and—"

"No!" she told him. "I've—I've changed my mind. I want no part of this arrangement."

Jack shook his head. "Well now, I'm afraid it's too late for you to back out now. You named your price. I'm obligated to pay your debt—no matter how long it takes."

She ducked around him. "I want you to leave."

"It's not that simple."

"Yes, it is," she insisted. Anger pushed its way through her churning emotions, a welcome relief from the embarrassment and humiliation.

He gave her another grin. "Did you know you snore when you sleep on your back?"

"Get out!" Rebecca grabbed a dish from the sideboard and hurled it at him.

He sidestepped the plate, and after one more long, knowing look he gave her a nod and disappeared out the door.

Rebecca burst into tears.

CHAPTER TEN

REBECCA MADE ONLY ONE appearance in the tea-room that afternoon. The women there clucked sympathetically over her supposed illness, which only made her feel worse. They'd also rushed to tell her the latest gossip. The stagecoach expected to bring Jack's company had been delayed.

The last thing she wanted to hear about was Jack Delaney. Rebecca left the tearoom.

The stores in Marlow would close soon but she needed to get out, get some perspective on things. Mostly, she wanted to push last night and this afternoon's confrontation with Jack out of her mind.

That proved impossible.

Crossing Main Street she saw him step through the bat-wing doors of the Lucky Streak, arms folded across his chest as he settled his gaze on her. His look—even from a distance—was so knowing it caused her steps to falter. Quickly, she ducked into Townsend's Dry Goods Store.

She forced her attention onto some newly arrived bolts of fabric, but almost immediately sensed a presence and looked up. At the end of the aisle stood Jack. A small, very private smile spread over his lips.

Rebecca flushed. The gall of that man! Looking at her as if he could still see her naked. She circled the aisle in the opposite direction and left the store.

The Pink Blossom Café, the First Union Bank, the other shops passed in a blur as Rebecca made her way to East Street and turned the corner. Was the man following her? Deliberately taunting her? Tormenting her?

She considered ducking into the odd little museum that had recently opened, but went into Norman's General Store instead. Norman Kirby nodded from behind the counter.

Rebecca wove her way down an aisle studying each item on display. She hoped something on the shelves might spark her interest, take her mind off her situation.

A warm chill slithered up Rebecca's spine. Her senses sprang to life. She looked over her shoulder. Jack stood behind her, so close that she felt his breath on her cheek. She hadn't seen him come in the store or heard his approach.

Rebecca braced herself for yet another penetrating look from him, or at least a smug grin. Instead, he leaned down and snored in her ear.

"Oh!" She pushed past him and out onto the boardwalk, threading her way through the last of the day's shoppers. The nerve of that man!

Anger roiled through Rebecca chasing away most of the embarrassment she'd suffered today. By the time she reached the tearoom, she'd calmed down. She went inside and found her aunt heading for the door.

"You'd better hurry," Virginia said, pulling her shawl on. "You know Mrs. Frazier doesn't like to be kept waiting."

"What—oh." Rebecca recalled then that tonight the ladies were meeting at Mrs. Frazier's house to plan the school's pie social. Rebecca was expected to be there.

"I can't go," she said, and truly meant it. "Please give the ladies my regrets."

"Get some rest," Aunt Virginia said and left.

Rebecca collapsed into a chair and braced her elbows on the table. She covered her face with her palms.

How could her business proposal have gone so wrong? It had seemed like a perfectly good idea at its inception. And why was Jack tormenting her so?

Time slipped by, the minutes—hours, perhaps—uncounted while she contemplated these weighty issues. No answers came to her, only the prospect of another night in Jack's bed. She'd have to manage it, somehow. She still wanted a child. That hadn't changed.

If only she could remember. Rebecca sat back in the chair. The tearoom had grown dark, lighted only by the two lanterns on the mantel. She scrunched her brow, searched her memory. One of the biggest moments in a woman's life and she couldn't recall any of it. How could that be?

The little bell above the door jangled and Lucy walked in. "What are you doing sitting here all alone?" she asked, easing into the chair next to Rebecca.

"Thinking," she said wistfully. "Why aren't you at Mrs. Frazier's meeting?"

"I had to prepare the food for Mr. Delaney's customers."

Rebecca fought back the urge to grumble under her breath at the mention of Jack's name.

"You know, he's a very nice person. Everyone in town says so—except for Mrs. Frazier, of course." Lucy paused before going on. "I want to talk with you about something."

The tone of Lucy's voice jarred Rebecca's conscience. She'd been so wound up over her own problems she hadn't considered that anyone else might have troubles, too.

"What is it?" Rebecca gave Lucy her full attention.

"It's about Raymond." Lucy folded her hands in her lap.

"Did you hear from him?" Rebecca asked.

She shook her head. "No. That's just it. It's been so long now and I haven't heard from him. No letters, no telegram. Nothing."

"Do you want him to come back?" Rebecca asked gently.

"Part of me wishes he wouldn't," she admitted.

"Is that because of Ian?"

"Ian...he's such a wonderful man—everything that Raymond isn't." Lucy pressed her lips together. "He meets me every night when I take the food to the Lucky Streak, walks me there and back just to make sure I'm all right. He says the kindest things, Rebecca. Nothing out of line, of course. But he makes me feel...special."

"You are special," Rebecca said.

Lucy was quiet for a moment, then drew in a breath. "I've decided to pursue a divorce."

"Raymond has abandoned you, Lucy. It's the only thing you can do," Rebecca agreed.

Long moments stretched in the silent room.

Rebecca didn't envy Lucy her problem. Though she wouldn't admit it, Rebecca was sure she was in love with Ian Caldwell. He was a good man. Lucy deserved a good man.

Drawing in a fresh breath, Lucy said, "So, what have you been up to lately?"

Events of the last twenty-four hours came back to Rebecca, full force. Her stomach twisted into a painful knot at the memory.

But she pushed it away and sat straighter in the chair. Lucy was the only person in the world she could ask such a personal question. If she didn't do it now, she might never do it. And she had to know.

"I need to ask you something," Rebecca said trying desperately not to blush. "But it's terribly personal…"

Lucy looked unconcerned. "Go ahead. I grew up on a farm with seven brothers. Believe me, nothing offends me."

"Is there a way to tell—I mean, are there physical signs if a woman has—" Rebecca stopped, unable to say the words aloud. She leaned closer and whispered into Lucy's ear.

"Oh, certainly." Lucy cupped her hands around Rebecca's ear and whispered back.

Rebecca's brows pulled together. "You're sure?"

"Oh, yes," Lucy assured her.

Rebecca nodded slowly. "Well, thank you. That certainly clears things up. A lot of things, actually."

"You're welcome," Lucy said, rising from her chair. "I'd better run along. I left two pies in the oven."

Rebecca remained in her seat, barely aware that Lucy had left, hardly hearing the door close behind her as her anger grew. All she could do was think. And all she could think of was Jack.

"Oh!" Rebecca sprang from the chair, snatched the fireplace poker from beside the hearth and hit the street. By the time she reached the Lucky Streak, she was boiling.

She blasted into the saloon, throwing open the bat-wing doors so hard they banged against the walls. The place was packed with men sitting at the gaming tables, standing at the bar. Conversation droned. A cloud of cigarette smoke hovered near the ceiling. The men nearest the doors did a double take as Rebecca strode in, the poker clutched in her outstretched hand.

"Where are you?" she screamed, striding forward. Men fell back out of her way. She brandished the poker. "Where are you, you no-good, low-down varmint?"

Rebecca spotted Jack seated with two other

men, their table littered with beer glasses, talking
and grinning.

"You!"

Jack looked up, saw her. The smile fell from
his face.

"You mangy dog!" Rebecca closed the distance between them. He jumped from his chair.
She swung the poker, sending glasses and beer
crashing to the floor. Every man in the place
turned to stare.

Rebecca circled the table, pointing the poker
like a sword. "You are lower than a snake!"

Jack held up his palms, backing away. "What
the hell's wrong with you?"

"You are *worse* than a snake! You're snake
spit!" With a two-handed roundhouse swing, Rebecca sliced the poker through the air.

The men scattered. Jack leaped backward.
"Put that thing down before somebody gets
hurt."

"Yes, Delaney, like you, maybe!" somebody
called from the crowd. Laughter broke out.

"I mean it, Rebecca," Jack told her. "Put that
down—"

She swung again, this time nearly catching the
front of his shirt. "You don't deserve to live,
you—you—oh! I don't know a word bad enough
for you!"

"How about skunk?" someone suggested.

"Thank you," Rebecca called. She narrowed her eyes at Jack. "You skunk!"

"You tell him, honey!" another man called.

"What the devil's gotten into you?" Jack demanded.

"You filthy *liar!*"

He froze. His face paled. "Oh. I—I can explain, Rebecca. Just put the poker down and—"

She swung again, this time at his head. Jack lurched forward and caught her hands. She held on, but he was too strong. Jack ripped it from her fingers. She lunged for it. He raised it high over his head out of reach.

He caught her arm and leaned down. "Go in the back room," he said quietly.

Rebecca glared at him, her blood still boiling. She didn't intend to do anything he suggested.

"Go on. Nobody here paid for this sort of show," he said, sounding so reasonable she wanted to hit him.

Reality oozed through her anger. He was right, of course, though it didn't suit her in the least. Rebecca glared at him one final time, jerked her arm from his grasp, put her nose in the air and marched through the swinging door into the kitchen. Applause and hoots of laughter erupted behind her.

Jack followed her into the kitchen. They squared off in the middle of the floor. She eyed the poker in his hand. Jack pushed past her to the back door, tossed it out into the night, then slammed the door shut.

"You lied to me!" Rebecca shouted. "You led me to believe you and I had—had—well, you know what I mean. You tormented me over it. And *nothing* happened!"

Jack just looked at her for a moment. "No, nothing happened. When I got there you were drunk. You passed out. I couldn't very well carry you home, so I put you in bed."

"Did—did you…ogle me?" she demanded.

"Hell, no! Do you think I'm the kind of man to go peeping under a woman's skirt when she's passed out drunk?"

"Then how did you know about my mole?"

Jack shifted uncomfortably. "Well, all right, when I was putting you in bed your gown came up a little and I saw it there on your calf."

"You pig."

"What the hell was I supposed to do with you?" Jack demanded.

"You could have put me in one of the *other* bedrooms!"

"Oh. Well, uh…"

"You lied to me, Jack," Rebecca said. "You

lied about everything. You made me think we'd—we'd—''

''Made love?''

Her cheeks flushed. ''Was it all just a game to you?''

''A game?'' Jack's expression tightened. ''*You've* got a hell of a lot of nerve asking *me* if this is a game!''

''You never intended to go along with our business arrangement at all, did you,'' she accused. ''You're welshing on your debt. Fine! If you won't give me what I want, I'll find another man who will.''

He shifted closer, anger drawing his brows together. ''Like hell you will.''

''It's none of your business. Not anymore.''

Jack closed his hand over her arm. ''I'm not going to let you—''

''Just try and stop me.'' Rebecca jerked away and stormed out the back door.

CHAPTER ELEVEN

OF ALL THE TALK that had circulated through the tearoom, none of it had been about Rebecca. Thank goodness.

Late afternoon, the tables were empty now. Rebecca had kept to the kitchen today as much as possible, affording her customers the opportunity to talk about her, if they chose. Yet peeking through the curtained doorway, straining for snatches of conversation, she'd picked up nothing to indicate she was today's topic of whispered gossip.

No one had mentioned last night's escapade at the Lucky Streak. So far.

With a sigh, Rebecca loaded dishes onto her tray and headed back to the kitchen. So many emotions churned in her, she wasn't sure she could capture and name any one of them.

"You've been quiet today," Aunt Virginia said, drying a teacup. "I'll bet I know what's on your mind."

Rebecca held her breath.

"Mrs. Wagner's millinery shop next door."

Rebecca heaved a sigh of relief. "What about it?"

"Didn't you hear? She's decided to close the shop and move to Keaton with her daughter."

Rebecca had kept her eye on Mrs. Wagner's shop for months, planning how she could expand the tearoom if the older woman decided to move. Today, she'd been so involved in her own problems, she'd completely missed the news.

"I'll help you with the dishes," Rebecca said, and picked up a dish towel, "then go talk to her."

"You really are distracted today," Aunt Virginia said, shaking her head. "Usually, business is *all* you think of."

Business had been her whole life for months now. It had been her future. It was still her future, she realized.

Business. Not a child.

Sadness gripped Rebecca's heart. After all that had gone on between her and Jack, she knew there was no way they'd continue their business deal now. And, despite the threat she'd made in the kitchen of the saloon last night, she'd never approach another man with the proposal.

So where did that leave her? Exactly where

she'd started. With a tearoom, a head for business, and a lonely future.

The kitchen seemed to close in around Rebecca. She untied her apron. ''Do you mind if I talk to Mrs. Wagner now?''

''That's fine, dear. I can manage things here.''

Rebecca slipped outside into the alley but didn't go to Mrs. Wagner's shop. She'd been inside dozens of times and knew exactly what renovations she'd make. Instead, she headed toward East Street. If business was to be her future, then she should pursue it. She rounded the corner and ran into Jack.

They both froze, staring into each other's eyes. Rebecca's heart thumped wildly, weakening her knees and causing her hands to tremble.

How could he have this effect on her? Still? After what he'd done, what she'd done? How could she want to throw her arms around his neck, in the middle of the afternoon, on a public street?

''Where are you headed?'' Jack asked softly.

''To see Seth Grissom,'' she said.

Jack's expression hardened. ''If you think I'm going to let you ask him to be a party to this ridiculous business proposal of yours, you can—''

"No," she said quickly. "I just want to ask him about doing some renovations for me."

Jack eased off a bit, but didn't look happy. "Keep away from Grissom."

"Why?"

Jack looked at her for a moment, then pushed his hat an inch higher on his head. "The men in town have been giving Griss a hard time about painting your store pink."

"Why on earth would anyone blame him? I'm the one—"

"Because that's the way it is," Jack told her. "Anyway, Griss isn't taking it so well. He keeps to himself now. It would be better if you just left him alone."

She realized then that she almost never saw Seth on the street. She'd assumed he was busy working, but now it seemed he'd become somewhat of a recluse. Thanks to her.

"Maybe I should go apologize," she said.

"No, Rebecca. Stay away."

She looked up at Jack. "I suppose all the men in town are talking about *you* now. After last night."

Jack waved away her words. "It doesn't bother me."

A long, silent moment passed as people hurried by on the boardwalk, horses and carriages rumbled through the street. Rebecca wondered if she'd ever have a moment alone with Jack again. If she'd ever have this opportunity.

"What was the real reason you wouldn't go through with our…arrangement?" Rebecca pulled up her courage. "Did you find me unattractive? Too outspoken? Too…old?"

Jack's frown deepened, his expression changing from confusion to hurt, then to anger.

"I've got a question for you," he said. "When you agreed to fix up my house, did you plan all along to use me to get yourself pregnant?"

Rebecca gasped softly and reeled back. She felt the color drain from her face. Jack's question was so far from her thoughts, it took a full minute for her to understand what he'd said.

"My gracious, Jack, no," she said, almost in a whisper. "I never considered the idea at all until…"

His expression softened marginally. "Until what?"

"Until I saw what a lovely home you had and it made me realize I wanted the same. But not just a house, a baby, too." Rebecca gazed up at him. "Do you really think I'd plotted and schemed against you this whole time?"

Jack didn't answer right away, making Rebecca wonder—for the first time—if maybe that's exactly what he thought of her. Her heart ached. Could he really have such a low opinion of her?

"Jack?" she asked, wanting an answer.

He glanced around, seeming to realize that they were still standing on the crowded boardwalk, then hooked her elbow and led her into the alley. A few minutes passed while he seemed unsure of what he wanted to say—or if he even wanted to say anything.

Finally, he looked down at her. "My mama died."

Rebecca drew in a quick, sharp breath as she saw the hurt in his eyes and remembered the pain of losing her own mother. She wanted to hold him, comfort him, but he went on.

"It was about five years ago," Jack said softly. "That in itself was hard enough to deal with, but then—then other women started showing up at our house."

"Women intent on pursuing your father?" she asked.

"Our family had money, good social standing. My pa was a 'good catch,' as the women liked to say." Jack's expression hardened at the bitter memories. "These women started taking over. Rearranging the furniture, hosting dinners, wearing my mama's clothes and jewelry."

"Oh, Jack, that's terrible."

"No, the terrible part was that my pa didn't do anything to stop them. He wouldn't listen— to me or my brothers and sisters. He was too busy working—or he just didn't care. I never knew which." Jack drew in a breath. "I took it as long as I could, then I left."

"That's how you ended up in Marlow."

Jack nodded. "And I swore I'd never let a woman—any woman—take over my life."

Instinctively, Rebecca latched onto his arm. "That's exactly what you thought I was doing. Oh, Jack, I'm so sorry. I never meant—"

He pulled away, then turned and disappeared around the corner.

Rebecca watched him go, something inside her tearing away with him. Tears welled in her eyes. She wanted to run after him. She wanted to tell him—

Tell him what? Rebecca gulped, forcing down her tears. That she was sorry? That she'd missed him? That the days spent with him had been wonderful? That her heart ached thinking of him?

Rebecca didn't know. Standing on the boardwalk, staring at the spot where Jack had disappeared around the corner, she didn't know what she wanted to tell him.

Not that it mattered. Jack, apparently, wasn't interested in hearing anything she said.

Not even that she loved him.

So, SHE'D RUINED the reputation of two men in Marlow.

Rebecca slipped out the back door into the dark alley, clutching her heavy canvas bag. Hopefully, after tonight, she'd redeem herself—in the eyes of one of them, anyway.

Only a few windows shone with lantern light as Rebecca made her way south on East Street. A cool breeze brought the sound of distant piano music from the saloons, an occasional laugh, and the bay of a dog somewhere in town.

Darting into the alley, she glanced around, then knocked on the back door of Seth Grissom's shop. She heard his heavy footsteps inside. The door creaked as he opened it.

Holding up the lantern, Seth glared out at her. He towered over her. His shoulders nearly touched both sides of the narrow doorway. For a moment Rebecca feared he'd close the door in her face, but he didn't.

She pulled a book from her bag and thrust it at him.

"It's an art book," Rebecca said. "I brought it with me from Baltimore."

Seth glanced at the book, then at her again.

"The Lucky Streak needs a painting behind the bar. You can use the models in the book as a guide," Rebecca said.

Slowly, Seth hung the lantern on a nail beside the door and accepted the book. He flipped it open and his cheeks above his full beard turned bright red.

"These—these women are n-n-naked," he stammered.

Rebecca's face heated, but she pushed on. "It's art."

He turned another page, his eyes bulging. "But—but they don't have on any clothes."

"Yes, I know." She closed the book, brushing her hands over his meatier ones, forcing aside her own embarrassment. "You did those fashion pictures for my tearoom, so I know you can paint something…appropriate…for the saloon."

Seth just looked at her, the red fading from his face.

Rebecca squared her shoulders. "Hopefully, your…donation…to the saloon will give the men in town something to talk about other than you and my pink store."

His expression softened as realization dawned on him.

"Thank you," he whispered.

Rebecca managed a small smile. "Just don't give the model in the painting my face, please."

Seth grinned, his beard and mustache parting to reveal gentle lips and gleaming teeth.

"These are my art supplies." She passed him her bag. "And tell Jack he should have a contest to name your painting. A nickel a vote."

"Yes, ma'am."

Seth stepped inside and closed the door as Rebecca hurried away.

DORIS TIDWELL BROKE THE NEWS. Rebecca nearly dropped her serving tray as she rushed through the tearoom.

"Lucy's husband came home last night," she said to her aunt at the stove.

Aunt Virginia nodded. "You should go to her."

Rebecca hurried down East Street and knocked softly on Lucy's door. After a few minutes it opened. Lucy glanced over her shoulder, then slipped outside and pulled the door closed behind her. She looked pale and drawn, tense.

"Are you all right?" Rebecca kept her voice low.

Lucy gave her a quick nod.

"Did Raymond find work?" she asked. "Or investments?"

"No." Lucy looked away. "I don't know what's going to happen, except...Raymond says he's home to stay."

Rebecca's heart sank. "What are you going to do?"

"Nothing." Tears pooled in her eyes. "Raymond is my husband and...and that's that."

Rebecca touched Lucy's hand. "If you need anything, let me know."

"I will." She swiped at her tears, then ducked into the house and closed the door.

Tears came to Rebecca's eyes as she walked down East Street. Of course, Lucy was doing what she thought was right. Raymond was her husband.

Ian Caldwell came into Rebecca's mind and a new sadness settled around her heart. Ian. He loved Lucy, genuinely loved her. How would he accept this news?

At once, Rebecca wanted to run to Jack. She wanted to lay her head against his broad shoulder. She wanted to hear his voice rumble in his chest as he spoke against her hair. She wanted to feel his big arms around her. She didn't care what they'd been through. She just wanted to be with Jack.

Rebecca turned the corner onto Main Street

heading for the Lucky Streak. Inez Becker fell in step beside her.

"Rebecca, I was just headed over to your tearoom," she said excitedly. "I have news."

"Everyone's already heard," Rebecca said.

"But that's not possible. I saw it myself, just now at the depot." Inez touched Rebecca's arm, stopping her on the boardwalk. "Mr. Delaney's company arrived. And it's not what everyone thought. Not investors at all."

Rebecca braced herself, not sure she wanted to ask another question.

Inez didn't give her the opportunity. "Mr. Delaney's company is a *woman*. I heard him call her by name. Emily. She's young and just lovely. Why, the way he fussed over her, I'd say she's his fiancée. Or maybe even his wife."

CHAPTER TWELVE

IF JACK HADN'T already heard the news, he could have figured it out from the look on Ian's face. Standing at the bar, Jack saw him push through the swinging doors and drop into a chair in a corner table. Jack got a bottle of whiskey and a glass from behind the bar and walked over.

"On the house." Jack put both on the table in front of Ian and sat down beside him. "Do you think Lucy will—"

"She'll stand by her husband." Ian scrubbed his hands over his face and slumped forward, bracing his arms on the table. "But I can't ask her to leave him. All I can do is be here when she decides she's had enough of that bastard."

Jack rose from the chair and clasped Ian on the shoulder. "Let me know if you need anything."

Ian just nodded. He pulled off his badge and dropped it in his pocket, then poured himself a shot of whiskey.

Jack ambled through the crowded tables and

leaned on the bat-wing doors. His gaze drifted to Rebecca's tearoom.

Dark, late, not a light on in the place, but he knew she was inside. A heaviness settled around his heart as he thought of Rebecca, then Ian and Lucy.

What would Ian give to walk to Lucy's house this minute, knock on her door and be invited inside? Jack could do that at Rebecca's place, if he wanted to. Problem was, he wasn't so sure she would invite him in.

He'd done a lot of thinking about Rebecca, about himself, about the two of them. He'd asked her flat out if she'd conspired to deceive him and she'd told him that she hadn't. She'd even apologized. Jack believed her.

But things still weren't settled between them. Now, seeing Ian's misery, Jack knew what he had to do. He pushed through the swinging doors and headed down the street.

Things would never be settled between him and Rebecca until he gave her what she wanted—truly wanted.

REBECCA STOOD at the window of the tearoom staring down the dark street at the Lucky Streak saloon. Light spilled over the top of the door and out the windows, bringing laughter and piano music with it.

Was Jack inside the saloon? Or was he home with Emily?

Rebecca's stomach twisted into a cold knot. All afternoon the tearoom had buzzed with excitement. Who, exactly, was Jack's mysterious guest? Was this Emily really his fiancée? His wife, perhaps?

No one had known the answer, and Rebecca couldn't bring herself to contemplate the question any longer.

With a heavy sigh, she turned away from the window. She'd changed into her nightgown hours ago, but couldn't sleep. With the lantern burning low on the bureau in her bedroom, she'd tried to read but couldn't.

All she could think of was Jack…of what he'd been through after his mother's death…of how he'd suspected her of the same despicable thing. She didn't blame him.

Slowly, she plodded into the kitchen. Food seemed unappealing, but at least cooking was something to do. A soft knock sounded on the back door. Lucy flew into her mind. No one else would come to call at this late hour. She opened the door.

Jack stood outside.

"We have some unfinished business," he said.

Stunned, Rebecca just stared as he moved past her into the kitchen, torn between throwing him out, and throwing herself into his arms. He reached over her head and pushed the door shut.

"Shh." Rebecca put her finger to her lips and nodded toward her aunt's closed bedroom door.

"I'm here to give you what you wanted," Jack whispered. "If you still want it."

Her heart fluttered quickly beneath her breast as she gazed up at him. How handsome he was. How she longed to be in his arms—forever.

Jack pressed his palm to her cheek, caressing it lightly. Rebecca's knees weakened at his touch. Yes, she wanted him, with all her heart she wanted him. But should she allow herself this one moment with him? Because that was all it could ever be. Just tonight.

He eased closer, his warmth robbing her of her strength—and threatening her good judgement.

"What about Emily?" she asked, managing only a whisper.

Jack frowned. "What about her?"

"She's home waiting on you, and you're here with me—"

"I don't usually ask my sister along when I visit a woman," Jack told her.

She gasped. "Emily is your—"

"Sister," Jack said.

Rebecca touched her hand to her chest, relieved. "I thought she was your fiancée, or even your wife, and—"

"Rebecca," Jack said softly, easing closer. "Sometimes—not always, but just sometimes—you think too much."

A whisper of laughter bubbled up inside her. "I do?"

"You do," Jack said gently. "And while we're on the subject, let's get something else straight. No, I don't think you're unattractive. No, I don't think you're too outspoken. And hell no, I don't think you're too old."

"Oh, Jack…"

He took her into his arms, pulling her tight against him. With a touch of his finger, he lifted her chin, then settled his lips over hers.

Rebecca melted against him. His warmth, his strength captured her, and she knew there was no place on earth she'd rather be.

He broke their kiss, but still held her close. "About this business deal of ours. I'm willing to hold up my end of our arrangement. But it's up to you. Do I stay? Or go?"

For so long she'd feared an empty, lonely future. That's why she'd proposed the business deal in the first place. Yet now that the opportunity was here, now that Jack had agreed to give her what she wanted, Rebecca didn't know if she could go through with it.

What sort of life would that be? A life without Jack himself? Her heart ached at the thought.

But she didn't know what the future held for her, she had no way of knowing for sure. All she knew was this moment. And at this moment, Jack was what she wanted.

''I don't want you to leave. I don't want to be anywhere but with you, Jack.'' She looped her arms around his neck. He lifted her into his arms and carried her into her bedroom, pushing the door closed behind him.

Jack laid her on the bed, then sat beside her. He stroked her hair, feeling its silkiness, then lowered his head and kissed her on the mouth. His lips trailed down her cheek and he buried his face against the curve of her throat. She smelled sweet. He claimed her mouth again, deepening their kiss until she parted her lips.

Rebecca gasped and threaded her fingers through his hair. Then she touched his arms, his chest, the heat warming her palms. He pulled off his clothes and tossed them aside, then stretched out beside her.

He kissed her as he unbuttoned her nightgown, then slid his hand inside. Rebecca moaned when he touched her breast, then gasped with pleasure as his lips followed. When he tugged at her nightgown, she raised her arms and he sent it flying.

Jack rose above her and slid between her thighs. He kissed her softly, tenderly as he made a place for himself there. Slowly, cautiously he moved. The rhythm caught Rebecca and she moved with him, unwilling to resist. She wrapped her arms around him and caught a handful of his hair as the pleasure broke within her over and over again. Jack called out her name, and he followed until he was spent.

"WE'VE GOT A PROBLEM," Jack said.

Her arms and legs entwined with his, Rebecca gazed up at his face in the dim light. After their lovemaking, they'd cuddled together, neither speaking until now.

Jack pushed himself up on his elbow. "I've been thinking about you and this business proposal, and I decided that you don't really want a baby."

"I don't?"

"What you really want is a family," Jack said.

A little smile crept over her lips. "How did you know?"

He waited a moment, then said, "Because it's

what I want, too. I just didn't realize it until recently.''

''What happened?''

''I was lonely. I missed my family. Even though my pa hadn't done what I thought was right, I still missed him.''

''So you wrote? Made amends?''

Jack nodded. ''And I convinced Emily to come out here. She'd been through a tough time with a man she thought wanted to marry her, but ended up walking out. She was ready for a change. I asked her to come out here, to start over. But mostly I was being selfish. I wanted some family close to me again.''

Rebecca touched her palm to his cheek. ''Family is important,'' she agreed.

Jack covered her hand with his. ''That's why I think you and I should be a family.''

Rebecca gasped. ''Are you saying—''

''I'm saying that I love you, Rebecca. I want you to marry me—if you love me, that is.''

She threw her arms around his neck. ''Yes, Jack, I do love you.''

He covered her lips with his and smothered her with a hot kiss, then lifted his head. ''And you'll marry me?''

She smiled. ''Yes, Jack, I'll marry you.''

''Good,'' Jack said, and splayed his fingers

across her belly. "Because there's no way in hell I'd ever let you move back to Baltimore with my baby inside you."

"I don't want to move to Baltimore."

"Good." Jack glided his finger along the curve of her jaw. "So, how old *are* you?"

Rebecca smiled. "I'm not getting any younger, that's for sure. In fact, if we want to have a baby, I think we should keep working on it."

Jack buried his lips against the curve of her neck. "Now *that's* the kind of thinking I like."

Dear Reader,

"Snow Maiden" is based on a Russian fairy tale and is inspired by my daughter. Ten years ago this month, my husband and I traveled to Russia to adopt our daughter. At the time she was five months old and living in an orphanage in a small town outside Moscow. To this day, I still remember the cold, the long trip over snowy roads and seeing her for the first time in her brown jumpsuit and red boots. Today she is a bright, healthy young lady who loves music and sports.

Over the years I've developed an interest in all things Russian—from the cuisine to the stories and the rich history. The snow maiden fable is one of my favorite stories. It tells the tale of Grandfather Frost and Mother Spring's daughter, the Snow Maiden, who yearns to leave her enchanted winter forest to live among the humans. The Snow Maiden does go to live in the village of humans and for a time she is happy. But when winter fades into spring and the hot sun shines down on her, she evaporates in the mist, never to be seen again.

I couldn't let a sad ending like that stand, so I took the bones of the tale, gave it an American 1880s twist and added an ending that I hope you will enjoy!

Mary Burton

SNOW MAIDEN

Mary Burton

Dedicated to the Families for Russian and Ukrainian Adoption, a nonprofit organization dedicated to increasing public awareness of Eastern European adoption, offering a network for adoptive families, preserving the heritage of adopted children and providing relief to children who remain in orphanages.

CHAPTER ONE

Denver,
December, 1884

SNOW CONJURED memories of home.

Sophia Petranova stared out St. Martin's stained-glass window at the flurries and let her mind drift to childhood days spent in Russia. She could almost smell her mother's *piroshki* baking in the oven, almost hear the hiss of her grandmother's silver samovar as it brewed black tea and almost feel the sable warming her legs as her father's sledge cut across the icy roads.

Almost.

Sighing, she turned from the window and looked up at the church organ's twenty-foot pipes. Her heart leapt in her chest when she imagined climbing the ladder behind the wind chests to the pipes and tuning the great instrument. Such was the work of an artist, a master, and though she had assisted her stepfather, Ivan

Alexandrovich, with the delicate task before, she had never done it alone.

The bell in the clock tower chimed three times. Ivan was over six hours late. Soon another sun would set and they'd lose another day of work. Time was running out.

"Sophia!" a familiar voice growled.

Whirling around, Sophia nearly wept with relief. "Ivan!"

"Yes, who else would it be?" Ivan grumbled in their native Russian. The old man staggered down the center church aisle uncaring that his boots tracked mud or that melting snow dampened his long graying beard.

"Where have you been?" Sophia said. She hurried toward him, and then froze when she smelled vodka on his breath. "You swore no drinking. You knew we had to work today."

Bloodshot, weary eyes stared at her. "We won't be tuning the organ. We are leaving Denver."

Alarm swept through Sophia. She'd been apprenticed to Ivan for six years and recognized the signs of trouble. "What have you done?"

Ivan's lips flattened into a grim line. "You always think the worst of me."

She struggled to keep her voice calm. Stirring his anger only gave him more reasons not to work. "How can I not? You waste so much time when you know Mr. Richmond will not pay us unless we finish the organ by Wednesday. We have only four more days, Ivan. Four days."

"Richmond." The name rumbled in Ivan's throat like an oath. "Peasant."

Richmond had visited the workshop of Charles Anderson where Sophia and Ivan had worked on the organ's construction. He'd been to the church every day during the installation process. Just a glimpse of the businessman's ghost-gray eyes had told Sophia he was sharp, cunning and missed little.

Thoughts of Adam Richmond always left Sophia edgy, restless. "Mr. Richmond is no peasant and this organ is our last chance to prove our worth to Mr. Anderson."

Ivan pulled a bottle from his pocket and uncorked it. "You worry too much."

Numbly, she watched him raise the bottle to his lips and drink. He closed his eyes and savored the vodka burning his throat.

She shoved her hands in her pocket, tugged at the threads unraveling into a hole. "That's what you said when we left Seattle and San Francisco."

The tall, burly man's eyes closed for an instant. "Always like your mother. Nag. Nag. Nag."

Frustration sharpened Sophia's words more than she'd intended. "We *need* this fee to get home!"

He continued as if she hadn't spoken. "Noble bloodlines, distant connections to the Czar." He snorted. "You think you are better than me, yet there's not a ruble to your family name. Worthless. My money put food in our bellies, brought us to America. You are as worthless as your mother."

Sophia's temper snapped. She slapped the bottle from his hand. The glass shattered on the stone floor and vodka trickled into the cracks. "Don't speak about my mother that way!"

Rage reddened his cheeks. "How dare you! If not for me, you'd have gone to an orphanage with all the other unwanted children."

Sophia tilted her chin back. For an instant, she was fourteen years old again, alone and desperate for the mother she'd lost. Old emotions drained her anger and choked off her breath. A moment passed before she regained her balance.

"We are wasting time," she said coolly. "We are staying in Denver. *You* are going to sober up and finish this organ."

He leaned toward her, his dark eyes intent on her face. "Stay if you wish, but *I* am leaving."

His determined tone raised more suspicions. "Ivan, have you been gambling again?"

His face tight with anxiety, he started down the long narrow aisle. "It does not matter."

"You *have* been gambling." Ivan's trail of gambling losses stretched from Denver to St. Petersburg. She hurried past him and blocked his path. He stood a good foot taller than she but she planted her hands against his chest and braced her booted feet. "Who do you owe?"

He hesitated, shrugged. "There are men. They say I owe them money."

Sophia stood rigid in disbelief. A door somewhere in the church opened and the wind outside screeched inside the barren hallways like the lament of an old woman.

Ivan wrung his hands. "It was not my fault," he said more to himself than her. "The cards were marked."

Her body felt numb. "Where did you get the money? We have none to spare."

"I was lucky at cards last week," he said quickly.

Breath hissed through her clenched teeth. "You are never lucky, Ivan."

The spark of indignation in his eyes nearly

made her laugh. "I'm down on my luck now, but I've been up plenty times."

"You had no money! How did you get into another game?"

"I will win it back. You'll see."

The last time he'd gambled he'd sold the chain to her mother's locket. She struggled not to scream. "Where did the money come from?"

He flinched. "The locket."

Sophia sank back as if he'd slapped her. "Mother's locket?"

"Yes."

The gold locket, small but intricately carved, held a miniature of her mother in the oval casing. Since Ivan had stolen the chain, Sophia carried the treasure with her. Two days ago she'd discovered the hole in her pocket and had decided to leave the locket hidden under the floorboards in her room. Somehow he'd known she'd left it behind. "That was mine."

"I needed it."

"It was all I had left of her. You *promised* you'd never touch it."

Sophia could barely think. She wanted to weep for everything she'd lost: her mother, the village she'd not seen in six years, and the home she'd dreamed of making when she returned to Russia.

Pressing her fingertips to her eyelids, she

willed her tears away. If she were ever to return
home, she needed the money from this job. And
to do that, she needed Ivan. She drew back her
shoulders. "You must help me finish the organ."

He shook his head. "*Nyet*. It was your hands
that carved the mahogany casing and aligned the
bellows. I was but an adviser."

She pushed a strand of blue-black hair off her
pale face. "I assembled pieces and parts. Your
experience will bring the organ alive. Please
Ivan, just another day or two."

"I don't have another day. I must go now."

Sophia dug her calloused fingertips into his
arm. "Who will explain your absence to the
church committee?"

Bitterness sparked in his eyes like shards of
ice. "The committee does not matter. It is Richmond that matters and he does not care about this
organ."

"What are you saying? He commissioned it."

"He now only cares about disgracing the minister. He meets with the committee today to destroy the project."

Fresh fears swirled in Sophia's mind. "How
do you know this?"

"I hear things."

"But why would he do such a thing?"

He shrugged. "Who knows? Who cares?"

Sophia's mind moved quickly as she regrouped. If they lost this job, it could be years before she had enough money to return home. "You must talk to the committee. Make them understand that they must build this organ."

"Nyet."

"Ivan, please stay! I'm begging you, please. Just this one last time. If I must I will tune the organ but you must make the committee understand that it has to be finished."

Ivan seemed surprised by her desperation. She'd never begged before. He opened his mouth, ready to summon his deep voice, once so full of pride and life. Instead, he swallowed the unspoken words, then turned away and staggered out of the church.

Sophia's bare fingers curled into fists. Hot tears tumbled over her cheeks and she was aware of only the sounds around her. The sound of children laughing in the chapel. The firm click of shoes down the hallway. A door opening and closing.

She started after Ivan and then stopped.

Adam Richmond stood on the shadow's edge, staring openly, almost rudely at her.

Richmond possessed an earthy, raw quality that belied his fine wool suits and Irish linen shirts. His presence commanded the attention of everyone and he moved with the natural-born grace of a hunter confident of his skill.

She reminded herself that he did not speak Russian and hadn't understood her conversation with Ivan. Still, he stared at her as if he was trying to peer inside her heart. A jolt of electricity shot through her body.

''Mr. Richmond, may I have a word with you?'' she asked in English.

''I've seen all I need to see.'' He abruptly turned and strode out of the room, dismissing her as if she were nothing.

The rejection stung more than it should.

Something inside her hardened, like ice in January. She would not leave as Ivan had. She would stay and make the church committee understand that the organ must be finished.

Adam Richmond be damned.

CHAPTER TWO

WHEN ADAM RICHMOND reached the door that led to the meeting room, he stopped and flexed his right hand, working the stiffness from his joints.

Though he didn't understand Russian, he recognized the anger and desperation in Sophia's hushed tone. Clearly, Ivan had told her he was leaving and she had reached the end of her tether.

Adam should have been happy.

But he wasn't.

Irritated that he was giving Sophia a second thought, Adam reached in his vest pocket and pulled out his gold watch. He glanced at the time then shoved the timepiece back in its place. Soon it would all be over. Ivan's failure would be complete and the troublesome Reverend Nelson would be without a parish.

And Sophia would be gone.

He had never planned on the unexpected pull he'd felt when he'd first heard her singing a melodic Russian folk song. Drawn by the sweet sound of her voice, he'd ventured from the meeting in the craftsman's office to the back workroom. There she'd sat on a stool, bent over a rich mahogany board carving a rose, unmindful of him or the half-dozen other workmen around her. She'd worn brown breeches, a white shirt cinched at her narrow waist and her hair in a thick braid.

Her eyes were as blue as a winter sky and they'd been filled with shining confidence and laughter. When her gaze had shifted to him, the laughter had faded and there'd been a flash of appreciation as her gaze slid over his body. The jolt of desire rocked him and left him hard and wanting.

Many a night, he'd dreamed of peeling the coarse fabric from her skin and making love to her. Many a night he'd wished circumstances were different.

"Sophia." He muttered her name like a curse.

Adam laid his palm flat against the door, needing to touch something tangible, real. Dreams were all fine and good at night, but in the clear light of day practicality reigned. Sophia didn't belong in his world. He had a family to protect and that was that.

Adam shoved open the door and walked into the empty meeting room. He stared down the length of a long, Spartan table encircled by eight straight-back chairs as he shrugged off his snow-dampened coat and laid it on the back of his chair at the head of the table.

Restless, he moved toward the window and looked out at a small courtyard. An inch of snow coated the ground. A row of naked Poplars dripped with ice.

The snow showed no signs of ending and judging by the heavy, gray clouds, there'd be close to a foot to contend with by sunrise.

Adam's jaw tightened. He should have been worried about the snow playing havoc with his construction schedules and the deliveries to his brick factory. If it continued at its current pace, he'd have to shut down operations. Instead, he worried about Sophia.

Snowflakes would be dampening the knots in her blue-black braid, coating the shoulders of her ragged sheepskin coat as she made her way toward her rented rooms on Blake Street. Soon she'd discover Ivan had fallen behind in his rent and they'd been evicted. She had no place to stay.

Adam decided that after this meeting he'd send a runner to Sophia with money. At least, she'd have some money in her pocket when she left Denver.

The idea of Sophia leaving Denver blackened his already foul mood.

This wasn't like him. Contact with women always stayed casual and brief. He'd given as good as he'd gotten, but he'd always been careful not to care too much.

And here he was worrying about a woman he barely knew.

"You look a million miles away, Adam," Claire Richmond said.

Adam turned to see his sister standing in the doorway. Her too-expensive boots clicked against the stone floor and her pencil-thin skirt rustled as she moved, reminding him that her outfit cost more than he'd earned the first months he'd owned the brick factory.

She kissed him on the cheek, then efficiently tugged off her gloves and tucked them in her reticule. Like him, she had a habit of arriving early.

"You looked preoccupied, worried," she said frankly.

For her sake, he smiled. It had been just the two of them for so long, protecting her was automatic. "It's my job to do the worrying. Not yours."

She lifted an eyebrow. "Well, I do worry. You spend so much time alone."

"I like my solitude."

"That may have worked when I was a child, but no more. You need someone in your life, Adam."

When I was a child...

Just eighteen and still so young, Claire knew little of the world or how it worked, yet neither fact tempered her confidence. So young. Adam chose not to remind her of those facts. He wasn't interested in an argument today.

"It's the snow and the holiday," she said unexpectedly. She looked past him to the window. Snowflakes stuck to the glass, clinging only for a moment then melted. "Both always put you in a foul mood."

"They don't," he said.

Her gaze lingered on the snowy view, the brightness in her eyes dimming. "They have the same effect on me. It reminds me of Mama and Rose. You know, I can barely remember what they look like now."

Unconsciously, Adam curled his fingers over the scars on his right palm. Twelve years had passed since the fire that had swept through their wood-framed house, killing their mother and sister. Adam had been trudging through the snow that day, returning from his shift in the factory when he'd seen the flames. He'd run as fast as he could through the white mire to reach them.

He'd clawed his way into the inferno, but the heat had burned his hand and seared his lungs almost immediately. It had been a miracle he'd been able to save six-year-old Claire.

Adam shook off the images. "I prefer to think about the future."

"You never speak of the past," she said quietly. "Have you forgotten them?"

So many times, he'd prayed he could forget. "I haven't forgotten a thing."

"What do you remember?"

Adam shoved out a deep breath. Any other day, he'd have steered the conversation to another topic, but today his emotions were tipped out of balance. "You and Rose had decorated a Christmas tree the day before. Rose strung berries and wrapped them around the tree. She also tore pages out of one of my books and cut them into stars."

Claire smiled, her eyes sparkling. "*I* stole the pages."

If only if it hadn't been so cold that day, his mother would never have banked the fire so high. If only he'd said no to the tree or hadn't stopped to buy toys for the girls. *If only.*

He wrenched his thoughts away from the past and focused on the reason they were here today—Harrison Nelson, the interim church minister.

Bright, young and full of ideas, the young Reverend Nelson had been the one who first suggested constructing the pipe organ. Claire had championed the project and convinced Adam to underwrite it. Nelson's status had risen among the vestry members and there'd been talk about making his job permanent.

Adam had been happy to indulge his sister, until a week ago when his butler had given him a letter intended for Claire. The letter had been from Nelson. It spoke of their love and plans to announce their engagement when the organ was completed and Nelson's position as minister was secure.

Adam's first impulse had been to have Nelson fired on the spot. He'd worked too hard to give his sister a good life to see it ruined by a man who worried more about emotions than practicality.

But Adam had learned long ago to play his cards close to his vest. So he'd kept his temper in check and begun to plot.

Openly withdrawing his support of the organ would ensure the project's failure, but Claire would never forgive him. Instead, Adam focused on Ivan Alexandrovich, who'd already proven he couldn't stay to a schedule. It didn't take much to learn that Alexandrovich, a once-great craftsman, had all but drowned his talent in a sea of vodka and gambling debts. All Adam had to do was call in the Russian's markers to send him running from Denver. With the organ unfinished, Nelson would be fired, leave town, and Claire would get on with her life.

A perfect plan, if not for Sophia.

The sound of voices and footsteps echoed down the long stone hallway. The first to arrive was Mrs. Dalrumple, one of the elite members of Denver society and a founder of the coveted Thirty-Six, a clique of whist-playing society ladies who ran the city's social circles. A tall, slender woman, her pinched features, tight graying chignon and silver-tipped walking stick made her look older than her forty years. She'd been the biggest supporter of the organ, telling anyone who would listen that Denver was finally starting to enjoy real culture.

Mrs. Dalrumple raised an eyebrow when she saw Adam. "You're the last man I'd expected here today. I'd think you had more important details to handle than this humble project of ours."

Humble. The organ had cost well over one thousand dollars of his money. "I want to make sure my investment pays."

Mrs. Dalrumple cleared her throat. "Reverend Nelson has assured me the organ will be finished by this Wednesday. He understands my Dora's hopes are set on playing at the Christmas Day church concert."

Adam was careful to keep all traces of emotion hidden. "Good."

Mrs. Dalrumple allowed Adam to pull back her chair. She sat and took extra time to arrange her skirts before she spoke. "I hope he's not too late. I've an afternoon tea to attend."

"He'll be here," Claire said, glancing at the door again.

Mrs. Dalrumple pulled spectacles from her reticule and put them on. "All here except Reverend Nelson and Mr. Alexandrovich."

Claire met Adam's gaze. "Just a minute or two more."

"I'm sure you're right," Adam said mildly.

The clock struck three before they heard the hurried click of boots echoing down the hallway. A harried and very out-of-breath Nelson appeared in the doorway. He shoved a lock of thick blond hair off his face. "I believe that church clock is fast. It seems I'm always in a race with the thing."

Young Nelson greeted everyone at the table but his gaze lingered a beat too long on Claire.

She dipped her head away from Adam as if to hide the blush in her cheeks.

Adam seethed.

Nelson's unsteady gaze met Adam's. "Mr. Richmond."

Adam shook the young man's hand, surprised Nelson managed a firm handshake despite his fine-boned fingers. "Nelson, good to have you here."

"Good to be here."

Adam sat at the head of the table and Nelson took the chair on his right next to Claire. Mrs. Dalrumple called the meeting to order. She offered a brief welcome then turned the meeting over to Nelson.

Nelson laid his long, slim hands on the table. "We have a bit of a problem."

Mrs. Dalrumple's mood soured. Adam nearly smiled.

"What kind of problem?" Mrs. Dalrumple asked, her voice stiffer.

"It seems Mr. Alexandrovich has disappeared."

Adam leaned forward, his chin resting on his steepled fingers. "What do you mean *disappeared?*"

Nelson's face reddened a fraction. "He and I were supposed to meet this morning. H-He didn't show. Miss Petranova was here most of the day waiting for him, but when I checked the sanctuary moments ago, she was gone too.''

The mention of Sophia's name soured Adam's satisfaction. ''This isn't good.''

Mrs. Dalrumple tapped her cane against the floor. ''I was counting on that organ, Reverend Nelson.''

''Th-There are other artisans. I've just come from Mr. Anderson's workshop. He will send another craftsman as soon as he can.''

''When?'' Mrs. Dalrumple said.

Nelson's lips flattened. ''January?''

Claire paled. ''There is no one that can come earlier?''

Nelson's gaze met Claire's. ''No.''

Adam kept his voice neutral. ''I thought you had this situation under control Reverend Nelson.''

''I—I thought I did,'' Nelson said.

''*Thought* doesn't cut it,'' Adam said tersely.

''This won't do at all,'' Mrs. Dalrumple said. ''I was counting on that organ being finished on Wednesday. Dora will be humiliated.''

Claire leaned forward. ''There must be someone in Denver who can finish the organ on time. It's nearly complete.''

Nelson looked at her, his pale eyes filled with disappointment.

"*I* will finish it." Sophia's clear, slightly accented voice rang out from the doorway.

CHAPTER THREE

SOPHIA KNEW that her unscheduled arrival would be a shock to the committee. However, when she looked into Adam Richmond's unwavering gaze her breath hitched in her throat. Surprise flickered in his gray eyes, and just for the briefest instant she imagined respect, before his full lips thinned into an icy frown.

Her hastily planned speech to the committee vanished from her mind.

His body was only inches from her and she could feel the energy radiating from him. His bold presence goaded her worries and her first inclination was to beg his forgiveness for her impertinence, as if he were the Czar himself.

But she didn't.

A flicker of annoyance ignited inside her. Sophia's mother had instilled an unwavering pride in her that had sustained her through poverty, the death of her parents and six years with Ivan. She scraped together her bits of courage. "*I* can finish the organ."

Reverend Nelson scrambled to his feet. "Miss Petranova, I've been looking all over for you and Mr. Alexandrovich."

Sophia moistened chapped lips. "Mr. Alexandrovich is not coming."

Nelson pressed his long, slender fingertips to his temple as if his head had started to pound. "When will he be back?"

Guilt tugged at her as she stared at Reverend Nelson. He'd been kind and had given Ivan more chances than he'd deserved. "He has—"

Richmond rose to his feet. "We want the truth this time."

Sophia faced him, stung by his words. "If you will just let me explain."

Richmond's steady regard reminded her that his goal was to derail the project. "As far as I'm concerned, he's fired and we have nothing more to discuss. Miss Petranova, you may go."

Sophia refused to back down when so much depended on this job. "Won't you hear me out?"

Claire Richmond jumped to her feet. "Really, Adam, let Miss Petranova speak."

Mr. Richmond didn't take his eyes off Sophia. "All we've gotten from Miss Petranova is talk.

It's time to face facts, hiring Ivan Alexandrovich was a mistake.''

Reverend Nelson's cheeks burned with color. ''The man came highly recommended and no one can argue with the quality of the work so far. Yes, he's been very slow, but the organ is almost finished, Mr. Richmond.''

Richmond shoved a hand in his pocket and rattled the loose change. He wasn't accustomed to being crossed. ''*Almost* doesn't count.''

Richmond's hostility stoked Sophia's temper. ''*I* can finish the organ by Wednesday. You must give me a chance.''

The lines etched in Richmond's face deepened. ''*A* chance, Miss Petranova? I'd say your stepfather used up any and all his chances. This job should have been completed weeks ago, yet here we stand. Now you want *more* time.''

Despite his quiet voice, his last words reverberated off the walls, making her flinch. ''I'm not asking for my stepfather, but myself. I am giving you *my* word that the organ will be finished by December twenty-fourth.''

Mrs. Dalrumple's icy gaze slid over Sophia, making her very aware suddenly that she still wore her dusty workman's clothes. She'd run all the way from the sanctuary and hadn't taken time to brush her hair or wash the dirt from her face and hands.

The matron tapped the silver tip of her cane on the floor silencing everyone. "Young lady, why on earth should we take your word? You are nothing more than the organ builder's assistant. All you've done is make up excuses for your stepfather's absences."

Trembling, Sophia took a step toward the long table. "I am sorry for my lies and will always regret them." She fisted her fingers. "I do not profess to know as much as Ivan Alexandrovich, but I do know this organ. I built most of it with my own hands and I can finish it."

Mrs. Dalrumple thrummed her fingers on the table. "We would like to believe you, Miss Petranova, but what guarantee do we have that you won't leave like your stepfather?"

Reverend Nelson turned to Mrs. Dalrumple, his body tense with hope. "I can say from first-hand experience, Miss Petranova works hard, sunup to sundown most days. And we have nothing to lose. Anderson Organ Builders have already said they can't send anyone here for several weeks. What would be the harm giving Miss Petranova another try?"

Claire glanced at her brother and then Sophia.

"I for one vote to support Sophia, Mrs. Dalrumple. Dora is so counting on the organ being ready for her musicale."

Mrs. Dalrumple touched the cameo on her collar. "Everyone is coming to hear Dora play."

Mr. Richmond shoved his arms in his coat. "Don't be fooled like my sister, Mrs. Dalrumple. Miss Petranova is better at selling than she is delivering. I don't want her failure to reflect badly on you or Dora."

"I truly admire Dora," Sophia said. "She's been nothing but kind to me and I want her to succeed and be the belle of the holiday season."

Richmond's laugh was low, bitter. He looked at Mrs. Dalrumple. "Be smart. She will make a fool out of you."

Nelson leaned toward Mrs. Dalrumple. "If I could vote, I'd give Sophia a chance, Mrs. Dalrumple. I believe in her."

The older woman stared at Nelson. "I might be willing to give her a try, but I'd want assurances."

Richmond pressed his palms on the table and leaned forward. "And where is Miss Petranova going to live while she does this work? Have you asked her that?"

Mrs. Dalrumple turned to Sophia. "Is there a problem with your room?"

The challenge in Richmond's eyes told her he knew more about her situation than she did. Most likely, Ivan hadn't paid the rent and they'd been evicted. It wouldn't be the first time they'd been thrown out on the streets. "I don't need much. A room at the church perhaps."

Mrs. Dalrumple frowned. "That's not appropriate, my dear."

"It's only for a few days," Sophia countered.

Nelson held up a finger as if an idea occurred to him. "A cot could be found. She could sleep in my office."

Mr. Richmond took Sophia's arm. His grip was gentle but unbreakable. "This is ridiculous. She can't live in Nelson's office. Let's face it, this is over."

"I have an idea!" Claire said, moving toward Sophia.

Richmond's glare would have intimidated the most battle-weary general. "Not now, Claire."

Claire faced her brother and as if he hadn't spoken and said, "Miss Petranova could stay with us!"

Sophia hissed in a sharp breath. Adam's expression looked murderous.

Claire ignored them both and turned to Mrs. Dalrumple. "It really is the perfect solution. We have plenty of room and our house is only four blocks from the church. *And* Adam can personally keep an eye on Miss Petranova."

Mrs. Dalrumple nodded. "It does sound like a good idea."

Mr. Richmond's face darkened. "Claire, you go too far."

Sophia pulled free of Adam's grip. Behind the anger in Adam Richmond's eyes, Sophia saw something else. Lust tangled with worry. "That is kind, but I can manage elsewhere."

Claire placed herself between Sophia and Richmond. "Any rooms you find are likely to be in the roughest part of town. Staying with us is the perfect solution."

She lifted her chin. "Thank you, but I will manage."

Claire placed Sophia's hand in the crook of her own arm. "Miss Petranova, may I call you Sophia?"

Sophia could see the trap being set but didn't know how to free herself. "Of course."

Claire patted Sophia's hand. "Sophia, the church is out of the question, you've no time to find another room and you certainly can't sleep on the streets. Say you will stay with us and put an end to this tedious discussion.''

Mr. Richmond stiffened. ''No!''

''It's only for a few days,'' Nelson said. His cheeks turned crimson but he didn't back down.

Richmond clenched and unclenched his fingers as if they were stiff. ''I don't like strangers in my home.''

Claire's gaze was pointed, direct. ''Adam, do you want this organ finished or not?''

Richmond stared at Claire as if carefully considering what he'd say next. Ivan's words rang in Sophia's head. Richmond didn't want the organ finished. For reasons Sophia could not explain, Ivan was right. And Richmond did not want his sister to know he was behind this debacle.

''Of course I want it finished,'' Richmond said calmly.

Claire arched an eyebrow. ''Then say yes.''

Nelson smiled. ''St. Martin's will be eternally grateful.''

Richmond's jaw tightened, released, tightened again. ''All right, Claire, consider Miss Petranova under my care. But understand this, Claire—I have now done all that I can to see this pet project of yours finished. Don't lay blame at my feet if she fails.''

Claire beamed. ''I wouldn't dream of it.''

Mrs. Dalrumple rose. ''Then the matter is settled. Miss Petranova will finish the organ by Wednesday in time for my Dora's concert.''

Triumph exploded inside of Sophia. She would finish the organ and she would see her dreams of returning home come true.

Then she lifted her eyes to Richmond.

His gaze was as dark as Satan's.

CHAPTER FOUR

SOPHIA GLANCED DOWN at her hands when the meeting room door closed behind her. They were shaking.

If she hadn't wanted to finish this job so badly, she'd have refused Claire's offer outright. Even now, she wondered how she could ever live under Adam Richmond's roof? Just the sound of his deep, raspy voice tugged at her senses and reminded her of unspoken desires she'd never allowed herself to entertain.

Sophia had stayed in her share of seedy rooming houses over the last six years. She'd heard enough bawdy talk to know what happened between when a man and women came together. In truth, she'd never understood what all the fuss was about or why proud women gave themselves to men when in the end their only reward was heartache.

Many men had tried to cajole her into their beds, but she'd turned them all down without a second thought. Yet, these last few weeks, when

Adam Richmond strode into a room her skin tingled, and she'd known true lust.

Sighing, Sophia pushed open the double doors that led to the church sanctuary. The massive stone room was finely constructed as if its builder were daring the heavens to tear it down. Lined in military fashion, pews flanked the left and right sides of the room and faced a wineglass pulpit carved out of cherry.

She paused at a baptismal font located in the back of the church. Running her hand over the white marble, she smiled, comforted. She didn't need to see the font's base to know that engraved into the pristine stone was the simple phrase—*Rose and Eudora, into the hands of the angels.* She'd discovered the words just days into the job. The font always filled her with peace.

She squared her shoulders. Only four days—and three nights—remained until the organ was to be finished. Enough time, even for an apprentice, to tune the organ, and very little time in the grand scheme of life. She would manage living in Richmond House. She'd heard it had seventeen bedrooms and hallways that stretched for miles. Enough space to ensure she never saw Richmond.

"A few days is nothing," she muttered. In a few days the organ would be finished, she'd have enough money to return to Russia and Adam Richmond would be no more than a distant memory.

Oddly irritated, she shifted her focus to the ten-foot-wide organ. Located behind the altar, the organ had been carted across town in five different crates. It should have just taken a week to assemble but with Ivan's absences, the assembly's pace had been slowed to a crawl.

Now as she stared at the magnificent instrument, she forgot all the troubles and gave in to pride. Savoring the scent of linseed oil, she admired her handiwork. Soon, her creation would come to life and sing like no other.

Expelling a breath, Sophia started down the center aisle, nodding reverently to the crucifix hanging behind the altar. She shrugged off her coat, a castoff of Ivan's, and laid it on an empty pew.

A couple of hours of daylight remained. Not so much time, but enough to get started. Sophia headed toward the organ when, outside in the corridor, she heard children's laughter. Smiling, she savored the sound of untrained, enthusiastic voices. She knew most of the children by name and had enjoyed watching them practice for the Christmas Eve pageant.

Their arrival nudged her away from her

gloominess. She looked forward to their afternoon practice. When the great door to the hall opened, she turned with a smile on her face, ready to greet the children.

Mr. Richmond stood in the doorway alone. His presence ate up the threshold and his dark gaze closed the distance between them. Her smile melted.

"You were expecting someone else?" he said.

She smoothed an unsteady hand down her breeches. "The children's choir," she said with a slow shrug.

"I sent them down to the chapel so that we wouldn't be disturbed."

A shivery sensation raced through her body. "We?"

"We've much to discuss." Richmond moved down the long aisle, his pace slow and precise. His gaze lingered on her for what seemed like hours, but of course was but a beat or two. His frown deepened.

She'd been foolish to think he'd allow this small victory of hers. "We have already discussed the organ."

"The committee discussed it. Now it's our turn." He sat in a pew, folded his arms over his chest.

Her hands trembled and she shoved them in her pockets. "What more is there to say?"

His smile was faintly mocking. "This organ is important to you, isn't it?"

"Yes." Richmond wasn't a man prone to small talk. She sensed a trap. "What point do you wish to make?"

Her directness seemed to please him. "How important is the *fee* you'll receive from this job?"

She froze. "Very."

He raised a dark eyebrow. "Is the fee more important than the organ?"

The trap was set. "I see the point of this now. Pride versus money—it's a very old battle, Mr. Richmond."

The smile disappeared from his face. "One that always has a winner."

"Yes." A bitter taste settled in her mouth.

"And if you had to choose between pride and money, Miss Petranova?"

She took a step toward him. "These last few years I lied often to protect Ivan. I hated every bit of it." Her voice was steady but inwardly she wanted to weep. "Today, when I made a promise to your sister, Reverend Nelson and Mrs. Dalrumple, I spoke from the heart, the truth. I will not break my word."

He rose from the pew. The flaps of his black overcoat billowed softly as he moved toward her. Sandalwood mingled with his own masculine scent. "Come now, Miss Petranova, it is just you and me now. No committee to impress. You can be honest with me. You don't care so much about this organ. You care about the fee. You want to return home, do you not?"

He was tightening a noose around her neck and she didn't know how to escape. "I would give almost anything to return home."

Unexpectedly, he took her hand in his and turned it over. Slowly, he traced the lines on her palm and circled her calluses. "I admire you, Sophia."

His touch kindled desire. "You are not here to tell me this."

"It's true nonetheless. I've watched you struggle with this project. Watched you work as hard as any two men to see this organ finished."

The fact that he'd noticed her pleased her. Yet, she wasn't blind. He was manipulating her. "Let us not play games, Mr. Richmond. The day is late and I am tired. What do you want of me?"

"What do I want?" He was silent for so long she thought he might not answer. Then he leaned forward until his lips were but inches from hers.

"It's not the kind of thing a man talks about in church."

His voice had taken on an edginess that sent shivers rippling across her skin. "Tell me."

"Since the day I first saw you in the workshop, I've imagined the scene a hundred times. Your black hair flowing over satin pillows, the candlelight flickering over your naked breasts and hips."

The sound of her own blood pounded in her ears. She'd never experienced such naked longing. Madness! "Mr. Richmond…"

He stroked the underside of her chin with his knuckle. "I want to kiss you."

Nyet! Yes. English mingled with Russian, common sense warred with desire. Her mind shouted warnings—run, he plays you like a puppet. Still, she couldn't move.

He traced her jawline with his fingertip. Heaven help her, she wanted him to kiss her. Just once. Just once. Without thinking she closed her eyes and tilted her head up in anticipation of tasting him.

The next few seconds stretched like hours as she waited. It took an extra beat for her to realize he'd taken a step back. A niggling unease blossomed in her soul and scraped across her nerves.

Then she opened her eyes and saw the arrogant smile on his face.

Sophia felt as if someone had dumped ice water down her coat. He'd been playing with her as if she were a foolish country girl. She wished with her entire soul that she could melt into the floor.

Mr. Richmond reached in his breast pocket and withdrew a slim wallet. "Don't misunderstand, Sophia. I do want you. But I learned long ago that desire comes second to ambition."

Her cheeks flamed. "Leave this place."

"Not until you hear me out."

"I want nothing from you."

"That wasn't true a moment ago," he said, his voice husky now.

"Get out!" Her voice echoed off the tall stone walls.

"I'll pay you three times your fee if you pack your bags and leave Denver today."

She flinched. "I don't want your money."

He counted out more money. "Five times your fee. You can return home in style."

He offered more money than she'd make in the next two years. If she relented, she could be on the next train to California, buy first-class passage to Russia and a small home near St. Petersburg.

And what of Reverend Nelson, Claire and Mrs. Dalrumple? Ivan had disappointed her so many times with his broken promises, how could she do this to those that had been so kind to her. "Keep your money, Mr. Richmond. I only want what I'm due—when the organ is finished."

His eyes hardened. "Once my offer is off the table, I won't make it again."

The idea of turning down so much money made her dizzy. "Good. You'd be wasting your time and mine if you did."

For an instant, she saw a flicker of respect.

But the moment melted as quickly as snow in August and all that was left was frustration burning in his eyes. He shoved the bills inside his wallet. "You're a fool, Miss Petranova."

She allowed a small smile. "My stepfather has said so often enough."

At the comparison, his expression chilled.

She looked up at him. "Tell me one thing, Mr. Richmond. Why go to the trouble to bribe me? Why not fire me outright?"

"I have my reasons."

The glint in his eyes suggested her words hit a raw nerve. "Ivan told me you wanted Reverend Nelson fired."

"You are on dangerous ground, Sophia."

"Dangerous ground?" She remembered the

way she'd been ready to give herself to him. "Perhaps you are right."

"This isn't over between us." His words were as sharp as steel.

He turned on his heel and started down the long aisle. Drained of all energy, she numbly watched him leave. When he passed through the doors, her knees buckled and she sat down on the bottom step leading to the altar. Her heart hammered in her chest and she cradled her head into her hands. "When did it all spin out of control?"

"By the way, Sophia," Richmond's deep voice had her head snapping up.

Color flooded her cheeks and she rose, ashamed he'd glimpsed her fear.

His gaze locked on her. "We serve dinner at six-thirty in *my* house."

CHAPTER FIVE

FOUR HOURS LATER, Adam stared out the tall windows, streaked with frost into the dark, snowy night. He'd found it impossible to concentrate on business or to wrestle free of the knots tightening his back muscles.

All because Sophia was late.

Cursing, he moved toward a small table where he kept his whiskey decanters. Filling a crystal tumbler, he raised the glass to his lips, and then realizing he had no taste for liquor, set the glass down. He glanced up at the clock on the mantle.

Six fifty-three.

Where the devil was Sophia?

Nelson locked the church every night at sunset so Sophia couldn't still be working on the organ. In good weather, the walk between the church and his house took ten minutes. In this weather, it could take twice that. Even allowing for a stop along the way, she should have been here by now.

Unless she wasn't coming.

He picked up the glass of whiskey, drained the contents, wincing when it burned his throat.

Adam had not intended to speak so frankly to her today. Nor had he expected her response.

But he'd been frustrated that the meeting hadn't gone as he'd planned. When he'd seen her standing alone in the church, an ache burned the pit of his belly. He'd never wanted a woman as he'd wanted her.

So, he'd spoken his mind, half hoping that if he voiced his desires it would loosen their hold over him.

It hadn't worked.

His frankness had stoked a fire in his gut. Whatever slippery grip he'd had on his control nearly vanished when she'd closed her eyes waiting for him to kiss her.

And he'd turned her down.

A decision he'd regret for a very, very long time.

Damn.

He didn't want Sophia finishing the organ, but he wasn't a monster. He didn't want any harm to befall her.

He shoved his fingers through his short-cropped hair and strode back to the window. The temperature had dipped below freezing and the storm had worsened with each passing hour.

Five more minutes.

He'd give her five more minutes and then he'd summon his carriage. He'd retrace the stretch of road connecting his house to the church. If she wasn't there he'd ride down Fourteenth Street past the capital to her boardinghouse.

Double damn.

The grandfather clock in the hallway chimed seven times. He turned, ready to summon his butler to fetch his coat, when a loud knock on the front door echoed through the house.

The instant the butler opened the door the air became suddenly charged. An excitement pulsed through Adam's body. He knew Sophia had arrived.

Adam moved closer to the study door, which stood ajar. He had a clear view of Sophia dressed in her sheepskin coat cinched at her waist. She pulled a wet scarf from her head, revealing wisps of blue-black hair plastered against her forehead. Her cheeks glowed red but her lips had a blue tint.

''Miss Petranova?'' said his butler, Fritz. The man's thick accent and blunt manner had many a guest complaining about his harsh and unwelcoming demeanor. The butler's tall, lean build, graying hair and crisp suits added to his standoffish mystique.

But Fritz was loyal. He did his job with unfailing efficiency and Adam had decided long ago that he wasn't interested in welcoming strangers into his house anyway.

"Yes." Her voice was clear, hesitant.

"You are late."

Sophia smiled at Fritz. "You have an accent. German?"

Fritz looked surprised. "Yes."

Sophia responded in German, asking him a few questions to which he replied. Adam didn't miss the hint of surprise in his butler's voice.

Fritz seemed to enjoy conversing in his native tongue. Sophia asked him several more questions. By the butler's softening tone Adam guessed that the man had fallen under Sophia's spell.

A savage jolt of jealousy ripped through Adam's body. He wondered how many men had fallen prey to Sophia's sapphire eyes and melodic voice. Over the years he'd escorted dozens of bland society misses, but he'd never felt so protective or lustful over a woman.

Adam stepped into the foyer. "Fritz, has our guest arrived?"

All traces of good humor vanished from Fritz's face. He efficiently took Sophia's coat and draped it over his arm. "Miss Sophia Petranova has arrived, sir."

Sophia still wore the breeches and loose shirt tied at her narrow waist. Each time Adam saw the breeches and the way they molded her hips, he grew hard. He tried to imagine what her lips tasted like and the feel of her soft, supple breast in his hand.

Sophia seemed to sense his thoughts. Her cheeks turned crimson but she didn't drop her gaze. "Mr. Richmond."

"Welcome, Miss Petranova. We were beginning to wonder if you were going to arrive."

"I had to return to my rooms and collect my belongings."

He noticed the small bag at her feet. "Won't you come into my study?"

She hesitated. "I don't want to trouble you."

He crossed the foyer and took her elbow. "No trouble at all. I've been wanting to have a word with you."

Sophia reached for her bag, but Fritz brushed her fingers aside. "I can take that."

"I can manage it," Sophia said.

Fritz looked offended. "Don't be absurd. I will put it in your room."

Sophia frowned, as if the idea of staying here still didn't agree with her. "Thank you."

As he followed Sophia into the library, Adam realized he felt off balance again. Even with the cold howling outside, he felt hot. He imagined himself threading his fingers through Sophia's black hair and unbuttoning the row of buttons between her breasts.

Adam gave himself a mental shake. Seducing Sophia was not the point of this meeting, he reminded himself. "Sit by the fire. Warm yourself."

She tensed. "I am fine standing."

It bothered Adam that she looked nervous so he managed a small smile, hoping she'd relax. "I won't bite."

She stared at him as if she were trying to read his mind. "That, I am not so sure of."

Despite himself, he laughed. The woman had spirit, which pleased rather than annoyed him. He poured her a brandy and handed it to her. "You're blue from the cold. It would not be good for anyone if you caught a chill."

She eyed him a second or two longer, then moved to the great hearth where a fire blazed. She set her glass on the mantle and stretched out her long slender fingers toward the flames and rubbed them together. "I did not think Denver got this cold."

"Normally, it doesn't. When we get snow it's

usually no more than a dusting and it doesn't last long.'' He set his untouched glass down. ''Perhaps you brought the snow with you.''

She faced him. ''You did not bring me here to discuss the weather.''

Directness was an uncommon trait in most women. He liked that about Sophia. ''No.''

She possessed a royal bearing. ''Then what?''

''Family.''

Her eyes narrowed suspiciously. ''I don't understand.''

''Behind you, on the mantle,'' he said. ''There is a black lacquer box. Open it.''

She stared to move away. ''If this is about money…''

''No money.''

Slowly she lifted the palm-sized box in her hand. She traced the mother-of-pearl flowers embossed in the top before she opened the lid. Inside the red-velvet-lined box were a handful of melted bits of metal. ''What is this?''

Sadness hammered him. ''They were jacks—the last toy I bought for my sister.''

''Claire?''

''Rose.''

Her confusion was evident as she gingerly touched each piece, then the stiffness drained out of her shoulders. *Rose and Eudora, into the hands of angels.* "You memorialized the font in the church."

It touched him that she'd noticed the font's inscription. Most people overlooked it. "She died twelve years ago in a house fire. What you hold in your hand is my last Christmas gift to her. They fell out of my pocket when I went in to save her. And they are all that I have left of her."

"Why do you tell me this?"

"So that you'll understand." The fire crackled and popped. A log tumbled backward sending a flurry of sparks up the chimney. "I brought my family to Denver after my father died of cholera so that I could build my fortune. There was little left in Virginia after the war and we needed a fresh start. I worked long days in the brick factory. My mother took in wash and cared for Claire and Rose.

"There was a terrible fire." He swallowed, his throat feeling as raw as it did that long ago day when he'd breathed in too much smoke. "Many homes were destroyed. I got Claire out and went back into the burning house. I pulled my mother out, but couldn't find Rose. Mother died within minutes crying out for her children."

Sophia replaced the box on the mantle without speaking. A tear escaped and she savagely wiped it away. "I am truly sorry for your loss."

"Claire is the only family that I have. I'd do anything to protect her."

Her eyes softened. "You love her. This I understand."

He paused, knowing now he took a great risk. He wasn't a man who liked revealing his cards before he had to. "What you don't understand is that Claire wants to marry Nelson."

Her lips tightened. "He is a good, kind man."

Adam swore under his breath. "He is weak. He can't protect her."

Her long pause suggested she didn't agree. "Your sister is a strong woman."

"She deserves better," he said tightly.

She didn't move, but he saw the stiffness return to her shoulders. Without him having to say anything, she understood his train of thought. "And if the organ is not finished, Reverend Nelson will be passed over. He'll have to leave Denver to find another job."

So perceptive, he thought. "This organ has turned into a sort of test laid out by the church vestry for Nelson. They want to know that he is a man who can build this church, make things happen." He leaned toward her. "If the organ is not finished, he will not be hired as the permanent minister."

She stepped back as if needing distance between them. His words had shattered their brief connection. "Why don't you trust your sister to make the right decisions?"

"I know what's best."

She shook her head. "You do not give her enough credit. Claire is not one of these silly girls whose head is turned by flattery."

"How would you know anything about Claire?"

She shrugged. "I am invisible to people when I work. They see the organ, sometimes Ivan, but never me. It gives me a chance to watch people. Claire handles fussy old women, the vestry, even the children's choir with ease. She doesn't need your protection."

He closed the distance between them. "You loved your mother?"

Sophia flinched. "Of course."

He gripped her small-boned wrist, amazed at the strength that radiated from her. "You'd have done anything for her?"

She lifted her chin. "Yes."

He wanted desperately to reach her, to make her understand. "I'm no different than you. All I want is to protect my family. Walk away from the organ, Sophia. You will be well paid for your time. Nelson will leave. Claire will be safe."

"You are wrong in all this, Adam Richmond. You hold on too tight and you need to let go."

No one had spoken to him with such frankness in many, many years. He wasn't sure if he liked it or not. "Are you going to help me or not?"

She was silent for so long he wondered if she'd heard him. "The organ will be finished."

This sparring game they played was getting very old now. "Crossing me is a mistake, Sophia."

"Then you must add it to my list of many."

Before he could fire back a response, she turned and walked out of the room with the grace of a princess.

CHAPTER SIX

SOPHIA'S KNEES TREMBLED slightly as she followed Fritz up the stairs minutes later. Remembering Adam's bright, gray eyes, wild with anger, had her wondering if she'd taken a tiger by the tail. The question was: did she have the strength to fight Adam Richmond or would it not be wiser to simply let go and run?

She wasn't afraid of him. His anger was a part of his passionate nature. He was a man who fought for his own. This, she understood.

No, what worried her now ran much deeper, beyond her own loyalties to Ivan, Claire and the pipe organ. Now, she worried about her heart.

If Adam had remained the cold, ambitious man who'd tried to buy her off earlier today, everything would have remained simple.

But when she'd held Rose's jacks in her hand and felt the heat of Adam's body next to hers, she'd realized that beneath the ice beat the heart of a man who understood family.

Sophia thought of her pipe organ. Her masterpiece. Her pride. Her path home. What had started out as so simple was now tangled and confused.

Her head started to pound. She passed by a Queen Anne chair in the upstairs hallway, upholstered in a rich silk. "Mr. Richmond doesn't strike me as a man who would want such a fussy house," she said in German to Fritz.

"He built this all for Miss Claire," the butler said.

Sophia pictured Claire, small-boned and so lovely. "He worries about her."

Fritz stopped in front of a massive oak door, turned the brass handle and pushed it open. "She is his life."

She envied Claire. It had been a very long time since she'd had family to worry over her. "She is no longer a child."

Fritz nodded. "Mr. Richmond has not quite figured that out yet. But soon I suspect he will no longer be able to deny it."

"She is strong-willed, no?"

Fritz allowed a small smile as he opened her bedroom door. "To say the least."

Sophia's response caught in her throat at the sight of the lavish bedroom. A massive four-poster bed, which was larger than many of the rooms she'd stayed in, took up only a small portion of the room. Covered with an ivory silk bed-spread embroidered with hundreds of white roses and lilacs, the bed looked softer than sable.

"This can't be my room," she said. "I thought I'd be staying in the servants' quarters."

Fritz looked a bit offended. "This is your room."

Reverently, she moved into the room. With trembling fingers, she touched the coverlet. Such luxury. Opulence like this had been a part of her world when she was very young but she'd almost forgotten such finery existed.

Tears raised in Sophia's eyes as she thought of her mother's last poverty-ridden years. She would have done anything to prevent her suffering. *Anything.*

Like her, Adam would do anything to protect his sister Claire.

She looked up and caught her reflection in a gilded mirror. She barely recognized the woman who stared back. Where had the carefree young girl of St. Petersburg gone? She swallowed the tightness in her throat.

Fritz moved past her through connecting doors that led to a dressing room. Two lady's maids were already in the room filling a large brass tub with steaming hot water. She ached to soak in the hot water and free her mind of her worries.

Her joy was short-lived, however, when it occurred to her that Adam Richmond did nothing without good reason. Every move was calculated. "Why this room?"

Fritz raised an eyebrow. "It connects to his."

THE IDEA OF STAYING in the room next to Adam's horrified and excited her.

Sophia tossed and turned until well past midnight. Every gust of wind outside, every creak in the house had her tensing and staring at the door connecting her room to Adam's. He wouldn't dare enter her room. Would he?

No matter how much she tried to rid her mind of him, she couldn't stop wondering what it would feel like to have Adam Richmond's long, muscled body next to hers in bed. Or to feel his full lips kissing her neck.

Sophia's blood pulsed. Her breath caught in her throat.

Of course, he never came.

And she woke to bright sunshine and a crashing headache.

"Such a fool," she whispered as she rolled over in the plush bed. To want Adam Richmond, a man who stood between her and her dream, was madness.

A brief knock sounded on her door. Squinting

against the sunlight, she pushed up on her elbow seconds before Claire burst into her room. Her golden hair was twisted into a knot on top of her head and she wore a green wool dress fitted with wide sleeves and trimmed with an ivory cording. "Good morning, Sophia! I hope you slept well."

Self-conscious, Sophia sat straighter. "Excuse my laziness," she said. "I never sleep this late."

Claire waved away her concern. "You're entitled. By the looks of those dark circles under your eyes, I'd say you haven't had a decent night's sleep in years."

Sophia remembered her reflection. "It's been a long time since I slept in such a bed."

"Reverend Nelson told me where you were staying before you came here." She shuddered. "I know that section of town. It's a wonder you slept at all."

She shoved a lock of hair out of her eyes. After her conversation with Adam last night, she wasn't sure what to say to Claire. A part of her wanted to warn her. Another part worried that Adam might be right. "Many a night, I slept with one eye open."

Claire studied the cloudy sky. "Well, you're safe now."

She swung her legs over the side of the bed. "Is it still snowing?"

Claire turned away from the window. "No, and hopefully we won't get any more."

Sophia rose, wrapped a throw blanket over her threadbare nightgown and walked to the window.

She adjusted her focus past the frosted glass to the freshly fallen snow then up to the thick, dark sky. "We will have more snow before nightfall. I can smell it in the air."

Claire groaned. "Wonderful. The Christmas season puts Adam in such a foul mood. Snow makes it worse."

"Why?"

"Because Mother and Rose died on Christmas Eve." Claire shook her head, as if banishing the memory. "I keep telling Reverend Nelson that beneath Adam's rough exterior is the heart of a kind and generous man."

Sophia's heart went out to both Claire and Adam. "You and Reverend Nelson are close?"

Claire hesitated. "We are good friends."

Sophia heard the hitch in the younger woman's voice. "I think more than friends."

Claire blushed. "Yes."

"He is kind, no?"

Claire approached, her face glowing with happiness. "I've never met a finer man."

Love. Sophia could see the love in Claire's eyes. Such affection ran deep. She suspected with or without the organ or the permanent job at St. Martin's, Claire would love her Reverend Nelson.

Sophia understood the depths of Adam's concern. This kind of love had the power to bring exquisite joy and crushing sadness.

Claire held up a petticoat, as if inspecting it. "I've seen the way you and Adam look at each other. You are good friends too?"

Sophia didn't mistake the true meaning. "No."

"There is a spark," Claire said. "I've seen the way he looks at you."

Sophia drew a deep breath. "I annoy him."

A teasing light danced in Claire's eyes. "You fascinate him. He's never looked at another woman like he looks at you."

The flicker of hope irritated Sophia. "Last night he looked as if he wanted to strangle me."

Claire laughed. "I don't think so." Then just as suddenly, frown lines appeared between her eyes. "I am glad there might be something between you two. I've worried that Adam will end up alone. Then you came along."

Sophia thought of the kiss he'd rejected and the money he'd offered if she left town. She was simply an obstacle blocking Adam from his goal. "I upset his nice neat world, that is all."

Claire laughed. "He's needed that world upset for a long time. Everyone bends to Adam. But you don't."

Needing to change the subject, Sophia turned her attention to the dress. "Who is this for?"

"You, of course."

She captured a piece of the silk between her fingers and savored its softness. "I don't understand. I must go to the church and work today."

"It's Sunday. When I saw Reverend Nelson at the sunrise mass, he told me he would be conducting services all day long. The church is always so much busier before the holidays. You won't be able to get near the organ until tomorrow."

Guilt jabbed Sophia. She had lost all track of time. "You should have woken me. I'd have gone to church with you."

"You needed the sleep so that you'd be bright-eyed for the party."

"Party?" She couldn't help but touch the soft silk of the dress.

"At the Dalrumples'. It's their annual Christmas celebration. You've been invited."

Self-conscious, Sophia released the silk. "It would not be right for me to attend."

Claire started to sort through petticoats and stockings. "You must. You love music and I

know you will truly enjoy this outing.'' She
tossed the stockings aside and took Sophia's
hands in hers. ''Please say you'll come.''

Sophia didn't know how to refuse. ''It has
been so long since I had time of my own.''

Claire smiled. ''Then it's settled.''

Beneath the laughter, cunning sparkled in
Claire's eyes. So much like her brother. ''I am
not accustomed to charity.''

Claire waved away her concern. ''It's not charity. I'm simply lending you a dress for the afternoon.''

''Why did you invite me here to stay?''

All innocence, Claire said, ''So Adam can put
his worries to rest about the organ. I want him
to know you better and to see you have grit.''

Sophia frowned. ''Grit? What is this?''

''A term my mother used to use. It means you
are tough.''

''Ah.'' In truth she didn't feel so strong now.
She felt adrift, frightened and more homesick
than she'd been in years.

''She would have liked you,'' Claire observed.

''Your *maman?*''

''Yes.''

Sophia felt a kinship with Claire. They had
both lost their mothers at young ages. ''It's hard
to lose one so close to us.''

Claire's eyes softened and she looked as if she'd say something more. But instead she straightened her shoulders. "Say that you will come."

Sophia did love music. "Yes."

Claire clasped her hands together. "Excellent! Now, we must get you dressed quickly. Adam is not a patient man."

Even the sound of Adam's name had her nerves jumping. "Excuse me?"

Claire moved toward the door, opened it, ready to make a quick escape. "I have persuaded him to join us today. Isn't that wonderful!"

CHAPTER SEVEN

THE NEXT HOUR WAS a whirlwind of activity. Sophia had little time to worry about Adam Richmond as she struggled with silk stockings, corsets and layers of undergarments. She'd been reared as a lady, yes, but six years with Ivan had left her more at home in peasant's clothes.

By the time the clock in the downstairs foyer struck eleven o'clock, Sophia was dressed in a brown velvet skirt with a matching fitted jacket and derby style hat. Her hair was styled in a jet-black crown of curls and pearl drop earrings dangled from her ears.

Her ankles wobbled when she started to walk in the high-heeled shoes. Muttering an oath in Russian, she concentrated on putting one foot in front of the other. Her next step wasn't better than the first, but as she moved down the hallway, her stride became more graceful.

Then she caught sight of Adam at the bottom of the stairs. Magnificent. Dressed in a black tailored suit and overcoat, he moved with straight-back precision, every step conveying confidence and purpose. She tripped.

Hearing her, he glanced up as he shoved his large hand into a leather glove. He froze and simply stared at her.

Sophia felt the distance between them shrink. His intense interest stirred excitement in her stomach.

She tried to will away the tension and descend the stairs with as much grace as she could summon.

To her great relief, she did not stumble again.

When she reached the foyer, Adam continued to stare, silent. Slowly he walked toward her. He circled, taking his time as he inspected every detail of her transformation.

Her nerves bunching, she glanced down at her skirts. "Is something wrong? Have I forgotten something?"

"Shh," he said.

Heat burned Sophia's cheeks as she tugged at her cuff. Unlike last night, his skin was freshly shaven and he smelled of sandalwood, hair tonic and man. "Claire lent me the outfit."

His voice sounded rough, unsteady. "Nicely done indeed. Nicely done."

Desire darkened Adam's gray eyes. Every

muscle in his body radiated with masculine awareness.

Sophia's fingers ached to touch him. So difficult to believe that in the beginning, she'd not seen past the ice to the heat.

All thoughts of the party, Claire and the rest of the world receded. For a heartbeat, there was just Adam.

Fritz entered the foyer, a coat in his hand. He cleared his throat. "Miss Claire insisted that I have you at the party by noon. The snow is slowing traffic, so I suggest you leave now."

Adam didn't move right away. "Where is my sister?" he said, his stare on Sophia.

"Miss Claire had to leave early. Something about refreshments," Fritz said.

Sophia's attention sharpened. "I thought we were all riding together."

Adam took the fur-trimmed coat Fritz was holding and held it out for Sophia. If he was annoyed, he didn't show any signs of it. "My sister is always full of surprises."

Sophia slid her arms into the silken lining of the coat. The coat, soft as down, enveloped her.

Adam leaned close so his ear brushed hers. "I think we can survive a carriage ride alone, don't you, Sophia?" Humor and challenge coated each word.

"That depends. What scheme do you have up your sleeve today?" she answered.

He laughed. "For today, none. I'm calling a truce. Those foppish society people mean something to Claire and she wants to make a good impression, so I am willing to play along for today. Besides, it is Sunday and nothing can be done about the pipe organ."

Adam looked years younger when he laughed.

"I still intend to finish it," Sophia said.

He smiled but there was a glint of steel in his eyes. "One day at a time, Sophia. One day at a time."

Adam guided Sophia out the front door. Cold December wind whirled around them as they moved down the wide marble steps and into his carriage.

Sophia sank into the plush seat. The walls were upholstered in royal-blue velvet and the lap blankets were made of the finest mink. She smoothed her hand over the seat and thought of the six years spent walking nearly everywhere.

The carriage dipped as Adam climbed in and took his seat across from hers. His knees brushed hers as he sat down, then draped the fur over her lap.

The carriage interior felt very small.

Adam pounded on the side of the carriage, signaling the coachman to drive. Within seconds, the carriage jerked, jostling Sophia's knees into Richmond's, and they were off.

Richmond considered her for a long moment, staring until her cheeks started to flush.

Sophia tugged at the lap blanket. "Claire is a matchmaker, I fear."

He folded his arms over his chest. "How so?"

She met his gaze. "She thinks if she wraps me in fancy clothes that somehow you will be more attracted to me."

"She's wrong."

Disappointment tore at her heart. "You don't like the way I look?"

"I learned long ago to look beyond the packaging, no matter how pretty." A grin tugged at his full lips. "I'd want you even if you wore flour sacks."

Sophia couldn't quite breathe.

Adam took her gloved hand in his, traced small circles on her palm. "I heard you pacing last night."

She swallowed. "You put me in the room next to yours. How was I supposed to sleep? You...you could have forced yourself on me."

His face tightened with anger and he dropped her hand. "I've never forced myself on any woman and when you come to my bed you'll come willing and wanting.''

Her mouth felt dry, her lips parched. ''Perhaps *after* the organ is completed we could spend time together.''

''I want to spend time with you *now*. If I had my way, we'd turn this carriage around and head straight back to my house. We'd spend the afternoon in bed and there'd be no talk.''

The idea of lying next to him made Sophia dizzy. Shivery sensations danced down her spine. His rock-hard body radiated a fire that left her breathless.

But as much as Sophia wanted to close her eyes and give in to the sensations, she didn't. This time, she drew back. ''Are you always like this?''

Her words surprised him, but he recovered quickly. Tossing his head back, he laughed. ''No. Thank God. Only you do this to me, Sophia. Only you.''

CHAPTER EIGHT

SOPHIA WAS GRATEFUL when the carriage stopped in front of the Dalrumples' house. She needed distance from Adam so that her reeling senses could clear.

Adam climbed down and held out his hand to Sophia. Accepting it, she looked up at the front doors decorated with twin wreaths entwined with crisp purple ribbons. "How lovely."

Adam didn't spare the house a second glance. "Yes."

She squeezed the folds of her fur-trimmed cape closed. "It's festive."

"The Dalrumples keep a tree in the parlor lit with candles," Adam said, his mood darkening. "If it were to tip over the fire could be devastating."

Sadness filled her. The fire that had killed his mother and sister had scarred more than his hand. "You always think the worst will happen?"

He took her elbow and guided her up the five stone steps to the front door. "Yes."

Her heart went out to him. "So much worry is no good, Adam Richmond. I know this."

He captured her gloved hand. "Give me a life with guarantees, and I'll stop."

"I have learned that you can no more control life than a river's course."

Adam clenched and unclenched his fingers. "You underestimate me."

Her response was cut off when the door opened and a butler welcomed them inside. Mrs. Dalrumple, who'd been speaking to another couple, stopped when she saw Adam and Sophia. Her questioning gaze lingered on Sophia and then her mouth dropped open. "Miss Petranova?"

Sophia thanked the butler as he took her coat. "Yes."

The other couple, hearing Sophia's voice, turned their gazes toward her. She knew them from the church; however, their shocked expressions told her they'd not recognized her at first either.

Mrs. Dalrumple studied her more closely. "I never would have guessed it."

Claire breezed into the foyer with Reverend Nelson behind her. Her smile widened when she saw Adam and Sophia together. She quickly gave her brother a kiss on the cheek then took Sophia by the hand. ''You've arrived just in time. My sad little voice is a poor accompaniment to Dora's playing. Say you will sing.''

''I don't know the words to your songs,'' Sophia said.

Claire tugged Sophia toward the parlor. ''I will help you with the words.''

As Sophia moved down the hallway, she glanced over her shoulder at Adam. He mouthed ''good luck'' as his sister whisked her into the music parlor.

HOURS LATER, standing by the spinet, with the music and songs swirling around Sophia, it was as if the past six years had never happened. Memories of home came alive and she glimpsed her old self.

Sophia tapped her toe in time to the music, aware that Adam rarely took his gaze off her. His presence left her slightly dizzy and made her question her plans to return to Russia.

When she finished singing ''Silent Night'' for the second time, the crowd begged for more. But needing a moment's respite, she graciously declined.

She glanced toward the chair Adam had claimed. He wasn't there. Disappointed, she moved up the stairs toward the ladies' sitting room that Claire had told her about.

The Dalrumples' upstairs hallway was papered in a soft cream-and-white striped pattern and decorated with portraits of the Dalrumple children— seven in all. Despite the expensive furnishings, this part of the house exuded an informality that appealed to Sophia. Moving down the hallway, she lingered at each portrait, noting the red highlights in each child's hair.

She hesitated in front of the last portrait, that of a young girl with cherubic features. She raised her hand to the face, but didn't touch. "To have such a family."

She'd been so focused on surviving these last few years, she'd dared not entertain dreams of children.

Swallowing a lump in her throat, she lowered her hand. She wanted a house. A husband. Children. Love.

Distressed by the intensity of her feelings, she moved away from the portraits and slipped into the ladies' room. She took a seat in front of a mirrored vanity, grateful to be alone.

Her flushed reflection and watery eyes glared back at her. "Adam Richmond's not offered you anything other than passion. You'd be wise not to forget that, Sophia," she whispered.

Sophia Petranova, she reminded herself, did not worry about what could not be. She concentrated on reality. And a life with Adam Richmond was only a dream.

Determined to distract herself, she uncapped a crystal perfume bottle and savored the lavender scent. She dabbed the stopper behind her ears and the underside of her wrists.

As she rose, ready to return to the party, a child's frustrated cry carried through the door that connected the sitting room to another.

"No nap!" the child shouted. A toy crashed against the floor.

Unable to resist a peek, Sophia cracked open the door and looked into the connecting sitting room.

What she found was a delightful nursery with walls painted robin's-egg blue. A thick braided rug warmed the floor, two low-lying double beds were against one wall and endless blocks and books peppered the floor. In the center of it all were a young boy and girl, about four or five years old, and a very frazzled nursemaid.

The nursemaid, who didn't look to be much older than a child herself, tucked a loose ebony curl back under her white cap. "That's enough out of you two. You'll be taking your nap now."

The girl shook her head, shouted "No," and popped a thumb in her mouth.

Sophia recognized the girl from the portraits as the youngest of the Dalrumple clan.

The boy looked at his sister and like her shouted, "No!"

The nurse started to pick up the blocks. "Ol' Saint Nick don't take kindly to boys and girls who don't listen. He'll be filling your stockings with ashes and coal if you don't mind."

The children's eyes started to fill with tears and Sophia took pity on them. "What's this?" Sophia said, walking into the room. Her skirts swished behind her as she maneuvered through the minefield of toys.

The nursemaid curtsied, her face crimson with embarrassment. "Pardon me, miss. We didn't mean to disturb you."

"You did not disturb me." Sophia chucked each child under the chin. The nursery smelled faintly of milk and sweet cakes and she felt at home, quietly relaxed.

Both children looked up at her, their eyes dancing with curiosity.

Sophia sat in a rocker by a fire crackling in the hearth. She patted her lap. "Would you two like a story?"

The nursemaid wrung her hands. "They're

sticky, miss. They're sure to ruin your fine dress.''

Sophia asked the nursemaid for a towel and beckoned the children closer. As she wiped their small, pudgy hands she said, ''You must promise not to ruin my dress. You see, it is not mine, only borrowed for today.''

The little girl wiggled her clean fingers. ''Like Cinderella?''

Sophia hoisted the child up on her lap. ''And who is this Cinderella?''

''She is a princess.''

Sophia laughed. ''Ah.''

The boy scrambled up on her lap. ''You look like a princess.''

Sophia brushed the bangs from the boy's eyes. ''Maybe for today, but most days, I am just plain and ordinary. Now tell me your names?''

The nursemaid answered for them. ''The girl is Georgia and the boy, Seth. They're Mrs. Dalrumple's youngest.''

''We're not big enough for Dora's party,'' Georgia said.

Seth studied Sophia. ''You talk funny.''

''I'm Russian,'' Sophia said. ''I come from a place very far away.''

Sophia settled the children next to her. ''Would you like to hear a story?''

Georgia gently touched Sophia's earring. "A Russian story?"

Sophia pretended to think. "I will tell you about the Snow Maiden. She was the daughter of woodland spirits and she lived in a winter wonderland far away from people."

"Was she pretty?" Georgia said.

Quick purposeful footsteps echoed in the hallway and before Sophia could answer the door the nursery opened. Adam stood in the doorway, filling the space with his wide shoulders.

Suddenly, Sophia felt foolish and clumsy as she stared into his dark gaze.

The lines of worry, etched at the corners of his eyes, faded. "I thought you'd left."

The nursemaid stood, her shoulders straight and stiff. "We didn't mean to keep her, sir. She was just telling the little ones a story."

"I shall be along in a moment," Sophia said.

"Don't let me interrupt."

"It's a story for children," Sophia said, sitting straighter. "You would not be interested."

"I would," he said easily.

Adam stepped into the room, closing the door behind him. He leaned against the wall and folded his arms over his chest ready to listen.

THE TRUTH WAS wild horses couldn't have dragged Adam away.

Seeing Sophia in the rocker with the children on her lap knocked the wind out of Adam. He'd never seen a more beautiful sight. The children adored her and she'd looked at home and relaxed with them. As he watched her, painful memories of the past faded. In their place, he pictured Sophia surrounded by their children, singing to them as they all stood by the Christmas tree.

"Was she pretty?" Georgia said.

"Who?" Sophia asked. She tore her gaze from him.

The children giggled. "The Snow Maiden."

"Oh yes, very lovely," Sophia said.

Sophia's voice sounded shaky, a little nervous. She was very aware of his presence. And the idea pleased him.

Sophia cleared her throat. "The Snow Maiden had skin as pale as the moon and hair the color of the night. Her gown was made of finely embroidered silk and trimmed with sable."

"What happened to her?" Seth asked.

Sophia lowered her voice. "One day while the Snow Maiden was playing with her friend the bear, she heard flute music coming from the world where people lived."

"People like us?" said Seth.

Sophia touched his nose. "Just like you." She thought a moment. "The Snow Maiden followed the sound of the music to the edge of the winter forest. From there she could see green meadows and the bright sun shining down. She had never seen green grass before and she wanted to run barefoot through it. But she was afraid. Then she saw a handsome shepherd playing his flute. It was his music that she'd heard.''

''What happened?'' Georgia asked.

Sophia hesitated. ''To know the answer to that, you must get in your beds and under the covers.''

A little coaxing had them both in bed with the covers pulled up to their chins. Sophia tucked the edge of the blankets under the mattress. ''The Snow Maiden and the shepherd became good friends and then she returned to the magical woodland. You see, she is the one who tells your St. Nicolas which boys and girls deserve toys.''

Adam suspected the fable had not ended so happily and that Sophia had rewritten the ending for the sake of the children.

''Are you the Snow Maiden?'' Seth asked.

Adam laughed when Sophia shrugged. He could almost see the children's minds turning with questions.

''We are *good*,'' Seth said quickly. ''And if you see St. Nick tell him that Seth Dalrumple wants a toy train.''

Georgia sat up. "And Georgia Dalrumple wants a doll with blond hair and a green dress."

Trying not to smile, Sophia kept her tone serious. "If I did happen to see St. Nick, I will pass on your requests. But you must promise to take your nap and not give nanny any more trouble."

Both nodded.

She touched them each on the nose. "Then I will see what I can do."

The children squeezed their eyes tight as if that would make sleep come faster.

Sophia said reluctant goodbyes.

Opening the door, Adam placed his hand in the small of her back and guided her into the hallway. "So what really happened to the Snow Maiden?"

Sophia glanced up at him, a bit surprised. "She fell in love with her shepherd. Love warmed her heart. But the love was too much for her. Like snow on a sunny day, she melted, never to be seen again."

Adam pulled Sophia into a secluded alcove. "Would you vanish if I kissed you?"

CHAPTER NINE

As Sophia stared into Adam's gray eyes, excitement left her speechless.

He dipped his head and covered her lips with his. At first, his kiss was tentative. But the feel of his lips and the taste of him set her senses on fire and she rose on tiptoes and wrapped her arms around his neck. A moan rumbled in his throat.

Adam wrapped his arm around her waist and pulled her against him. She curled her fingers into his hair and abandoned herself to the moment until the sound of laughter on the staircase reminded her they weren't alone.

Sophia froze.

Adam drew back, muttering an oath. He took her hand in his. "Let's get out of here."

"Where are we going?" she said breathlessly.

"Back to my house."

Adam made hasty goodbyes for both of them to Mrs. Dalrumple and Claire and soon they were in his carriage. Neither spoke or touched one another during the carriage ride to Richmond house.

Both understood that once released, their desire would wash over them like an avalanche.

Sophia tried to let her mind drift—to ignore the *tap, tap, tap* of Adam's long fingers against the leather seat cushion, the scent of his cologne mingling with tobacco, and the way his throat moved when he swallowed. But try as she might, she couldn't let go of the fact that soon he'd be her lover.

Nor did she fool herself. She wanted this. She understood that whatever happened between them might not last beyond tonight. It was a risk, yes, but one she knew she must take.

At Richmond House, Adam escorted her up the front steps and opened the door.

In the foyer, he gave her coat to the butler. "Fritz, Miss Sophia is done for today. When she's ready for dinner, she'll order a cold tray for her room."

Sophia barely registered Fritz's reply before Adam turned to her and mouthed the words, "Five minutes."

Filled with anticipation, and a good case of nerves, Sophia climbed the stairs and entered her room. She unpinned and brushed her long ebony hair until it crackled and glistened, then changed into the pale-pink silk wrapper she found in the armoire.

Seconds later, Adam opened the door connecting their rooms. He'd shed his tie and jacket and rolled up his sleeves to his elbows.

Gas lamps flickered, casting shadows on his angled face. His gaze slid to her neck. A rush of heat flooded her veins and suddenly the air around her felt thick. She could barely breathe.

"You're beautiful," he said softly.

"So are you." Her voice sounded as if it belonged to someone else.

Adam pulled her to him and kissed her. His scent and heat enveloped her. She slid her fingers through his thick hair, fisting handfuls as he banded his arms around her narrow waist and hauled her against him. His chest and body were firm, taut with wanting.

Then, with a groan, he scooped her up and carried her to her bed. He laid her down and covered her body with his, kissing her lips, her neck as his hands pushed open the lacy folds of her wrapper. When her breasts were exposed, he suckled her pink nipples until she arched her back.

Letting her body fully enjoy Adam's touch heightened her own desires. She spread her legs, allowing him to press his erection against her nakedness. His kisses, the way he cupped her breasts with his calloused hands, left her breathless. Her stomach tightened; her heart pounded.

Adam raised his head. "I've never wanted a woman like I want you, Sophia."

She smiled, trailing her long fingers down his back. Grabbing a handful of his shirt, she pulled it free from his waistband. He rose and pulled the shirt off, then kissed her again, his passion as hot as the summer sun.

In the dim snowy light, she stared at the lines around his eyes, deepened by desire, and marveled at her womanly power. She brushed her fingers over his buttocks, smiling when she felt his muscles tighten.

He tugged at the sash belting her robe. The cool air rippled over her body, triggering elation and a flicker of embarrassment. Her experience with men had been minimal. She sailed into uncharted waters. Suddenly unsure, she tensed.

Confused by her unexpected hesitation, Adam frowned. "What's wrong?"

She met his gaze. "This is new to me."

Understanding dawned in his eyes and he smiled. "I will show you the way."

Adam slid his fingers between her legs. Immediately, her heart raced and the blood in her body pounded with an unknown anticipation. He stroked her until moist heat dampened his fingers. Sophia tottered on a thin line between pleasure and pain. She moaned his name.

He kissed her again and she could feel his erection pressing against her. Instinctively, she opened her legs to him.

Adam shifted his weight, positioned himself over her then came into her with explosive force, pushing through the tightness in one swift move. She gripped his back, sucking in a breath as her body adjusted to him.

Adam stilled after his first invasion. He kissed her and waited until she grew accustomed to him. Finally, pain gave way to a hotter heat and she began to move beneath him.

He matched her tempo in a timeless dance until his thrusts became a frenzied assault. Her own desire climaxed in a blaze of heat and Sophia called out his name. Adam thrust one last time and spilled his seed inside her.

Afterward, he lay back against the pillow, his chest heaving as if he'd just run a mile. Sophia spooned her body against his and touched his cheek, rough now with unshaven beard. The fire he'd aroused in her still warmed her limbs. For the first time in her life, she understood total joy, fulfillment and love.

And she could almost pretend it would last forever.

"I've heard you're a Russian princess? Is that true?" Adam said just after midnight. He tore off a piece of chicken from the cold plate Fritz had left earlier and fed it to her.

Russia felt very far away to Sophia. "Russia has many princesses."

He lay on his side and rested his head on his palm. "So you are a princess?"

She leaned back against the plumped pillows as if she were telling one of her fairy tales to the children. "My mother used to tell me that once our family was second only in power to the Czar. We had chests filled with rubies, we drank out of gold cups, and we wore the finest sables and minks."

He traced her naked thigh with his finger. "What happened?"

"My grandfather wanted more. He wanted not only the wealth of a Czar but he wanted the power as well. And he tried to take it. Of course, he did not win. He was executed and our family was stripped of its power and wealth. I was about eight when this happened. Everyone, including Papa's family, cut us off and we were exiled to the country. Papa tried to make a go of the land, but he knew nothing of farming or hard work. He died when I was ten."

"That explains why you handled yourself so well today. As if you were born to wealth."

She laughed. "You can thank my *maman* for my manners. She refused to let our change in station alter her plans for me. She trained me in the ways of the court, hoping one day I'd make a good marriage."

"Why did she marry Ivan?"

"He was different then—a master craftsman who was respected by all. He had some money and he liked Mama's old connections to the Czar. She was lonely."

"And they married."

"Yes."

"How did you end up in America?"

"Ivan hoped if he and *maman* petitioned the Czar for forgiveness, they could revive some of the old glory. This did not happen and Ivan was bitterly disappointed. He began to drink more." A sigh lifted her shoulders. "When my *maman* died of the cancer, Ivan's debts began to mount. We came to America to escape them."

His jaw tightened as if he didn't like the story. "He will come back for you, won't he?"

"No, not this time."

He traced the line of her jaw with his fingertip. "Does that bother you?"

She shook her head. "I've known for some

time he'd leave me. It's for the best. We both will move on with our lives now.''

Adam kissed her shoulder. ''I have something for you.'' Unmindful that he was naked, he rose and disappeared into his room. When he returned he carried a small black box. ''This is for you.''

Suspicious, she smoothed her hand over the soft exterior. ''What is this?''

''You will be pleased.''

She cracked open the lid. Inside nestled in silk was her mother's locket, polished and cleaned with a new gold chain threaded through the clasp. Tears sprang in her eyes. ''Where did you get this?''

He kept his expression hooded. ''One of my contacts bought it from Ivan.''

Reverently, she clicked open the locket. The portrait of her mother stared back at her. Her heart clenched with joy.

''At first I thought it was a picture of you,'' he said gruffly. ''Then I realized it had to be your mother.''

A tear slid down her cheek. ''This means more to me than I can say.''

''We're very much the same, Sophia. Family is everything.''

''Yes. Family first.'' She kissed him on the lips. ''Thank you.''

He cleared his throat. "I want to take care of you now. I want to build you a fine house and wrap you in silks."

She closed her fingers over the locket. "I don't need these things."

He kissed her hand. "What do you want?"

You. "A simple home, children, laughter."

"I will give you all that if you'll let me. Stay in Denver, Sophia."

He'd not spoken of love, but she knew she had enough for both of them. "I love you," she dared to whisper.

Happiness softened the lines on his face, but he did not answer in kind.

Sophia cupped his face and pressed her lips to him. Soon, their bodies were entwined and they made love. His lovemaking was just as passionate and intense as the first time, but this time he took his time, savoring every inch of her body.

Hours later, Sophia awoke to the morning sun shining in the window. She lay on her side, her body cradled in Adam's arms. As much as she wanted to stay in bed and make love to Adam all day, it was Monday and she had to finish tuning the pipe organ.

It took every ounce of her willpower to rise from the bed and dress. Adam awoke as she laced up her second boot.

Sophia smiled at him, knowing there'd never be another man for her. "Good morning."

He swung his legs over the side of the bed. "Where are you going?"

"To the church. If I leave now, and if I am lucky, I will have the organ finished by sundown."

All traces of good humor vanished from his face. "After last night, everything changed between us. We are on the same side now."

Confused by his shift in mood, she shoved her arms into her sheepskin coat. "We are."

His shoulders stiffened. "Then why are you going to finish the organ?"

Her body stilled. "I gave my word."

He stood, took hold of her arms. "I want to build you a beautiful home, shower you with silks, give you children. But you must not finish the organ, otherwise Nelson won't leave Denver. Do this one thing for me and you will have me forever."

She jerked free. *"This one thing...?"* Her heart contracted as if the life were being squeezed out of it. "These things you will do for me as long as I do as you say."

He jabbed his hands through his hair. "Sophia, you've seen enough of the world to know nothing's free."

Her heart shattered in that moment. "I thought what we had was different."

"It is, but you must be practical."

Sophia felt as if the earth was shattering under her feet. Pride kept her shoulders back. "I must finish the organ."

All the warmth drained from his body. What remained was the cold, chiseled man she'd met just days ago. "Either you are with me or against me," he said tightly.

Shock and a wrenching sadness sliced her heart. Such a fool she'd been.

Through the blur of tears, she summoned the strength to turn and walk out the door.

CHAPTER TEN

ADAM STARED out his bedroom window and watched Sophia walk away. The sun was already turning warm and turning the ice to slush.

Like the snow on a sunny day, she melted never to be seen again.

Sophia's tale of the Snow Maiden had been a grim harbinger of today.

Without her, the house had taken on an eerie silence and for the first time in a very long time, he felt utterly alone in the world.

After what he had said, he knew she wasn't coming back to him. Her pride and sense of honor wouldn't let her. Both were just two reasons why he loved her so much. And why he'd lost her.

The pipe organ, ousting Nelson didn't matter anymore. What mattered was Sophia.

He quickly dressed and thundered into the foyer. "Fritz! Get my coat!"

Almost instantly, the butler appeared with

Adam's coat. Adam slid his arms into the coat with the butler's assistance.

"I'll summon the driver," Fritz said.

Adam accepted his leather gloves from Fritz. "Don't bother, I can move faster on foot."

Adam jerked open the front door. To his surprise he found Claire and Nelson standing there, ready to enter.

Claire glanced up. "Adam, I didn't expect you home this time of day."

Nelson too looked surprised but he recovered first. "Mr. Richmond."

"Nelson, Claire. I don't have time to talk now. I'll be back soon."

Nelson cleared his throat. "Mr. Richmond, we have other news for you."

With great effort, Adam stopped and turned. "It'll have to wait."

Claire tugged off her glove and held out her hand to him. A shiny gold ring banded her ring finger. "We got married last night!"

He mouthed the words, "I'll be damned."

Nelson rushed to say, "We were married in a small chapel on the edge of town." The young man stared him squarely in the eyes and there was no hint of apology or fear. Claire stared up at her new husband, her face beaming with adoration.

Swallowing a lump in his throat, he held out his hand to Nelson. "Take care of her."

Nelson's expression registered his shock but his handshake was firm. "I will."

Adam kissed his sister on the cheek. "Be happy."

She clung to him, choking back tears. "I will." When he released her she stared up at him, worried. She touched his face, then squeezed Adam's hand none too gently. "We just passed Sophia on the street. She was crying."

Adam's gut twisted into knots.

"You've got to set things right with Sophia," Claire said.

"I intend to do just that."

SOPHIA'S MIND WAS muddled with sadness and grief when she stepped into the church sanctuary. She shrugged off her coat as she looked at the pipe organ.

It was stunning. Its polished mahogany and walnut trim and brass pipes glistened in the bright sunlight shining through the stained glass windows. Joy and pride mingled with loss and sadness.

Adam.

Suddenly her legs wobbled and she sank down on the organ's bench. Her eyes filled with unshed tears. "How many tears before the pain eases?" she whispered.

The sanctuary door banged open. "Sophia!" Adam's rich voice reverberated off the walls.

Sophia stood and faced him. The closeness they'd shared had vanished. "I intend to finish the organ."

Desolation deepened the lines on his face as he strode toward her. His gaze didn't waver from her. "I was wrong." His hand under her chin, he tipped her head up. "I'll help you finish the organ."

Confused, she stepped back. "Why are you saying this to me now?"

"I love you."

She stood very still. "I fear your kind of love, Adam. You say you love Claire, yet you've done all you can to keep her from the man she loves. Your love comes with conditions."

"Claire and Nelson were married yesterday."

His news shocked her. She searched his eyes for the anger. There was none. "What are you going to do about it?"

"Nothing."

Warily, she moved a step closer. "You will not try to destroy what they have?"

He shook his head. "No. I'll always be there for Claire if she needs me. But she's made her choice." He took her hand in his. "Marry me Sophia, today."

She wanted to fling herself into his arms, but she held herself back. "I will not change for you. I will be a very willful wife."

"I wouldn't have it any other way." He held her hand tighter. "I'll take you to Russia if that's what you want. I'll track Ivan down and ask his permission. I want to do this right." For the first time, Adam Richmond seemed to struggle for words. "I should have a ring. There should be roses."

She'd never been filled with such joy. "I don't need any of those things." She wrapped her arms around him, savored his scent. "All I want is you."

"You'll marry me?"

"Yes, most definitely yes."

He kissed her until she was breathless. "Then I'm taking you home. Nelson's got a job to do. Let's get that organ finished."

Georgette Heyer is
"…the next best thing to reading Jane Austen."
—*Publishers Weekly*

GEORGETTE HEYER

POWDER
AND PATCH

Featuring a foreword by
USA TODAY bestselling author
Susan Wiggs

Cleone Charteris is an English belle who yearns for a refined,
aristocratic husband…but ends up loving rogue Phillip Jettan instead!

Available in February 2004.

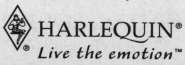

HARLEQUIN®
Live the emotion™

Visit us at www.eHarlequin.com

PHGH602

HEAD FOR THE ROCKIES WITH

Harlequin Historicals®
Historical Romantic Adventure!

AND SEE HOW IT ALL BEGAN!

COLORADO CONFIDENTIAL

**Check out these three historicals
connected to the bestselling Intrigue series**

CHEYENNE WIFE
by Judith Stacy
January 2004

COLORADO COURTSHIP
by Carolyn Davidson
February 2004

ROCKY MOUNTAIN MARRIAGE
by Debra Lee Brown
March 2004

Available at your favorite retail outlet.

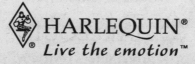

HARLEQUIN®
Live the emotion™

Visit us at www.eHarlequin.com

HHCC

From Regency romps
to mesmerizing Medievals,
savor these stirring tales from
Harlequin Historicals®

On sale January 2004

THE KNAVE AND THE MAIDEN by Blythe Gifford

A cynical knight's life is forever changed when he falls
in love with a naive young woman while journeying
to a holy shrine.

MARRYING THE MAJOR by Joanna Maitland

Can a war hero wounded in body and spirit find
happiness with his childhood sweetheart, now that she
has become the toast of London society?

On sale February 2004

THE CHAPERON BRIDE by Nicola Cornick

When England's most notorious rake is attracted to
a proper ladies' chaperon, could it be true love?

THE WEDDING KNIGHT by Joanne Rock

A dashing knight abducts a young woman to marry his
brother, but soon falls in love with her instead!

Visit us at www.eHarlequin.com

HARLEQUIN HISTORICALS®

HHMED34

If you enjoyed what you just read,
then we've got an offer you can't resist!

Take 2
bestselling novels FREE!
Plus get a FREE surprise gift!

Clip this page and mail it to The Best of the Best™

IN U.S.A.
3010 Walden Ave.
P.O. Box 1867
Buffalo, N.Y. 14240-1867

IN CANADA
P.O. Box 609
Fort Erie, Ontario
L2A 5X3

YES! Please send me 2 free Best of the Best™ novels and my free surprise gift. After receiving them, if I don't wish to receive anymore, I can return the shipping statement marked cancel. If I don't cancel, I will receive 4 brand-new novels every month, before they're available in stores! In the U.S.A., bill me at the bargain price of $4.74 plus 25¢ shipping and handling per book and applicable sales tax, if any*. In Canada, bill me at the bargain price of $5.24 plus 25¢ shipping and handling per book and applicable taxes**. That's the complete price and a savings of over 20% off the cover prices—what a great deal! I understand that accepting the 2 free books and gift places me under no obligation ever to buy any books. I can always return a shipment and cancel at any time. Even if I never buy another The Best of the Best™ book, the 2 free books and gift are mine to keep forever.

185 MDN DNWF
385 MDN DNWG

Name	(PLEASE PRINT)	
Address	Apt.#	
City	State/Prov.	Zip/Postal Code

* Terms and prices subject to change without notice. Sales tax applicable in N.Y.
** Canadian residents will be charged applicable provincial taxes and GST.
  All orders subject to approval. Offer limited to one per household and not valid to
  current The Best of the Best™ subscribers.
  ® are registered trademarks of Harlequin Enterprises Limited.

BOB02-R   ©1998 Harlequin Enterprises Limited

PICK UP THESE HARLEQUIN HISTORICALS® AND IMMERSE YOURSELF IN RUGGED LANDSCAPE AND INTOXICATING ROMANCE ON THE AMERICAN FRONTIER

On sale November 2003

THE TENDERFOOT BRIDE by Cheryl St.John
(Colorado, 1875)

Expecting a middle-aged widow, a hard-edged rancher doesn't know what to do when his new cook is not only young and beautiful, but pregnant!

THE SCOUT by Lynna Banning
(Nebraska and Wyoming, 1860)

On a wagon train headed to Oregon, an independent spinster becomes smitten with her escort, a troubled army major.

On sale December 2003

THE SURGEON by Kate Bridges
(Canada, 1889)

When his troop plays a prank on him, a mounted police surgeon finds himself stuck with an unwanted mail-order bride. Can she help him find his heart?

OKLAHOMA BRIDE by Carol Finch
(Oklahoma Territory, 1889)

A by-the-book army officer clashes with a beautiful woman breaking the law he has sworn to uphold!

Visit us at www.eHarlequin.com

HARLEQUIN HISTORICALS®

HHWEST28

What happens when a pirate
falls in love with his captive?

BEAUVALLET

GEORGETTE HEYER

Featuring a foreword by
USA TODAY bestselling author

Heather Graham

While sailing the waters of Spain, notorious pirate
Sir Nicholas Beauvallet takes the lovely
Dona Dominica de Rada y Sylva as captive...
and vows to win the heart of the Spanish beauty!

Available in March 2004.

HARLEQUIN®
Live the emotion™

Visit us at www.eHarlequin.com

PHGH604

PICK UP THESE HARLEQUIN HISTORICALS
AND IMMERSE YOURSELF IN THRILLING
AND EMOTIONAL LOVE STORIES
SET IN THE AMERICAN FRONTIER

On sale January 2004

CHEYENNE WIFE by Judith Stacy
(Colorado, 1844)

Will opposites attract when a handsome
half-Cheyenne horse trader comes to the rescue
of a proper young lady from back east?

WHIRLWIND BRIDE by Debra Cowan
(Texas, 1883)

A widowed rancher unexpectedly falls in love with
a beautiful and pregnant young woman.

On sale February 2004

COLORADO COURTSHIP by Carolyn Davidson
(Colorado, 1862)

A young widow finds a father for her unborn child—
and a man for her heart—in a loving wagon train scout.

THE LIGHTKEEPER'S WOMAN by Mary Burton
(North Carolina, 1879)

When an heiress reunites with her former fiancée,
will they rekindle their romance or say goodbye
once and for all?

Visit us at www.eHarlequin.com

HARLEQUIN HISTORICALS®

HHWEST29

England, 716—a time of power and passion, corruption and courage, violence and vengeance...

helen Kirkman

FORBIDDEN

He belonged to her....

He was a slave constrained to do others' bidding. She was a lady who was bent on revenge. They were worlds apart, yet together they found a passion so intense, so unlikely that it must be forbidden....

Coming to stores in March 2004.

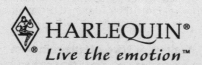

HARLEQUIN®
Live the emotion™

Visit us at www.eHarlequin.com

PHHK629